HARSH LINE

AN URBAN FANTASY

ANN GIMPEL

CONTENTS

HARSH LINE

CATACLYSM SERIES, BOOK ONE

An Urban Fantasy

**By
Ann Gimpel**

Tumble off reality's edge into myth, magic, and Armageddon

Copyright Page

BOOK DESCRIPTION, HARSH LINE

My very existence is under attack. I've kept a low profile, told myself the craziness sweeping the world would pass me by. Yeah, it was wishful thinking, actually an outright lie, but it's kept me sane.

I've been hiding out forever in one guise or another. Currently, I run a nightclub. *Ascent* is an "ask me no questions, and I'll tell you no lies" haven. For everybody. I'm a Vampire. Far be it from me to judge.

My closest ally is a shapeshifting dire wolf. I adopted him when he was a scrawny puppy, but I'm getting ahead of my tale.

The fragile détente between supernaturals and humans has crashed and burned. I can't avoid the truth any longer. Lucky for me, mortals don't know exactly what I am. When I moved to Seattle, some vampiric sixth sense urged me to play my cards close to my vest, but I'm done burying my secrets.

And my power.

It's past time for supernaturals to get over their stupid infighting. Meh. So what if Witches hate Druids? Or Fae never deal with Sorcerers? We have to pull together, or we'll have no chance at all.

Not that it's likely, but if any mortals see the light and sign up for our side, we'd damn well better welcome them.

I'm Ariana Hawke. No more skulking in the shadows for me.

BOOKS IN THE CATACLYSM SERIES

Harsh Line, Book One
Warped Line, Book Two
Broken Line, Book Three

AUTHOR'S NOTE

Part of me can scarcely believe I'm writing this series. Vampires have been the bad guys in my Bitter Harvest series and my Gatekeeper series and several others. Not so in the Cataclysm books.

Maybe I named the series what I did because turning Vampires into heroes was cataclysmic for me. Mortals are a sketchy lot. When the reality of magical beings got a little too close, they banded together and fought back. Silly of them, huh? Even an army of humans isn't a match for a couple of determined magic-wielders, but they're going to have to figure that out on their own.

Ariana is a great heroine. I'm excited to tell you her story. And Conan is perfect. He reminds me of my own wolves: noble, principled, and courageous as hell.

CHAPTER ONE, ARIANA

"*Y*ou shorted me again." Standing straight, I locked gazes with the liquor distributor for my nightclub.

"You've miscounted...ma'am." Defiance fairly dripped from the burly driver as he dared me to contradict him. Greasy black hair was stuffed beneath a dirty baseball cap. He had dark eyes, a million wrinkles, and a beer gut hanging over his too-tight jeans.

Ha! I could rip him limb from limb with one hand tied behind my back, but no reason to let him know that. "Shall we count them together?" I adopted my best dumb-female mien. Not easy because it was so not me.

"Maybe some other time." He thrust an invoice at me with a pen clipped to the board beneath it. "Running late."

"I'll just bet you are. Look, Roger. Either we count them, or you can take the whole mess back to your truck. And I'll find another distributor."

A shocked look bloomed on his beefy face. Red splotches marked both stubble-coated cheeks. About six feet two, he was the same height as me, but he outweighed me by a good hundred pounds. "I don't have time to do that, either," he sputtered. "You'd better sign off on the fucking shipment."

I waited, but he stopped shy of tacking "bitch" onto the end of his statement.

I glanced at the invoice, snatched up the pen, and scratched corrections onto the sheet. I wrote in a new total, signed it, and handed it back to him. "There you go, bud."

"But—but you can't just write down any amount you want."

I shrugged. "Just did." I crossed my arms beneath my breasts and shook strands of black hair out of my face. "Two choices, Rog. Accept my figures—and I did count the boxes as you carted them in here. Or take everything back to your truck."

"I didn't see you count nothing."

"Yeah well, I did. You shorted me the last two times, and I don't trust you."

He stared at me, mouth opening and closing like a gutted fish as his pea-sized brain absorbed he'd have to come up with the difference for the cases he'd clearly sold to some black market trader.

"What's it going to be?" I pressed. "I'm a busy woman. A while back, you said you didn't have time to count the cases, so presumably you have a schedule as well."

He turned on his heel and stalked out of my back room. It opens onto an alley, and I pulled the heavy, wooden door shut, dropping an aluminum bar into place to secure it.

Breath hissed from between my clenched teeth. I'd stayed out of the slice of daylight cutting through my open door, but my skin still had a burned feeling. I'm a Vampire. One of the old ones, so daylight isn't the scourge for me it is for the newer batch, but it's still not pleasant.

I can go outside during the daytime, but I view it as a last resort.

Being my usual, methodical self, I recounted the cases of booze. I'd been right on with my tallies. Five hundred and twenty-three bucks of my order was missing. Either the bastard driver was skimming off the top, or the liquor distributing company was purposefully shorting me. Regardless, I'd give the distributor—Northwest Spirits—a call to alert them.

My money was on Roger, not the huge distributor. Northwest Spirits had a reputation to uphold.

A low growl wafted from the corner of the stockroom where I parked my Harley. Except it only looked like a motorcycle. I covered the distance from the door to the corner and asked, "What do you think?"

"Ripping his fat throat out is too good for him."

I tossed a leg over the bike and settled onto the plush leather seat. "It may come to that," I muttered.

Beneath me, the motorcycle illusion shimmered and shifted until I was astride Conan, a shapeshifting dire wolf I've been hanging around with for the past 500 years or so. He snarled, but I didn't take him seriously. I did dismount, though. He's good with me on his back when he's masquerading as a bike, or at least he tolerates me.

It's the only time, though.

I walked around until I faced him and buried my fingers in his lush black-and-silver pelt. Amber eyes regarded me with their usual inscrutable lupine expression. As if I were prey. Or could be.

Back in the day, we used to hunt together. I got the blood. He got everything else. Not that we'd given up hunting, but we had to be far more discreet. He laid his muzzle on my shoulder; I scratched his ears.

"We should leave." Capable of speech in wolf form, his words came out garbled, but understandable.

"Where would we go?" He and I had had this conversation before. Many times.

A frustrated growl rumbled from his throat. I let go of him, walked to a chest freezer, and pull out a cow's leg bone with a good bit of meat still clinging to it.

"Buying me off?" Bitterness lined Conan's question, but he snatched up the treat and proceeded to annihilate it. Powerful jaws crunched through bone as if it were made of cardboard.

I left him to it and trotted out of the storage room and into the huge main section of *Ascent*, a nightclub I own. Buying it might not have been one of my better ideas, but it was my baby. Win, lose, or draw. Unlike some bars, we didn't open until seven in the evening. I had zero interest in pandering to stone-cold alkies, the ones who substituted booze for breakfast.

Besides, being open when it was light out held obvious problems for me.

I went to work tumbling chairs back onto the floor from where the cleaning crew had balanced them on tables and thought about Conan. By virtue of a rare genetic mishap—and intervention from a gifted mage—he'd become an extraordinary type of shapeshifter, capable of any form he wanted to adopt.

The genetic part was supposition on my part, mostly because Conan was one of a kind. I've lived a long time, and I've never seen another supernatural creature anything like him.

I came across the wolf when he was a gangly puppy. Hiding at the bottom of a shallow well in a small village in the Carpathian Mountains, he'd been in bad shape. My heart had gone out to the scrawny pup. Vampires don't keep pets, except as a blood source, but something about Conan drew me. Magic ran strong in him, and I couldn't walk away from his plight.

For the first few months, his survival had been nip and tuck. I'd had to keep all the other Vamps away from him, for one thing. And then, I'd had to locate a Sorcerer who understood the small wolf's brand of power. The Sorcerer hadn't wanted to work with me, but I can be persistent.

Vampires are gifted with persuasion, or we'd have faded out of sight long ago. I gave the Sorcerer my word I wouldn't harm him, and I didn't. Long story short, the wolf and I have been together ever since. Not because of magic, but because of loyalty to each other.

Saving someone's life creates a solemn bond, especially for me since ending lives is more my style. Or it used to be. Now I sneak blood from slaughterhouses—and the occasional morgue. It's not any more appealing to me than that frozen bone was to Conan, but we have one another to bitch to.

Misery loves company.

We do still hunt from time to time. Fresh animal blood beats dead human blood every time.

He's been bringing up leaving more and more often, but everywhere except maybe the north and south poles are war zones. I suppose we could get by in a frozen wasteland, but it would be lonely—and cold.

The wolf had dreamed up turning into a motorcycle as cover. When it looks like I'm riding it, I'm really riding him. He's damned fast, and creates realistic motor sounds. He's never admitted this, but I think he has fun with that illusion. It gets him out into the world with me.

Even though he could craft a human form, he never has.

I stood back and surveyed my club with its scarred wooden floor, round tables, and staunchly made chairs. After a few brawls where customers had broken cheaper seats, I'd spent the money for ones resistant to damage. Several large windows ran the length of the nightclub. A raised dais near the back hosted occasional live music.

Unlike many establishments, I served everyone. *Ascent* was a place no one talked about what they were. A spot where humans and magic-wielders established détente. I have very good ears—it's part of my Vampire magic. At the first hint of trouble, I make certain the parties take it outside.

A key slotted into the front door lock, and Ruby Brighton hustled inside, relocking the door behind her. "Hiya, boss," she called cheerily and headed for the bar.

"Hiya back." I waved.

Ruby's rainbow hair hung to shoulder level. Today it was red, blue, and violet. The violet matched her eyes. Ruby was Fae, and hundreds of years old. Like so many ancient beings, she looked about thirty-five. Today she was garbed in her usual black slacks, white shirt, and leather vest. She far preferred bare feet, but I insisted she wear shoes. Fae blood is...unpredictable, and the bar floor often has bits of broken glass.

If someone pissed her off, her blood might shape itself into a weapon. Shoes were a simple solution.

Everyone who works for me has some variety of magic. I've tried mortal employees, but they're too damned fragile. Always one excuse or another for why they can't do something.

"We're out of port and scotch. Did the shipment come?" Ruby quirked a black brow my way.

"Yeah. Fuckers shorted us again. This time, I spoke up."

"Really?" She blew out a noisy breath. "How'd that go?"

"Predictably. Roger played dumb. I scribbled in the number of crates he delivered, initialed it, and wrote in the amount I actually owe."

"Mmph. You planning to call the company?"

"I am, indeed."

"Who else is working tonight?" she asked.

I smothered a sigh. Immortals had their own set of challenges as employees. Some didn't get along very well with others. It made crafting the schedule an ongoing dilemma. Of course, most magical beings loathe Vampires. Somehow, I'd managed to move past that with my staff. The ones who couldn't suck it up were long gone.

I rattled off a spate of names. *Ascent* is a big place. We can seat a couple hundred, and we're often full. Full enough to keep three bartenders, a few circulating waitresses, and a bouncer busy.

I'd just turned around, intent on helping Ruby haul liquor crates from the storeroom to behind the bar when the fine hairs on the back of my neck quivered. "Did you feel that?"

Ruby slitted her eyes. I both felt and saw power shimmer around her, turning the air a delicate silver. Fae magic smells like wildflowers soaked in Irish whiskey, alluring as hell.

"Crap," she cried, dove across the room, and threw her body over mine. We crashed to the floor the same moment as the biggest of half a dozen windows exploded, shattering and littering my freshly mopped floor with a million bits of glass.

Fuck. Please let this be a random event and not my bar specifically targeted because someone figured out what I am.

"Let me up." I struggled beneath Ruby, but she's as strong as I am.

"Not yet," she said.

"But we have to go after whoever did this."

She rolled off me. "You're not thinking. What were you planning? If you sink your fangs into someone's neck, they'll discover what you are."

She didn't have to say the rest. *Ascent* would be finished once it became public knowledge a Vampire owned it.

"All right, all right," I groused. "But I'll be damned if I cower on the floor like a ninny."

Conan loped in from the storeroom, huge jaws snapping. Saliva spooled from his jowls.

"Ooooh. You're so beautiful," Ruby cried and tried to hug him.

He shook her off and glared at the busted window. "Who?" he growled.

"We don't know, sweetie," Ruby told him.

"Erm. Maybe we do," I muttered. "I did a fine job pissing Roger off. Probably cost him a few hundred bucks. And maybe his job—once I'm done talking with his employer."

Half of me had been expecting another blast until I looked around and saw the small boulder someone had chucked through the window. I got up and walked over to it. "Pretty low-tech," I mumbled.

"Sounding more and more like Roger," Ruby said. "The original low-tech dude."

A quick glance at the clock over the bar told me it was five thirty. "I'm going to call Northwest Sprits," I said, "and then I want to go for a little spin. You up for it?" I asked Conan.

"And if I'm not?" he growled.

"I'll take the car."

"With me in the back. You are not going alone." The wolf shook himself from head to tail tip.

"If you're coming anyway, I'd rather ride you." Licking my lips, I grinned at him. "Maybe we can do a little hunting."

"I hate mice," he informed me loftily.

"How about a nice, fat sheep?" Ruby squatted next to him.

"Don't," I snapped. "You'll get him all excited for nothing."

Him and me both. I was hungry. I hadn't fed for the last two days. Vampires don't have to eat often, but we do need food occasionally. Blood from living creatures was so much better than the horrid crap I pilfered from a nearby slaughterhouse. I had to do a whole lot of fantasizing to get morgue leavings down without heaving them back up.

Conan whined. My stomach growled.

To divert myself, I dug my cell phone out of a pocket, scrolled through contacts, and called Northwest Spirits. It was late enough, I didn't expect to do much more than leave a message, but the gal I usually order from picked up on the second ring.

We had a decent conversation. She at least sounded sympathetic. I offered to take pictures of today's delivery to verify my side of things, but she told me it wouldn't be necessary.

"Well?" Ruby asked after I hung up.

"I got the impression this wasn't the first complaint they've fielded about Roger," I told her.

"Interesting."

Conan trotted to the door. His brand of power made a whistling noise and smelled like rain-wet rocks. I wasn't surprised to see the Harley where the wolf had been. Silver and black, just like Conan, the bike glowed invitingly. Nothing like magic to dress something up.

"I'll get the door," Ruby offered. She patted the bike on her way past it. "Someday," she said, clearly angling for a ride.

"Tell her only you," the wolf said into my mind.

"I heard that, sweetie." Ruby grinned. It made her look

about sixteen with her hanks of parti-colored hair. "Can't blame a gal for trying. I'll get a leg up on clearing all that glass away."

She raised her hands. Magic crackled from them, and the glass swirled upward, forming a column. Once it was all flowing the same direction, she cracked a portal, and the remains of the window vanished.

"Too bad replacing it isn't that simple." She made a wry face and cut the flow of magic still shimmering around her. "What do you want to do for tonight?"

"Plywood?"

"Works for me," she said. "I'll get the guys on it as soon as they come in."

"We should have enough in the back from last time," I told her.

Ruby let her glamour fade. For a moment, she looked ancient and furious with her red wings, pointed ears, and golden eyes with vertical pupils. "Mortals are scum." She spat the words.

"Not all of them." My words surprised me. Vampires don't usually stick up for humans.

She sidestepped my palliative observation. "I say we replace all the glass with something that doesn't break."

"Go for it."

"Really? Last time you said it would be too dark in here."

I shrugged. "I'm a Vampire. Dark is where I live."

I grabbed my full-face, metallic-blue helmet off its hook near the bar and straddled the Harley. Its faux engine was already purring. No keys for this bike. No fuel, either. Made it an ideal road companion. Nothing to lose, and no reason to stop. Ever.

"We'll be back by opening time," I told Ruby.

"No rush," she called above the escalating roar of the Harley's engine.

Like I said, Conan has a hell of a good time with his motorcycle imitation. He reminded me of a little boy going vroom-vroom-vroom as he slid a toy truck across the floor.

"Where are we going?" I switched to mind speech.

"Where else? Sheep hunting?"

Aw crap. *"Um, Ruby was only kidding."*

We skidded out the door and made a hard right into the never-ending flood of traffic on Mercy Street. Horns blared. I hunched my shoulders and ignored them. Like I could control Conan even if I tried. The sun was down. Soon it would be full dark. My fangs wanted to drop, but I held them back.

A wild, feral part of me longed for ascendency. I was sick of adapting to the modern world. Fuck all of it. For once—for tonight—it could adapt to me.

An enthusiastic woof deep in my mind told me my wolf was with me 100 percent of the way.

CHAPTER TWO, ARIANA

We wound our way into wooded foothills beyond the Seattle metropolitan area. *Ascent* was located northeast of the city in Kirkland, a suburb east of Lake Washington. I'd flirted with buying a club in Seattle proper, but this was better. Meant I didn't have to deal with the incessant bridge traffic in and out of the city. After a brief stint on a major highway, Conan took to back roads.

I didn't ask again where we were going. Being out of the bar with the wind rushing against me was wonderful. I resented the fuck out of the law that said I had to wear a helmet, but I only resented it at night. During the day, it was essential.

I muffled a snort. Can't have things both ways, and some rules are both blessing and curse. Anyway, the last thing I wanted was for some do-gooder cop to flag us down because my hair was floating in the breeze. My bike wouldn't stand an up-close inspection. And I didn't want to have to answer questions like where the ignition was.

Another niggling point was my registration was forged, and my license plate bogus, but everything looked good. Unless someone ran them through some database or other. If that happened, the jig would be up.

I could just see Conan shifting into something lethal and making short work of a highway patrolman who'd only been doing his job. The wolf and I had had that discussion a time or two, but my puny arguments hadn't exactly convinced him. What would probably end up happening would be I'd exercise a smattering of Vampire mind control, convince whomever that they'd never stopped me, and hope like hell the officer hadn't kept a digital record of my bogus license plate.

If I got really lucky, I could finesse everything before the dude felt threatened enough to pull his gun and shoot me. Not that bullets would make much difference, but they would identify me as an immortal.

We've turned into the enemy in what's starting to look like an all-out war. Granted mortals outnumber us millions to one, but we don't die easily. It gives us somewhat of an edge. Still, concentration camps designed to stymie our power have been cropping up. I helped blow up two in this region—and not all that long ago—but mortals are busy building replacements.

Conan's pace had slowed. I glanced around us at an unbroken vista of evergreens and brushy undergrowth. If ferns aren't Washington's official plant, they should be. We'd been bumping along dirt roads for a while when the wolf pulled to one side. His transitions are fast. One moment, the Harley was between my legs, the next the wolf was.

I kicked my leg over his back and unbuckled my helmet.

"You were serious about hunting," I said.

"You bet I was." He tilted his head, nostrils flaring. "Just smell all that game."

I scented the air. Sure enough, the rich tantalizing smell of blood reached me. Saliva flowed; my fangs dropped. No reason to hide them all the way out here. Conan loped through the trees. We'd find each other. I wasn't concerned about keeping precise tabs on him.

I enjoy hunting when I'm not quite this hungry. My compromise was to crouch and loose a volley of persuasion. Small rodents heeded my call, and I took care to kill them cleanly. Quick. Painless. I made certain they were gone before I fastened my fangs over their vessels and drained them, saving the carcasses for Conan.

Back before humans declared war on those like me, I'd had another option. The government had packaged up pasteurized blood and sold it. No one talked much about what kind of blood—and some batches had been better than others—but that project had died along with the détente between humans and magical creatures.

I took a break from feeding and rolled back onto my haunches. Four rabbits, three squirrels, and a marmot would hold me for now. No reason to run through more than the wolf was likely to eat. Warmth rustled through me. It had been a long while since I'd drunk almost-living blood, and it was so much more satisfying than stuff that had been dead for days, weeks, or maybe years.

There'd been a time when only blood from living, breathing humans would do, but I'd lowered the bar. A lot. I've never been much for turning mortals, though. Frankly, it never made sense to me. It's not like Vamps have ever been welcomed in polite society, and the more of us there are, the stronger the competition for food.

Only about half a century had passed since those with magic declared our emancipation from skulking in shadows. Lots of us—like Witches, for instance—had been convinced it was a horrible idea. We chalked up their worries to them being in the crosshairs at events like Witch trials.

They'd shaken their heads and told us we'd be sorry. Turned out their prophecies had been far more accurate than our Pollyanna vision for a bright future hand in hand with mortals.

Conan sidled close, silent on his large paws. His snout was smeared with blood, and he looked pleased with himself. Without being directed, he bent to the pile I'd left for him.

"What'd you find?" I asked.

"*A young wild pig.*" Because he was busy eating, he switched to telepathy.

Annoyance washed through me. I didn't want to come across as a poor sport or anything, but I couldn't stop myself from asking, "Why didn't you call me. I adore pig."

He crunched down the rabbit hanging from his jaws and tipped his head up. "Not sure what you want to do about this, but I didn't call you because the carcass had already been drained."

It took a moment for the implication to sink in. "By another Vampire?" Disbelieving, I sought confirmation.

"Yes. At first, I wondered if it was a ritual sacrifice. But then, I saw fang marks—and smelled Vampire." He shook himself. "I ate fast and hurried back to tell you."

I opened my mouth to say he should have called me right away, but shut it before I said something I regretted. I hadn't been in any kind of shape to do anything before I'd fed, and the wolf knew it.

I waited until he was done mowing through the pile of dead rodents, and then followed him to where the pig had been. Only bones were left, but I sensed Nosferatu. Not close, but another Vampire had been here.

Contrary to popular belief, there aren't all that many of us, especially not in the States. I've had Vampire acquaintances, but we're never friends in the sense of chatting each other up or sharing meals. Blood has always been a precious commodity. For the same reasons I never made new Vampires, I also wasn't interested in alerting others to my food sources.

"Well?" Conan prodded me with his snout.

"Well, what? You already smelled Nosferatu all over the carcass."

"Are we going to do anything about it?"

I buried a hand in the wolf's thick neck ruff. His outer fur was rough, but beneath, the strands were warm and silky. "If we take time to track the other Vampire, I may not make it back to *Ascent* tonight."

"What's more important?"

I honestly didn't know. It wouldn't be like locating a long-lost relative or something, but I was curious.

"Did you know others from your pack were nearby?" Conan persisted.

I twisted my mouth into a sour expression. No matter how many times I'd explained things, my sidekick viewed the world through his unique lens. In his world, pack was everything. I assumed I'd become his pack only because there weren't any other dire wolves. We'd run across wolf shapeshifters, but they weren't the same as Conan.

They didn't accept him, and he'd snubbed them right back.

The Sorcerer who'd nurtured his magic, coaxed it into full bloom, had told both of us he was special. At the time, it hadn't sunk in how lonely he'd be.

Long years had brought that point home to roost. No wonder the wolf got excited about potential packmates for me. It was as close as he was likely to come to adding to his circle.

"What do you want to do?" I asked. We were a team, and this wasn't only about me.

"Go after the Vampire before the trail grows cold."

I nodded. I'd figured as much. "He may not welcome us, assuming we can find him," I cautioned.

"What makes you so certain it's male? I can't tell from the scent."

Conan's question brought a smile to my face. "I'm not. Shall we?"

I have a good nose, but the wolf is a far superior tracker. I let him take the lead. Beyond not welcoming us, the other Vampire might not let us catch him—or her. Supernatural strength and speed are part of our makeup.

An hour passed. And then another. I got a definite feel for the other Vampire, and he did not want us to catch him. "Hold up," I told Conan.

"Why? We're getting closer." He did stop, flanks heaving, tongue lolling. Much like when he turned into a motorcycle, he was enjoying himself. Wolves lived to hunt, and elusive prey were their favorites. Made the denouement that much sweeter.

I puffed out an unneeded breath, followed by another. They formed clouds in the chilly night air. "Not that much closer. He knows we're after him."

"So? We'll win."

I shook my head. "Nope. We won't. He's playing with us. He just fed, so he doesn't have anything better to do."

Conan tilted his head to one side and regarded me with his amber eyes. "If we leave, we'll never find him."

I held a hand up and projected my voice. "My name is Ariana Hawke. I'm just like you, but you already know that. Supernaturals sticking together is critical now that humans are out to annihilate us. You can find me at *Ascent*. It's a nightclub I own in Kirkland on Mercy Street just past the corner of Warren Way."

I organized my thoughts. No reason to turn this into a soliloquy worthy of Eugene O'Neill. "I'm the only Vampire there," I continued, "but other immortals work for me. I can't say we'll welcome you, but at least you'd be with others like yourself."

Not much more to add, so I turned to Conan. "We can leave now. We've done all we can."

His forehead scrunched in disappointment, but he didn't

argue. We retraced a more direct version of our steps until we returned to the dirt track. "What'll it be?" I asked.

"Can we split the difference?" He understood what I was getting at and sent a hopeful look my way. He hated teleporting—unless he controlled the spell.

"Sure. I'll get us back to the highway, and then you can take over."

He swiped his tongue up my face, starting with my chin. While he was pretending I was a puppy who needed cleaning, I built a hasty spell, visualizing a darkened glade not far from the main road into Kirkland. We'd no sooner touched down than the Harley took shape, engine thrumming.

I kicked a leg over the bike, and we headed for home. Words crowded through my head, but I didn't give voice to any of them. I was sorry Conan was alone, but there wasn't anything either of us could do about it. Unlike wolves, Vampires are the farthest thing from pack creatures on Earth. The only reason we ever formed seethes was so Vamps who'd turned a bunch of minions could keep a close eye on them—and work on empire-building.

"Do you think he'll accept your invitation?" Conan asked.

I tried to put myself in the other Vampire's position. "Uh, probably not."

"I don't understand. He's alone."

"Yup, and he likes it that way." I started to remind the wolf I was dead, same as all my ilk, but I didn't. That part creeped him out. Our partnership was...unusual. If I hadn't rescued him, ensured his survival, we'd never have ended up together.

On the other hand, if he hadn't wanted to be found, I'd have walked right by his hiding place.

That we'd remained together was one of the unsolved mysteries.

We rode the rest of the way back to *Ascent* in silence. The front of the nightclub was crowded with a glut of cars and motorcycles, so we went around the back. The booming beat of raucous music—heavy on bass—thumped against my ears. It was only about half an hour from closing time, but it appeared the club had had a prosperous night despite the ugly chunk of plywood plastered over the broken pane. I hoped someone had called a construction company and gotten on tomorrow's schedule.

A quick flick of magic twisted the deadbolt and safety bar locking the back door; they snicked open. We rolled inside, but the wolf was changing even before we cleared the lintel. The feel of living flesh, warm and furry, was more satisfying than the illusion of metal and leather, but I knew the rules.

I only got to ride the bike, so I swung a leg over the wolf's side, landing lightly on my feet as I sent still more magic to shut and lock the door. The storeroom was dark, but I could see fine. So could Conan.

"I'm going to check on everything," I told him.

He stuck his muzzle into my armpit; I raised my arm and draped it around his neck. "I will be here until people leave this place," he told me.

"I know you will." I scratched his head. While I

appreciated his watchful eyes—and threatening teeth—I didn't need a bodyguard, but I'd never tell him that. For one thing, I didn't want to hurt his feelings. For another, I valued his loyalty.

I'd learned a lot from my years with the wolf. He's softened some of my less savory Vampire traits, taught me how to care and be cared for in return. Hard to say which of us has benefited more from our association, but I suspected the winner was me.

I laid my head alongside his and held him close, breathing in the clean, animal scent that always clung to him. We stood like that for a few moments before I crossed to the small sink in a corner of the storeroom. I did flip on a light then and took a quick peek at my face.

Yup. Blood had worked into the corners of my mouth, and flecks dotted my cheeks and chin. I wetted a rag and cleaned myself up while encouraging my fangs to retreat. Once I was decent, I hung my jacket over a hook, double-checked my clothes weren't bloody, and headed for the door leading into *Ascent*.

If the music had been loud on the other side of the stout door, it was deafening in the club. My ears are far more acute than mortal ears, so I spaded a bit of magic over them. A quick glance told me we'd exceeded the fire department's maximum capacity tacked beneath my business license. Both official documents sat under glass near the front door.

What the hell?

It was a Tuesday night. Why would we be this crowded? We never drew crowds like this unless it was a weekend and we were hosting a popular musical group. A closer look revealed mostly mortals—except for my staff.

I walked through the swinging partition that led to the order prep area and busied myself filling drink requests. Ruby and Dee had their hands full. "Hey. You're back!" Ruby shouted over the din.

"*I am.*" Mind speech worked ever so much better under these conditions.

She picked up on my cue. "*You were gone a while. Did you come across anything unusual?*"

"*You might say so, but we'll talk later.*"

Dee nudged me. "Hiya, boss! Busy night." Black hair in a geometric cut framed her stark cheekbones. Olive skin, black eyes, and pronounced bone structure confirmed her Native heritage. Medium height, she was thin with ropy muscles that hinted she might be stronger than she appeared. Ragged jeans and a red T-shirt emblazoned with a Witch on a broom and the words, "My Other Car Is..." covered her lean frame.

A necromancer, she was a Witch who dealt with the dead. It was a long-running joke between us that centered on me being dead and her frustration at her inability to exert even the slightest control over me.

Except she'd known from the beginnings of her power that Vampires were way outside her wheelhouse. Hence, the joke. We thought it was a hoot, but I was certain mortals wouldn't appreciate it.

"Any idea why we're so full?" I slapped two Singapore slings on the bar and a shot glass of rum.

"Yeah. *The RoughShod* got shot up a couple of hours ago. We ended up with their customers as well as our own."

My eyes widened. *The Roughshod* was a bar one block down. It catered to a slightly different crowd. Worry slithered through me. "*Shot up by whom?*" I was back to telepathy.

"*Two rival bike gangs.*"

It explained all the motorcycles crammed in front of *Ascent*.

"*Don't look so worried, boss,*" Dee went on. "*Percy checked everyone at the door, and we have a passel of guns locked in the side room. Knives too and brass knuckles.*"

Annoyance joined my concern. This was precisely why I didn't encourage the outlaw bike clubs to frequent *Ascent*. I tried to create an atmosphere that was too tame for their liking. Not that motorcycle gangs had a corner on the violence market, but I'd been more than happy when they preferred *Roughshod* over my place.

Percy, my bouncer, shut off the music. Before conversations could drown him out, he shouted, "Closing time. Finish your drinks." The music started up again.

Nearly seven feet tall, Percy was built like a tank. An old-world Sorcerer, he had power to burn and could back up his imposing physique with magic if he had to. So far, it hadn't come to that. People took one look at him and decided to do what he said. Bald, blue-eyed, and garbed in a tartan and a linen shirt, he might have dropped in from an earlier era. One I and the rest of my staff remembered, but my patrons probably assumed Percy had crafted his unique appearance after watching too many *Highlander* movies.

I kept an eagle eye on the line of departing customers, breathing easier as they shuffled out the door. Percy had them line up so he could return their weapons. My jaw gaped at the variety—and sheer numbers—of firearms and knives. We may have lost a window tonight, but it could have been ever so much worse.

"What happened?" Ruby tossed glasses in the sink, adding a flush of magic to the mix as she washed them.

"Did something happen?" Dee glanced from one to the other of us as she capped liquor bottles. "I thought we got off clean tonight."

"We did," I assured her.

"We're closed," Percy bellowed in his no-nonsense voice. The one imbued with compulsion no mortal could disregard.

"Save it for the sheep," a rough male voice growled. "The lady invited me."

I vaulted over the bar. No reason to hide my athletic ability from my staff. They all knew about me. Somewhere between calling mortals sheep and his comment about being invited, I knew who had to be pushing his way past Percy.

"It's all right," I told the Sorcerer. "I did invite him."

Although I had no idea it was a him.

The Vampire sort of oozed through the door in a flood of nacre-and-black-tinged magic. Feet planted shoulder width apart, he raked me with his green eyes. Copper hair swept back from a high forehead and spilled down his back in a cascade of waves. About my height, he had impossibly broad shoulders, narrow hips, and long legs encased in beige khaki pants. A black linen shirt covered his torso, and his feet were laced into scuffed brown boots. Like many male Vampires, he was so beautiful, it was hard to look at him. Movie-star good looks coupled with Vampiric power were an impossible combination to resist.

As the other Vamp took me in, probably searching his memory to see if we'd ever met before, he shifted to full Vampire knock-your-socks-off presence. He smiled, displaying fangs.

"I'll save you the trouble," I barked. "We've never met, and you can reel in your compulsion. It won't work on me."

"You belong with your own kind," he said flatly. "I'm here to escort you to more appropriate surroundings."

"Um yeah. I don't think so."

He'd never shut off his persuasion; its focus narrowed to me and me alone. I kept my feet right where they were, but it wasn't as easy as I'd have liked.

"I outrank you," he said. "We're leaving."

No one's ordered me to do anything for centuries. I forgot about being polite and stripped off the gloves. When I opened my mouth, I felt the press of fangs against my lower lip.

"The only one leaving would be you," I said flatly.

"You invited me. You cannot refuse me."

I made a rude sound. "Watch me."

Meanwhile, Ruby, Dee, Percy, and the three waitresses— a coyote shifter and two Fae—formed a line between me and Vampire No-Name. I felt rather than saw the magical shield they erected.

"Whoever turned you left out essential lessons." The other Vampire spun on his heel, clearly intent on leaving.

"Not quite yet." I employed compulsion of my own. "I have questions."

"What if I don't have answers?" he shot back without turning around.

"We'll see," I said and wove my magic in with Percy's and Dee's. Between all of it, the Vampire stepped in a jerky circle until he faced me again. He was so reluctant, his boots gouged my wooden floor.

"That's better," I purred. "Let's get a few things straight. Vampires haven't endorsed a hierarchy in several hundred years. Why the hell would you believe you outrank anyone?"

CHAPTER THREE, ARIANA

*F*unny what you look for. I searched for bloodstains while I waited for him to come up with an answer but didn't find any.

Conan padded into the bar, growling, as he strode to my side. "That's him," he said, totally unnecessarily.

The other Vampire's eyes widened. "So you were what I sensed out there."

The wolf growled louder. Hackles raised the length of his back and across his shoulders.

"I'm guessing he's the mystery thing that happened while you were gone." Ruby jerked her thumb at the newcomer.

"Yeah. I knew it was another Vamp, but that was about it. Until now."

Conan glided closer to the Vampire, snuffling like a mushroom-sniffing pig.

"That's it, wolfie." The Vampire sank into a crouch and opened his arms. "Come to Daddy."

I almost told Conan not to get too close, but he could take care of himself without input from me. Plus, he'd lived with a Vampire his entire life. I was confident he was more than a match for the smiling Nosferatu with his arms spread wide.

The dire wolf's unique blend of magic sheeted from him. Where he'd stood, a reddish jackal squatted on its haunches, sharp teeth showing as he chittered and snarled.

The Vampire nearly fell over. He scrambled upright to mask his shock. "What other tricks can you do, mate?" he muttered. Before he'd sounded sort of American, but the question betrayed Scottish roots.

I positioned myself next to Conan. "He's capable of infinite forms. Two questions, and then you're free to leave."

"I'm free to leave now." He fixed me with a stare that had no doubt obliterated hundreds of mortals' free will.

I rolled my eyes and raised an arm, index finger extended. "Sorcerer. Fae. Fae. Fae. Witch. Shifter," I said as I pointed to who owned each type of magic. "If you think you're a match for them all, have at it."

His eyes might have widened fractionally, but we Vamps are masters at concealing our emotions. Ha. That would presume we had any, which most of us don't. If it hadn't been for Conan, I'd be just as oblivious and uncaring as the rest of my kinsmen.

People have muttered about Vampires pissing ice water forever—and with good reason.

I gave the fact my "guest" was outnumbered and outgunned a moment to sink in. He could probably teleport out of *Ascent*. Maybe. Percy might be able to stop him, but I wasn't certain of it.

"For starters," I said conversationally, "I gave you my name back in the woods. What's yours?"

"Hawke, right?" At my nod, he went on, "Are you affiliated with Clan Hawke from Cornwall?"

"Aye, that I am," I reverted to the British accent that's never entirely left me. "Vampires broke away from our clan affiliations two hundred years ago, though."

"Some Vampires."

Breath hissed through my teeth. "Your name. Now."

"If the lady insists." A rakish grin made him even more stunning.

Conan chittered and shrieked in jackal-ese, no doubt telling him to get on with things. Perhaps missing the extended vocal range he had as a wolf, he shifted back.

"Damn, he's quick," Ruby murmured.

"Ya think?" Selene, the coyote shifter, shook her head. Strawberry curls bounced around her shoulders. Petite, with the same russet coloring and brown eyes she had as a coyote, she stared adoringly at Conan. Something about the dire wolf was irresistible. Even more so than a Vampire in full prey-mode.

I clapped my hands smartly together. "Focus, people."

I moved closer to the other Vampire. "Ariana from Clan Hawke requests the pleasure of your name." My appeal was formal and couched in terms no Vampire should be able to refuse. We may not have much of a social structure, but once upon a time, we did maintain a hierarchy of sorts.

He inclined his head. "Finally. One of us remembers better times. I am Nickolas Giovanni."

I didn't bother masking my surprise. "Clan Giovanni vanished at the front end of the 1600s."

"We wished others to believe so."

I pressed my lips into a tight line. "Are the other two clans are still active?"

"Is Clan Hawke?" He answered my question with one of his own.

"Not that I know of. Until we ran cross you earlier, I was certain I was the only Vampire on the West Coast."

"But surely, Clan Hawke remains in Cornwall or the Carpathian region...?" Nickolas pressed.

I shrugged. "Not in Cornwall. I left the Carpathians a long time ago. Never went back."

The four Vampire clans consisted of Tremere, Ravnos, Giovanni, and Hawke. I hadn't thought about any of them in forever. "Even when we organized into seethes based on clan affiliation," I said, "all we ever did was fight each other over territory."

"We did a wee bit more than that. Blood was plentiful. Mortals feared us—"

"Hold up right there." I punched the air in front of me for emphasis. I was pretty sure I knew where Nickolas was heading with this. "Just so we're clear. I have less than zero interest in returning to the way things used to be. I left Sibiu with no intention of ever returning. In case you missed it, we don't like each other. You're nothing but competition for limited food."

He furled copper brows. "Then why did you tell me where to find you? I assumed you wanted to renew your acquaintance with your own kind."

"Assumptions are like assholes. Everyone has one." I narrowed my eyes. "I told you who I was and where I work for two reasons. Conan and I could have stayed out there all night tracking you. It was wasted time; we'd never have located you."

"And the second reason?" Nickolas crooked two fingers my way.

"You may have missed it, but humans have declared war on immortals. Now is a time for us to stick together regardless of what kind of magic we wield."

The shock rolling across his even features was genuine, and immediate. Quite a show of emotion from a Vampire. "But we have never worked with anyone outside our own ranks," he protested.

"Speak for yourself," I retorted. "I have the answers I need. You're free to go."

"Just like that?"

"Yup. Just like that. It's been a long night."

Conan had moved to my side and stood with his shoulder pressing into my arm.

"I have a question before he goes," Ruby spoke up.

"Go." I nodded her way.

"Are you by yourself?"

I offered her kudos. It was something I should have thought to ask.

Nickolas hesitated for so long, Percy dropped a truth net over him, not even trying for subtle. The Vampire hissed with displeasure but didn't attempt to dismantle the weave. Perhaps he realized its magic was beyond him.

"Apparently, that question was too hard," I said. "Let's spin it this way. How many other Vampires are with you?"

"Two."

"We didn't smell them." Conan head-butted my side.

Nickolas shrugged. "Not my problem."

"Where exactly are your compatriots?" I asked, almost certain they had to be some distance from where he'd drained the pig.

"What difference would it make if you knew?" He held his ground, standing straighter.

Conan growled, a low vibration that set my teeth on edge and made me glad he was on my side. I replayed Nickolas's seeming surprise when I'd mentioned the war with mortals.

Settling my hands on my hips, I frowned. "You didn't know about mortals targeting us, did you?" After a brief hesitation, he shook his head.

"How could you not know?" Ruby demanded. She'd dropped her glamour, and her red wings quivered with indignation. "We're all in danger—unless we come out swinging and kill every mortal who crosses our path."

"It won't help," Percy's deep voice rumbled. "I don't fancy watching my backside for the next fifty years. Whole lotta humans out there. More than enough to make us heartily sick of killing."

"Fifty years wouldn't make a dent," Ruby muttered and

sent a pointed look at Christa, one of the other Fae who worked at *Ascent*. She'd dropped her glamor as well and looked even more alien than Ruby with silver wings dappled in jewel tones. Her skin was dusky, her eyes milky white. When I'd first met her, I'd assumed she was blind, and she was—in human terms. Christa assessed the world through her psychic senses, which were far sharper than my own.

Dressed in the goth garb she favored, black garments swathed her tall, spare frame. Bronze earrings dangled from many ear piercings, and impossibly high glittery heels added to her height. Never mind they didn't match the goth motif at all. Curly black hair tumbled halfway down her back.

Christa gave an almost imperceptible headshake. If I hadn't been looking right at her, I'd have missed it. I made come along motions with one hand. "Spill. What did you see in your mirror?"

Christa glanced skyward. "It's not a mirror. I'm scarcely the wicked queen in Snow White. And nothing certain."

"But you saw something," I persisted. "You're a seer for chrissakes."

Conan walked to her and nuzzled her shoulder, offering encouragement. She sank her long-nailed fingers—sporting black nail polish—into his rough outercoat.

"It doesn't look good," she offered up after a lengthy pause.

Yeah. Tell me something I didn't already know. I didn't want to take the time to dredge more out of her. It was pushing three in the morning. Nights were my playtime, but everyone else needed to get some sleep.

Besides, we were getting off track.

Nickolas looked from one to the other of us almost as if he hadn't seen an immortal other than a Vampire in a long while. I took a stab at getting closer to the truth. "You've been in stasis, haven't you?"

He nodded slowly. "Just woke a week or so ago."

"I've heard about that," Percy said, "but I didn't realize you could control coming out of it." The Sorcerer was looking at me, not the other Vampire.

"Stasis has a few different options," I told him. "In this instance, I bet they set a rough time clock, but the shortest option is something like twenty years."

"We've been in hiding for over a hundred," Nick said.

"Why?" Ruby asked.

"Why would you think?" he countered. "We were under attack. I and two others traveled to the western regions of North America intent on...augmenting our clan with fresh energy. Hadn't been here long before dark Sorcerers hounded us. We tried many things to dissuade them, but they were intent on our blood for ritualistic pursuits. Stasis was a last resort, not one I would have chosen willingly."

"I see," Ruby murmured.

Nickolas set his mouth in a tense line. "Appears to have worked. The bastards haven't come after us."

"Like I said," I cut in, "until you showed up, I haven't seen another Vampire in a very long time. If you've been out of commission for so long, why that whole song and dance about reuniting me with my own kind?"

Percy apparently decided the truth spell wasn't needed, so he withdrew it. Nick stood straighter. I wasn't sure if the vote of confidence heartened him or pissed him off. Or if he just didn't care.

"A while back, you said we were done," he countered. "I'll be on my way."

Anger flashed through me, and I sprang to a position between him and the door with the wolf by my side. "I asked you a question."

He shrugged. "Coming here was a mistake. I misread your invitation."

"If you assumed I needed saving, then you did, indeed." An idea socked me in the midsection, and I jabbed an index finger his way. "You're the Master for Clan Giovanni. You assumed you'd drag me into your seethe."

A muscle beneath one of his eyes twitched. Beyond that, his expression could have been etched in granite. When he spoke, his words held a stiff, formal tone. "I was planning to extend you the *honor*"—he stressed the word—"of offering you a place with my kin."

He was serious as sin, and I should have just walked away. Instead, I burst out laughing. In between gales of mirth, I managed to squawk, "What? You think I was just turned? That I don't know better?"

Before I got myself under control, the air around him took on a liquid, glistening aspect. "Do you want me to hold him here?" Percy asked.

"Nope. Good riddance." I dusted my hands together about the time Nick vanished from the room.

"What the hell did you say wherever you found him?" Ruby demanded.

"Yeah. Inquiring minds want to know," Dee chimed in. "From the looks of things, you offered up hot sex."

"Meh. Mostly, I wanted him to know this was a haven for immortals." I blew out a tight, totally unnecessary breath. "So much for trying to be kind and supportive."

"I don't care if he just woke up. How could he not know about the war?" Percy mumbled and started chucking chairs on tables. The cleaning crew would show up around six in the morning.

"Where are the other two?" Conan circled back to the problem that bothered him. Why we hadn't smelled them.

"Obviously, a long way from where we were," I told the wolf.

His upper lip twitched in the beginning of a snarl as he muttered, "Tell me something I haven't already figured out on my own."

"What was so funny?" Ruby trotted nearer, with Dee so close they could have been glued together.

I was still chuckling. Vampire humor was never funny to anyone else, but I tried to explain anyway. "He played the oldest card in the deck. Tried to convince me he was doing me a favor when his seethe has been out of commission forever. It would have been closer to the truth if he'd said his clan needed an infusion of Vampires and asked for my help."

"What happened to yours?" Ruby asked quietly, tacking, "Your clan," onto the end of her sentence on the off chance I hadn't understood her.

"You never talk about them," Dee added.

"Observant of you." I toned down the acid laced into my words. "I don't talk about them for good reasons, and I'm not going to start now. I left my clan to keep Conan safe—among other things—and never looked back. The world has changed since then. A whole lot. Clan Hawke isn't around anymore. Not in the way they used to be, but that's true of all Vampires. I blame it on mortals. Even before the two big wars, bands of them fancied themselves Vampire hunters and went after us like we were prize game trophies."

I stopped long enough to take a superfluous breath, hoping it would mitigate the outrage turning my blood molten. "We call ourselves immortal, but there are ways to kill all of us. Nothing like standing in the dirt looking at heads that used to belong to a man you loved or a woman you called friend."

Ruby patted my arm. "It's okay, Ari."

"Yeah. No need to tell us more," Dee said.

"It is not okay." I could barely get the words out. My fangs had dropped. That more than anything told me my emotions were on the edge of spiraling out of control. I couldn't let that happen. If it did, I was likely to bolt out the door and jump the first mortal who crossed my path.

It sounded like a wonderful idea. Night still reigned, and I know how to kill. Quick. Clean. Quiet. None of this making-new-Vampires crap. Whoever designed that system had shit for brains.

Before I did something I was sorry for, I made shooing motions with both hands. "Go home. We're done for tonight. Did someone call a glass company?"

"You agreed to replace the windows with something that wouldn't break," Ruby reminded me.

"So I did. Well, did you call someone?"

She nodded. "Yeah. A contractor. It won't be as quick as dropping a new window in, but he promised to show up tomorrow around ten to bid the job."

"I'll be here to let him in," Percy assured me.

The corners of my mouth almost, almost formed a smile, but not quite. At least the fury ripping through me was subsiding. "Try not to scare the dude half to death," I cautioned.

"Thought I'd borrow Conan," Percy said, deadpan. "Between the two of us—"

"Anyone would go running for cover," I cut in.

"Do you want to take care of it?" One of Percy's black-and-silver brows shot up, forming a question mark.

"That would be a no. I'd have to be all covered up. The dude would peg me as a junkie or victim of some dread disease."

"Eh, you don't look all that bad in daylight," Ruby said. "A wee bit on the pale side..."

The tension that had been thick as thieves in the room frittered to nothing as my colleagues left in small groups chatting among themselves. After checking the plywood, I added a layer of magic to make it more tamperproof and double-checked the drop bar that locked the front door. I sealed it in its cradle more securely, adding magic for good measure. Usually, I'm not this paranoid, but Nickolas was like as not the master over Clan Giovanni. He hadn't denied it earlier. Regardless, he knew about *Ascent* now, and I did not want to show up here tomorrow to find he'd moved a critical mass of Vampires into my club.

He'd mentioned two associates, but where there were two, there could be more.

Conan padded after me as I restocked the booze, tossed empty bottles and cans into recycling bins, and dragged everything to a collection site at the end of the alley. I rarely spent time thinking about my Vampire beginnings, but something about my exchange with Nickolas brought everything roaring back.

The horror.

The fear.

The unbelievable, unrelenting pressure to drink from my own master. I didn't want to think about Mistral—hadn't given him any airtime in centuries, but there he was, front and center in my mind.

All of it. How he'd lied to me, seduced me, made me believe he loved me... But I'm getting way ahead of myself. If I was going to do this, I'd damn well do it in order, and then I'd bury the whole mess back where I'd kept it all this time.

Nothing in those memories but pain. Vampires are supposed to be immune from it—in every form, physical and mental—but I never was. I don't perseverate over shit like I did as a human, but neither did my propensity to spin events a million ways entirely disappear.

Isn't that the way of it, though? The things you wish would quit plaguing you never truly do. Mistral told me I was lucky.

Breath steamed from my teeth, making clouds in the chill night air. I don't have to breathe, but I like to. There's something comforting about it, something normal. Funny the things that are tough to let go of, even after more years than I can count. I dumped the last load of bottles in the glass recycling bin and walked down the alley.

Conan stuck to my side through every transit from club to dumpster and back, and I was grateful for his not-so-simple animal presence. Even if someone was considering fucking with me, the wolf was quite the deterrent.

I was almost back to *Ascent*, thinking about how Mistral had been the lucky one—even though he was permanently dead—when three thugs melted out of the shadows with Roger squarely in their midst.

"We have a score to settle. Bitch," one of the men said.

I glanced from one to the other. They were built like Roger: big, burly, fat, and out of shape. I caught the flash of brass knuckles and laughed.

"You won't be laughing when we're done," Roger sneered.

Deciding they weren't worth wasting words on, I flashed out a high side kick, courtesy of martial arts training, and connected with the man who'd called me a bitch. I felt his shoulder dislocate and kicked his useless arm to make sure it stayed out of joint. My reward was an outraged yelp as he barreled toward me.

Conan leapt on Roger, driving him to the ground.

"Don't kill him," I cautioned.

"Don't ruin my fun." With a deep, guttural growl that should have made any human's blood turn to ice, Conan closed his jaws over Roger's upper arm. I heard the bone snap and a shrill, pain-laden shriek before I settled in with my victim. Man number three was nowhere in sight.

What a craven fool. Willing to fuck with a woman, but

only if he figured he'd prevail. Yup. Roger definitely ran with the winners. When I was done with him, he'd be crippled and out of a job.

My fangs wanted out, but I kept them under wraps. No reason to reveal myself. If I did, I'd have no choice but to kill both these bozos—or turn their brains to mush. I could blow off steam without exposing what I was.

CHAPTER FOUR, ARIANA

The man bucked and heaved beneath me. I'm sure he couldn't figure out how I held him down with so little effort, and I wasn't about to give away any secrets. I may have resented the fuck out of being turned, but there were a whole bunch of parts of being a Vampire that I'd come to value.

Strength and speed sat at the top of the list. Immortality ran a close third.

Taking my time, I pushed on his other shoulder, keeping up the pressure until I felt ligaments and tendons rip. A high, thin shriek of pain was followed by him twisting his head and burying his teeth in my lower arm. I gripped his jaw and forced his teeth apart, moving my arm out of reach. He did not want to drink from me.

Vampire blood would make him crazy. Crazier than he already was.

Drinking from those like me only works if we've already drained our victims.

"Fuck you, you goddamned slut," he screeched. "How'd you do that? What kind of fucking black martial arts voodoo is that?"

I smiled sweetly and hoped to hell my fangs were behaving. I couldn't feel them, but it didn't mean they hadn't begun to erupt. A side-handed slice finished off his other shoulder. He yelped.

"Ready to give up?" I inquired.

Conan joined me and growled at my victim. "Good boy," I said cheerily. "Ready for another one?"

"I—I fucking quit." The man spat bloody phlegm from his mouth. It bubbled on his lips where remnants of my blood ate holes in his flesh. He'd wonder why his mouth looked as if someone had come at him with a burning cigarette butt.

Conan snarled, upping the ante. My wolf was quite the bully boy at heart.

"Alrighty," I purred. "I'm going to get up. And then you are going to hightail it out of here and never return. Do we have an agreement?"

He nodded once, terse and curt. A quick scan of his thoughts reinforced he couldn't wait to get away from me. I rocked back on my heels and rolled to my feet all in one relatively fluid motion.

The man had a hell of a time getting up since his arms were useless. Finally, he turned onto his belly and sort of figured things out from there. I could have helped—it would have hurried his egress—but I didn't want to make things easy for him.

Grunting from what must have been agony shooting through both shoulders, he shambled down the alley at something approximating a trot. Roger lay sprawled on the ground, his limbs at crazy, unnatural angles, but there's not much honor among bastards. His buddy didn't give him so much has a backward glance.

Roger lay face down. I nudged him in the ribs with a boot. He groaned. Fine. He'd get up at some point. I squatted in front of him and got hold of a hank of hair. Once I'd lifted his head out of a pool of vomit, I said, "Listen, and listen good. You will never come back here. If you do, what happened to you tonight will look like child's play. Got it?"

He cracked one blood-crusted eye open and glared at me. I gave his head a shake for good measure. "I asked you a question."

When he didn't answer, I dropped his head and stood. I'd said what I needed to. He'd been warned. I was partway down the alley when he rasped, "You're one of them supernaturals. Gonna turn you in."

The laughter I'd been sitting on ever since his ridiculous attempt at an attack burst out of me. Once I could talk, I said, "Yeah? How's that going to go for you? You planning to tell the authorities you stalked me—a woman alone—because I caught you skimming from my business? If anyone's going to be turning someone in, I'd say this cuts the other way. I already spoke with them, but your employer will hear from me again come morning."

I slipped my phone from a pocket and took a quick picture of him. Proof if I needed it. And then, I thought better of my bravado. Last thing I needed was a tussle with the special ops forces every branch of law enforcement has formed to hunt down paranormal creatures. Bending over him, I dropped a hand on his head and shot a sloppy burst of magic through his brain. He'd forget a whole lot. All of tonight, and probably the previous few days.

Pfft. He was lucky I didn't kill him. I would have if I hadn't called in my shortage problems to his employer. Between that and his corpse near my club, I'd be a prime suspect for questioning. Better for everyone to think he drank away what was left of his brain.

I walked backward, keeping an eye on him. He'd just pushed to a sit when Conan and I turned into *Ascent's* back door. I slid it shut and threw both the deadbolt and the drop bar.

"Thanks for not killing him," I told Conan.

"I know the rules," he said, sounding hurt. "You considered it. Before you fried his mind."

"I did." No point lying to the wolf.

"What stopped you?" Conan tilted his head to one side.

I shut my eyes for a long minute. When I opened them I said, "Too many potential problems. We couldn't have left his body so near the club. If we'd moved it, we'd have risked him leaving DNA in my car. Plus, it's too close to daylight for me to go traipsing around the city with a dead body in tow."

Conan growled and raised a few hackles. "He doesn't deserve to live."

"Yup. I know."

At least the wolf didn't go off on a tirade about how stupid modern laws were. It was one point where we were in total and absolute agreement. My first stop was the sink where I scrubbed my hands and face, rinsing blood off them. I'm picky about my food, and I wouldn't have dined on Roger or Mr. No-Name-Thug if they'd been the last two humans on Earth.

By the time I was drying my hands on paper towels, Conan had laid down on the wooden floor and was regarding me, head cocked to one side. "Ready to go home?" I asked him and waited.

Sometimes he stayed at *Ascent*. Hell, sometimes I did too, but I wanted a spot where I didn't have to watch my back. Roger might be out of commission, but by the time I'd understood I needed to obliterate his memory, the other dudes were long gone. They were wild cards at this point. I had no idea what they'd do, especially once they figured out Roger's brain had turned to pablum.

I wasn't worried about bluffing my way through a visit from the local cops. They all knew me and appreciated that I ran a tight ship, one not requiring their intervention. Unlike the biker bar down the way that had erupted into a gunfight earlier this evening.

RoughShod had been a perennial problem for the Kirkland PD. I'd heard them complain about it more than once. Yeah, the local cops weren't the issue. It was the paranormal special ops dudes I worried about.

"Well?" I asked Conan.

He stretched out his front legs and got up. I took it as a

yes-I'm-ready-to-go gesture. He didn't show any signs of turning into the Harley, so I started patching a teleport spell together.

"Why not take the car?" He pricked his ears forward.

"We can do that," I agreed and snatched up a set of keys from a board on the far wall. My black Toyota 4-Runner was parked in front, straddling a no-parking zone. Like I said, the cops like me, and it was the best place to leave my car where it wouldn't be bothered.

I cracked the back door and followed the wolf through, locking it behind us. The night air was welcome, cool and damp. Morning wasn't far off, which meant we had to get moving. A quick transit of the block brought us to the front of my building; I hit the clicker to unlock the hatch. Conan jumped inside. I followed him, but courtesy of the driver door. A few clicks and pushes, and the hatch slithered down. The wolf was uncharacteristically quiet, but he'd tell me what he was thinking eventually.

Not much traffic at four in the morning. I started on the freeway and then traded it for winding streets into foothills to the east of Kirkland. We made decent time and were home in about forty minutes.

"Going hunting," the wolf said when I opened the hatch for him.

I wrapped an arm around his neck and gave him a quick hug before he melted into what was left of the night. From long habit, I sent power spiraling outward. Satisfied no one had been here, I redirected my magic to carve through wards around my home. Not much reason to lock anything.

Unwanted company would be sliced to ribbons by my elaborate system of protections.

I'd had this place built to my specifications over fifty years before. Buried in a thick evergreen forest at the end of a long, bumpy road riddled with potholes, it didn't exactly scream "welcome stranger." To anyone.

I got my mail at *Ascent*, and insofar as I knew, the address for my home had escaped inclusion in any database.

I'd had to wipe a few memories once the house was finished, but it was a small price to pay for privacy—and silence. One of my requirements was no one talked about my home to anyone. Impossible to enforce over the long haul; ergo the memory eradication. Lucky I'd had the place built before the digital age took off. No handy cell phones to snap photos in those days.

Built of wood and stone with very small windows, it reminded me of crumbling manor houses dotting the Old County. A raised veranda ran the length and breadth of the house, and it had a full basement. Critical for those rare days when sunlight filtered through the trees and made me uncomfortable.

I walked inside, inhaling the scents of wood and leather and wax. Wood from a fireplace and leather from shelves and shelves of ancient books. Wax from the candles I favored for light. I had my own library, gathered through the long years of my life, and it was more precious to me than almost anything.

Except Conan.

The books and scrolls and the wolf had been the only constants of my existence. They'd been enough to keep me from falling into the pit most long-lived Vampires succumb to. The one where all they think about is blood. I like to believe I haven't become a ruthless, heartless motherfucker, but I could be deluding myself.

Not killing Roger had been a struggle. The only thing stopping me had been the logistics of hiding what I'd done. Conan had been absolutely right about that piece of scum taking up too much air.

More laggardly than usual, the door finally swung shut. Residual magic powered it, and it knew to close once I was inside. It would open again for Conan when he returned.

The main floor of my house is one large room with a bedroom and bath at the far end. They have doors, but they're the only two inside my abode. I do have a kitchen; it gets very little use. I can eat if I choose, but regular food holds scant appeal. I lit a fire in the grate the old-fashioned way. Once it caught, I walked to the bathroom, kicking off clothes as I went. I'd pick up the mess sometime before I went to work tonight.

After running a bath, I sat in the tub as it filled. Antique and made of copper, it was luxurious by today's standards. I'd found it moldering at the back of a used furniture shop. It had a few dents, but nothing held heat quite as well as copper. I didn't shut off the taps until water licked my chin. Silence settled around me, soothing in its own way.

Something was bothering Conan, but I'd never drag it out of him. Not until he was ready to talk. Maybe Roger's threat had struck a chord—and his compatriots were running around free—but we'd been living on borrowed time forever.

Sooner or later, supernaturals would have to fight back.

We'd lose—because there were so many mortals—but the war would drag on for centuries. A line from an old song about not counting the dead when you had god on your side stuck in my head.

God was a joke. There was no such thing, at least not for Vampires or Fae or Shifters or Sorcerers. Not in the way humans envisioned a deity. Plenty of gods exist. All the pantheons are replete with them, but they're living, breathing—unlike me—people. I've met a few over the years of my life. Liked some better than others. Regardless, in the wake of full-out war, the tally sheet of dead mortals would be long and grim. Killing didn't bother me, but mowing through the weak for nothing rankled.

I tipped my head back and washed my hair with a mint-vanilla shampoo that I love and then got out of the tub. It would be full daylight by now, but neither my bedroom nor bath had windows. The contractor had argued with me when I was building the place. I'm sure he thought I was some sort of crackpot.

A few rolls in the hay had shut him up. He'd have stayed with me forever after that, courtesy of vampiric magnetism, but I'd chased him away along with everyone else. Soon as the place had been signed off on, no one remembered anything about any of it. Not the planning. Not the building.

I'd devoted a few nights to tracking everyone down. Conan helped locate one or two elusive roofers. In the end, once I was certain we'd gotten to everyone, I'd breathed a metaphorical sigh of relief. I was far more careful with those workmen than I'd been with Roger. I took my time and plucked specific memories. They'd have wondered where the last month went, but they'd get over it. And I'd paid in cash. It saved me a few bucks and ensured there wouldn't be a paper trail.

I chuckled. My seemingly unending bundles of hundred-dollar bills must have made me look like a mob boss —or a drug dealer.

Out of the tub, I wrapped one towel around my hair and another around my body. My phone trilled from the spot I'd dropped my jacket, and I hustled to it, interested to see who was calling. It was still quite early by human standards. Supernaturals keep odd hours. Most of us require very little sleep, or none at all.

By the time I located my coat and then the phone, it had quit ringing. When I stared at the display, it obligingly told me the call had come from a private number.

Mental eye roll.

Nearly everyone I know has private numbers. We all carry a love-hate relationship with modern contrivances, and cell phones are the absolute worst. Only reason I kept mine on at all was in case someone needed me at *Ascent*. And the closest I've come to guilt-tripping my staff into keeping theirs on is while they're actually at work.

No one wants to be bothered during their personal time.

It's added to my scheduling woes since if someone can't make a shift, I have a hell of a hard time reaching potential fill-ins. I narrowed my eyes at the phone, willing the message indicator to ding.

It didn't.

Fine. Couldn't have been that important.

I plugged the phone into its charger and walked into my

bedroom, shutting the door behind me. Muted light was trickling into the house. Not enough to bother me, but I preferred none at all. I could have sealed the shutters, but this was simpler.

Simple sounded pretty damned good about now.

Paneled in imported cherrywood, my bedroom is lovely, soothing, personal. Antique carved furniture lines the walls, including the bedframe, three dressers, and two armoires. I lit a brass-and-porcelain kerosene lamp, enjoying the play of its glow reflecting off the wood.

The altercation with Roger had spiraled out of control, not because of me, but because he was a self-righteous dick who didn't like to lose. I wasn't too worried about his friend spilling the beans. Roger wouldn't remember anything, and it would make the other fellow's story a much harder sell.

Unless Thug-Number-Three got into the act. He could corroborate whatever the dude with the dislocated shoulders had to say.

I hung my towels on hooks and dragged an old faded T-shirt over my head. Soft and comfortable, it hit me mid-thigh. Another sideline benefit of being a Vampire is I don't get cold. The fire I'd lit in the main room was for ambience, not heat. Eventually, I'd wander out there, close the shutters, and add wood to my dying fire. Maybe I'd pour myself a glass of wine.

My bed beckoned; I sank into its many layers of feather mattresses, pulling a cozy duvet over myself. Kind of like with the copper tub, no one had ever improved on ticking stuffed to the brim with a mix of duck and goose feathers.

Contrary to popular beliefs, Vampires do not cart their coffins around to sleep in.

Who the fuck knows how those rumors get started and then grow until they become urban myths. Maybe it was the combination of Vampires and legends, but Mistral flashed across my mind's eye again. Second time in just a few hours.

I closed my teeth over my lower lip hard enough to draw a bead of blood. Why was I thinking about a dead Vampire? One I'd beheaded myself. It hadn't been one of my finer moments, but it had proven how strong I'd become...

Not willing to fall headlong into that particular set of memories, I pushed them aside. Killing Mistral had freed me, but I could have accomplished the same thing with a whole lot less drama.

Conan wasn't back yet. I considered raising him with telepathy but left him alone. Just like me, he needed a certain level of privacy. It was odd he hadn't returned though. He'd said he was going hunting, and all the game scattered once darkness ceded to the next day.

My eyes, which had been hovering at half-mast as I lolled in bed, snapped wide open. I grabbed handfuls of the comforter so violently it ripped in two spots. Conan had gone after Thug-Number-Two. I felt certain of it.

Tossing the duvet aside created a mini-snowstorm of feathers from the holes I'd made. I was on my feet and heading for a dresser to find something clean to wear when I stopped dead. What exactly was I going to do? Knowing Conan, he'd probably turned into a bird—a big one—and flown back to *Ascent*. From there, he'd have followed the scent track.

Didn't matter where the thug was. Conan could turn into a cockroach if he needed to and get inside anywhere, including a hospital emergency room. I retraced my steps and curled up in the nest I'd made in my bed.

Nothing I could do but muck things up at this point, and I'd have a hell of a hard time traveling anywhere until the damn sun went down. The moment I shut my eyes again, Mistral roared to life. Beautiful and terrible with stunning blond curls that framed his perfectly proportioned face. Silver-blue eyes, a high forehead, and a squared-off jaw made him irresistible—even before I recalled his broad-shouldered, slim-hipped build.

Clearly, the not-so-instant replay wasn't going to stop nagging for attention. My mountain retreat dropped away. In its place, a similar stone abode deep in England's coastal range in Cornwall took shape. The ancestral home of Clan Hawke, it was where I'd been turned.

Recordkeeping had been hit-or-miss in those days, but it was somewhere around 1200 A.D. I'd been thirteen, and my family sold me to Mistral. It sounds harsh, but such practices were commonplace then. My family actually hung onto me far longer than many would have. Female children weren't worth much. Just another mouth to feed, and Mistral had paid handsomely. I assumed I'd share his bed and work in his sprawling household in a huge lodge sitting atop a hill.

If my duties had stopped with sex and work, I'd have been dead these past 800 years and then some, but they didn't. I'd loved Mistral once, worshipped him, but that was before I understood what he was.

And what he truly expected from me.

By then, it was too late. I was complicit to my eyeballs, and the only way out was deeper in. Bloodlust is overpowering for new Vampires in ways mortals can't understand. All I could think about was the next infusion of blood, but I'm getting ahead of myself...

CHAPTER FIVE, NICKOLAS

Fury streamed through me, scorching and vital, as I teleported away from that goddamned nightclub. I'd read the woman's invitation all wrong. What the fuck was the matter with me, anyway? Was I still shaking off the effects of being asleep for nearly a hundred years?

I smothered a grunt. I'd been sucked in by delight at finding another like me. All Vamps carry an unearthly beauty, but she was incredible. Nearly as tall as me, she had a lean, curvy figure with breasts that stood out even beneath her coat and a high, tight ass. Dark hair cascaded to waist level. Her eyes were liquid pools of a clear, pure blue. I'd been surprised to see her wolf sidekick, and even more nonplussed when he'd begun changing forms. Vampires don't keep pets.

Was he some sort of closet lover? Given his ability to shapeshift, I could easily see him adopting a human form—and fucking her. Jealousy rippled through me; I chopped it off at the roots. Ariana had little use for me. She'd made that abundantly clear.

I'd been drawn in by her husky, compelling voice when she'd stood half a league from me in the forest and invited me to her home. This time, I didn't bother to hold back the disgusted snort that wanted out. I'd assumed I'd show up and we'd fall into each other's arms. Vampires love to fuck. It's our second favorite pastime after eating.

My cock twitched, rising in agreement. I pushed it to a more comfortable position and told it to retreat. Nothing for it to be hard for, no matter how much I wished there were.

The clearing where I'd killed the pig formed around me. Between the wolf and the woman, nothing much was left of my prey. Didn't matter. I'd indulged in the part I wanted, but it would have been comforting sitting with the hog's bulk—if anything but bones had remained.

Vampires aren't monsters. When I was latched onto the pig, love for the creature bloomed within me. An element in my saliva soothes my victims. Once they stop struggling, I latch onto their minds and assure them their passing will be easy, that their death serves a higher purpose.

Both those things are true, and I'd eased the hog across the veil as gently as I knew how. In the end, he'd clung to my reassurances, and in an odd way I missed him. But then, I felt the same way about every creature who died at my hands.

I was always careful not to be greedy, to only feed when I absolutely had to. Control was one of the sideline benefits of growing old as a Vampire. Not that my physical appearance changed. It never would. I'd always look the age

I'd been when one of the female Vampires from Clan Giovanni turned me.

I shook myself out of my thoughts. Sitting next to the remains of the pig was an indulgence. What I needed to do was get moving before night vanished.

Maybe I should round up Lorenzo and Clive, the two Vamps who'd shared my long sleep. We'd kicked it around and decided it was best to split up. At least, until we got the current lay of the land. Vampires have never exactly made the revered creatures list. It appeared things had worsened while we were checked out.

Ha. Worsened was seeming like an understatement.

What the Hawke woman and the passel of other supernaturals had inferred was that war had finally broken out between us and humans. Eh. Vampires have always had a *de facto* war going with mortals. They're drawn to us, and they hate us for it, unless they become one of the fortunate chosen ones.

Very few humans make the cut. Those who are invited to join our ranks have been extended a great honor. Honor... Damn. I choked on my thoughts. When I'd voiced a similar sentiment—about honor—to Ariana, she'd tossed my words back in my face. Not that I was offering to turn her. She was already like me. But I stood ready to include her in my clan.

Except she had a clan affiliation of her own, one she appeared to have eschewed. Had she known Mistral, founder of Clan Hawke? Probably not. She'd have to be very old to remember him. Not that we don't live a long time, but Mistral predated me by at least two hundred years. One of his minions had slain him, raised a blade against his master and lopped off his head. None of us spoke too loudly about that event. It was unthinkable, horrific. Clan Hawke had nearly disbanded over it.

The rest of us had kept our distance. A whole lot of distance.

I'd learned about Mistral in Vampire school. Once the worst of the bloodlust became manageable, our master taught us about the Vampire clans and our long, proud history. It was when I'd heard about Mistral—but that lesson was whispered and brief. Whoever killed him had covered his tracks well.

Good thing. Other Vampires would have chased him down and made him suffer. We have an established social structure, and it's not to be trifled with. I'd be lying if I didn't admit to a few rough years after I was first turned. The same anger and resentment that plagues most new Vampires rode me like a deranged hag.

But things improved around the time the bloodlust stopped dogging me. After that, I settled into the fold. Lots of perks—the modern term made me smile—to being a Vampire. Once every set of beating jugular veins didn't make me want to jump whoever owned them, I was able to appreciate the new me.

I squatted on the ground next to the collection of pig bones, idly turning one over and over between my hands. How could the woman not care about her clan? Worse, how could she have taken up with other supernaturals? We were mortal enemies, and Sorcerers were the reason I'd ended up choosing stasis.

Vampires are essentially loners. If we had to be with

anyone, our preferred companions were other Vampires. From the moment a master turned you, you became part of something bigger than you were. Some of us valued that. The smart ones.

My fangs had dropped; I urged them to retreat. I'd misjudged the woman. Badly. Revealed myself for nothing. Worse, I'd alerted Lorenzo and Clive about her. They'd ask if I'd found her. The simplest course would be for me to lie. I was the closest thing to a master Clan Giovanni had, and the others wouldn't question me. Nor would they suspect I hadn't been truthful.

The more I thought about it, the better I liked a simple untruth. Not being forthright with the other two went against the grain, but not as much as exposing what an idiot I'd been.

Dawn was nearly upon me. I'd run into my companions eventually. We hadn't been here long enough to build a shelter, so I called up an image of the cave we'd occupied during our stasis. It was perhaps ten leagues from here, well into a mountain range that ran north-south through territory that had turned into Washington state. When I'd gone to sleep, the countryside hadn't had a name.

During the brief time since we'd woken, I'd read everything I could get my hands on. We'd filched clothing from a place called the Salvation Army, teleporting inside once they'd closed. Lots to choose from, and most of it was nondescript enough no one would ever accuse us of being thieves.

Pfft. There'd been so much junk in the used clothing store, I'm certain no one even noticed the few things we took.

Garments had certainly taken a turn for the worse, replacing quality with quantity. The rough cloth encasing my legs was scratchy, and the workmanship lacking.

The clearing faded, replaced by the quiet darkness of a cavern. I'd found it quite by accident, realized it would be perfect for our needs, and done the spade work to prepare it for a long stay. The hardest part had been shielding it from the black Sorcerers who were out for our blood. Literally. They'd found some secret formula, fueled by Vampire blood, that would make them virtually invincible.

At least that was their story.

We never believed it.

I settled in on a large flat rock, leaning my back against a wall. Sprinkles of magic reflected off generous quartz crystals, providing muted light. I hadn't laid eyes on Lorenzo or Clive since we parted ways. Tilting my head to one side, I counted nights and came up with twelve.

We didn't have a specific plan to come back together. If another night or two elapsed while I got my story about Ariana straight, I wouldn't complain. I should have asked more questions in the nightclub. Like was this war widespread or limited to the States?

Perhaps returning to northern Italy would be the wisest move. Someone else would have set themselves up as master during my long absence, but I'd beat the crap out of them and reestablish myself as king of my clan. Reality nipped me in the butt. I'd try to best them, but there was always a possibility I'd lose and have to content myself with being their second.

It didn't sit well.

I'd never planned to remain on the west side of the Atlantic Ocean. Vampires loathe water, but that's a tale for a different day. Despite our issues with oceans and ships, we'd booked passage to New York City, and then teleported across the continent in spurts. What had begun as a reconnaissance to locate promising new Vampires had switched to a survival exercise when a group of black Sorcerers discovered us and shackled enough of our magic we couldn't teleport back to a port city for our return journey.

I'd picked a good long timeframe before waking to ensure the dark mages would have given up. It appeared my strategy had worked. Although, when I'd seen the Sorcerer at *Ascent*, I'd been certain Ariana's invitation had been a trap.

Until I scanned the big man and didn't find a trace of black magic within him. He was powerful as fuck, but his magic was clean, without taint.

A swoosh of magic presaged Clive's appearance. In the moments before I knew it was him, I leapt to my feet, ready for damn near anything after misinterpreting Ariana's invitation. For all I knew, one of the Fae from the club had tracked me.

Or the damned coyote shifter.

A swirl of golden hair and the comforting scents of Vampire, sweet and musky, brought breath whooshing from my lungs. I don't have to breathe, but I'd sucked in a good old lungful of air, anyway, testament to how rattled I was.

I had to get over whatever this was.

"Hey, mate." Clive shimmered into full corporeality.

"Wasn't certain I'd find you here." He'd never fully lost an upper-crust British accent, despite years living in Italy.

"Hey, yourself," I retorted.

Dressed in clothing nearly identical to my own, he turned in a full circle, scanning the cave with his dark eyes. "Where is she?"

"Where's who?" I did my absolute best to project confusion despite knowing exactly what he was getting at.

"The woman, mate. The one you told us about. I'm surprised Lorenzo didn't beat me here." He patted the front of his purloined trousers, his intent crystal clear. Sex is playtime for us. Very few Vampires pair off, human style. Clive was well within his rights to imagine we'd share the woman. I'd assumed much the same.

But that was before I'd seen her.

The jealousy that had dogged me earlier, when I'd assumed the wolf was my rival, roared back. I ignored it and shrugged. "Never found her."

"Really?" His shoulders slumped, and he stopped rubbing his cock through his pants.

"Nope. She led me on a merry chase, that one. I went where she said she'd be but didn't find anything. Just a deserted cottage." So long as I was at it, I laid it on thick.

"But if we return to where she spoke with you, surely we can track her energy," Clive persisted.

I shook my head. "Already thought of that. It's where I just came from." I was still holding onto one of the pig bones, and I dropped it on the cave floor.

"Damn it." He sank to a crouch. "Long as I'm here, I may as well report in." He raked his fingers through his long hair, moving it behind his shoulders. "This is a very different place from when we went to sleep. It's strange and crazy. I think we should return to the seethe."

"Much has changed," I agreed. The master Vampire mantle dropped over my shoulders. Now was a time to take charge, provide leadership. "We haven't been here long enough to make any major decisions."

"But we were trying to leave when those black Sorcerers made it impossible. At least, they appear to be gone."

"Yes, they do, but we may have other problems." I'd decided to share a smidgeon of information without revealing its source.

"Like what? Mostly, I've been feeding and regaining my strength."

"I've been reading," I told him. "As much as I can find. Unlike clothing, libraries have improved. Humans have declared war on those like us. What I haven't been able to glean is if this war is worldwide or just here."

Clive frowned. It added a few creases to his perfectly proportioned features but left his eerie beauty untouched. "I'm not seeing how that's any different. Other supernaturals always had it in for us, and we've never made the cut in human society, either."

"The difference is"—I paused for effect and to ensure I had his full attention—"supernaturals have banded together. Against humans who are tossing us into iron-lined prisons."

He barked a short burst of laughter. "You can't believe everything you read, mate. We've never been welcomed by other immortals. They think we're trash."

"They probably still do," I agreed. "Circumstances make for odd bedfellows."

"I can see mortals rising against supernaturals. What I can't envision is them winning. We have all the advantages on our side."

I narrowed my eyes. "Over the short haul, yes. Playing a long game tilts the field in their favor because there are so many of them, and the more we kill, the harder they'll try to defeat us."

"Mmph. Conclusions like that would fall into your court." Clive retreated to being my subordinate. "Since there's no woman and no possibility of leaving, I'm going back to where I've been spending my days. Call me if something changes."

I almost asked him where exactly that was but didn't. I could find him if I needed to. While we keep new Vampires on a short leash, we've never hunted in packs. Our particular brand of mesmerism works best one-on-one.

"Keep your ear to the ground," I cautioned him. "The more we can find out about this war, the better."

"Will do. Good hunting, mate."

"Same to you. Another few days, and we'll be back to our full strength."

He stretched upright and clapped me across the back. "I'm nearly there now. Feels good."

He developed an insubstantial aspect as he summoned a teleport spell and vanished from the cavern. I stared at where he'd stood for a few moments feeling slightly chagrined for lying to him, but not all that bad.

Settling in for what was left of the day, I plotted my next

moves. I'd return to *Ascent* and ask the questions I should have asked before. Armed with information, I could plot the best course for Clive, Lorenzo, and me.

Part of me hated to show up in the nightclub again, but I didn't have much choice. I could cull through newspapers until my eyes burned from the strain of reading a language that had gone through a major overhaul since I'd learned it and not find what I needed.

Nothing like harvesting information directly from the source. Ariana had invited me to *Ascent* because she believed our kind had to stick together. In my lexicon, "our kind" meant Vampires. In hers, it meant everyone who wasn't mortal.

Did it include the horrific Sorcerers who'd tried to imprison Clive, Lorenzo, and me and steal our blood? I'd have to tread carefully, not show too much of my hand just in case they were still an active force in the supernatural community.

I returned to my flat rock and leaned my back against an upright stone, trying to wrap my mind around the idea of a community of paranormal creatures. It felt right that all the ones in *Ascent* appeared to work for Ariana, but I had a feeling they were far from indentured labor. How in the fuck had she forged a relationship where she called the shots, but they retained most of their independence?

Clive had understated the point when he labeled this world as strange.

I shut my eyes to rest them. By this time tomorrow, I'd have answers. Maybe not all of them, but enough I'd never have to show my face in *Ascent* again.

CHAPTER SIX, ARIANA

J'd put on a brave front the day Mistral sent a man for me. I wasn't important enough to merit a horse or even a cart. After a rather tearful farewell where my mother didn't want to let go of me, I trudged down a muddy lane trying not to think I'd never be back. I had the patched skirt and tunic on my body. Nothing else. My family were peasants, and we didn't keep possessions in the same way even today's homeless do.

No shopping carts full of prized objects.

It was how things worked back then. No belongings and nothing like visits to your family on holidays. Once you were bought and paid for, your new master owned you. I suppose I was fortunate—tried to tell myself that as I avoided the worst of sharp stones that would have cut my bare feet. I'd lived over half my life with my family. I'd be fourteen soon, and no one lived much past thirty. No matter what happened with Mistral—a man I'd never met—I'd make the best of things.

Everyone in the village knew him by name, by reputation. He was powerful. Larger than life. He kept many women, but his manor house wasn't overflowing with children. Or if it was, they never came into the village. One favored rumor was he murdered them before birth using arcane magics. People also whispered about how he'd grown rich. It wasn't from the hectares of fields around his home that were never tilled, but from illicit trade in forbidden objects. No one went into too much detail about exactly what those objects might be.

We—my taciturn escort and I—wound our way down a steep hill and through the village. It was market day, and many of the merchants hawking their wares called out to me. I waved back, not trusting myself to speak. Surely by now, they all knew I was Mistral's latest acquisition.

Gossip traveled fast in those times.

For once, it wasn't raining. We navigated an even steeper hill on the village's far side. After a few more ups and downs, I was tired and thirsty. I'd never been so far from home before, and I was beginning to be afraid the man in front of me wasn't from Mistral after all.

"How much farther?" I asked, but he didn't answer me.

The sun was setting when I caught my first glimpse of a wall twice as tall as me. Built of mortared stones, it went on forever, as far as I could see in both directions with no visible gate. Something about that wall, with its black-and-gray mottled rocks made a narrow spot form in my throat. A chill washed through me, and not because the day had grown cold.

The man turned then, and I got a good look at his face. Until now, all I'd seen was the back of his black robe, sashed in red, and his long brown hair caught up in a bit of leather. He looked a great deal younger than I expected. Not much older than me, and he was pretty. Almost like a woman with high, arched cheekbones, beautiful lips, and pale-blue eyes.

Blinking, I stared at him. "We have arrived," he told me and removed the sash holding his robe together.

I girded myself for a quick fuck before he turned me over to Mistral. I'd known I had to lose my maidenhead sometime, but I hoped it wouldn't be out here in the dirt with a stranger. Rather than grabbing me, he wound the sash around my eyes.

"I need to see to walk."

He didn't say anything, but I wasn't expecting him to. Prickles surrounded me, first cold and then hot, and then cold again. I shivered and tried to run away, but my limbs were paralyzed. When I understood I couldn't move, I panicked and began shrieking.

He wrapped his arms around me, and I fought harder. "Control yourself. This part will be quick," he said right next to my ear.

Full-blown terror took over, and I squealed, "What part? Is this when you kill me?"

"Only if you misbehave. Quiet."

I could do that. I knew how to be quiet. Swallowing great, gulping sobs, I vowed to not utter another word. He'd meant what he said. The part about only killing me if I misbehaved. I had no idea why I believed him. Maybe because I had no choice.

The prickling intensified. A floating sensation added to it, but then everything stopped abruptly. He unwound the sash from around my head, and I stood blinking stupidly at the wall.

Except I was on the inside now.

Shudders wracked me. I couldn't stop shaking. I may have peed myself. It was so long ago, I don't remember. Why hadn't we walked through a gate? My escort yanked my arm none too gently, and I fell in behind him again.

This side of the wall contained lush gardens, each more beautiful than the last one I walked through. Filled with exotic plants and blossoms the likes of which I'd never dreamed existed, they went on and on. A house constructed of white-gray stones rose behind the gardens. Three storied, it was beautiful, graceful, and terrifying.

I'd never seen anywhere this grand. Not even the local duke's palace. I hadn't exactly seen it, but I'd peeked through holes in the wall with some of the other village children. Everyone important lived behind walls. As if they needed a place to get away from the rest of us.

So they could pretend we didn't exist.

I reached behind me and plumped my pillows higher. I always spent a lot of time with the early part of my memories of Mistral and his house. I was still an innocent then. And I'd remained so for the next few months. By then, I understood well enough I'd been shanghaied into a house of Vampires. No one hid that part from me. I figured it out my first week in the manor house. It explained why there were no children.

Vampires were dead. They could do a whole lot of things, but producing babies wasn't among them. It also explained why I'd had to pass through the wall magically. There were no gates. Not even one.

Mistral wanted to make certain no one stumbled onto his grounds without his say-so.

I fast forwarded to the day I actually met the man who would turn me. I'd been living in the compound for a couple of weeks then. The other women, some Vampires, some not, had cleaned me up and cut my hair. Not short, but to waist level. I'd always assumed nightwalkers were a myth, something adults threw in kids' faces to keep them in line.

If they were real, I supposed they'd drain me and leave me for dead.

I kept expecting it to happen, but it never did. One morning, I was cleaning my assigned section of the building when a man glided close. I ignored him, intent on the floor I was scrubbing, when he closed a hand over my shoulder and hauled me to my feet.

I kept my gaze firmly on the floor. Was he Mistral? If not, who was he, and what did he want? Not questions I could ask. I was nothing, the lowest underling. Those like me didn't get to ask questions.

"Look at me," he ordered after a few moments had passed.

I did, and it was a struggle not to gasp. He was the most

perfect man, the most beautiful creature I'd ever laid eyes on, with a corona of fair curls and silver-blue eyes. Heat blazed through me. Desire stronger than I'd ever felt. He'd mesmerized me, but I didn't know it then.

All I knew was I wanted to be naked in his arms. Suddenly bold, I reached for the sash holding his white robe closed, desperate to see what lay beneath.

He smiled, and it lit his face from within, making him even more irresistible. "I shall take you, little bird. But not quite yet. Mostly, I wished to make your acquaintance."

Without another word, he let go of my shoulder and strode away, leaving me alone in the corridor. I stuffed a hand between my legs and rubbed myself like a madwoman until sensation crashed through me. It was convenient I was alone, but I'm not certain I could have restrained myself even if I'd been surrounded by a roomful of people.

Mistral had that effect on me.

And he knew it, the bastard. He used me shamelessly. Or maybe the shame was all on me since I never even tried to resist. He was my first love, and I longed for him, yearned for his touch and resented the fuck out of every other woman he gifted with his hot, hard cock.

When he offered me the gift of eternal life, I dove in headfirst. Anything that would bring us closer. Damn I was young and stupid. Not that I've ever regretted my decision, but the first couple of years were hard. I spent most of them in Mistral's bed where he fucked me senseless to keep my bloodlust in line.

When he wasn't fucking me, he fed me from his wrist, infusing still more of his power. All that one-on-one time was how I became so strong, and what led to me killing him. Roll the clock forward a couple of hundred years, maybe four hundred to be more precise. Modern life was catching up with our medieval village. Mistral and Clan Hawke's seethe had to work harder and harder to remain invisible. Horses and carriages made it simple for people to find our compound and walk round and round our wall hunting for a way inside. We had to practice stealth to find blood to sustain ourselves, often resorting to draining cows and sheep.

A few of us were caught, beheaded, and burned.

Mistral was infuriated, but there wasn't much he could do without revealing himself. As things stood, those who knew about him viewed him as an eccentric who chose to climb in and out of his realm.

Part of the manor house included an elaborate basement system, one plenty large enough for Vampires to bide during the day. We didn't require much sleep, so most days we fucked the time away. I enjoyed watching, but I never joined the fuckfests. In my mind, I was Mistral's woman. Too bad he hadn't read from the same playbill.

One spring, he was gone for a good long while. Over a month. I pined for him. Yearned for him. We talked telepathically most days, but it wasn't the same as having him by my side. If I'd listened, I'd have heard him tell me Vampires didn't pair bond. I brushed off his warnings, and it was a mistake.

A huge one.

He returned from his time away with a woman by his side. Young and beautiful, she gazed at him with the same adoration I felt. Jealousy speared me so deep, I didn't even wait until we were alone to yell at him. How dare he? He was mine.

"I'm no one's," he'd told me. "And neither are you. Run along, Ariana. I need time with Becca." Wrapping an arm protectively around her, he'd walked toward his chamber.

I could have screeched strings of epithets, but darker thoughts converged. I'd show him. Was this how he rewarded years of love and loyalty? Centuries? His mistake was he thought he knew me, and my strength was I knew him too well. After thousands of times making love, he didn't have a move I wasn't familiar with.

I crept into the armory and took a silver blade. It burned my hands something fierce, so I wrapped the hilt in linen, which helped a little. The armory was pure vanity on Mistral's part. Vampires have no need for weapons, but he'd always been fascinated by knights and all their regalia.

And supremely confident in his control over his minions.

Armed with a blade, I took my time. Swathed myself in invisibility and waited in the far corner of his chamber. Pain stabbed me far worse than my abraded palms as he did the same things with that wretched upstart bitch he'd done to me. Cooed at her, told her he adored her, that she was fresh and young and perfect. It was all I could do not to puke when he started in about her breasts.

Fuck! She wasn't even a Vampire, but I saw how enamored she was with him, how she fell for every golden word that dripped from his perfect lips. One of the advantages of being turned is emotions are simplified. Rather than the unpleasant mix mortals deal with, my emotional life had been reduced to love, hate, and blood-hunger.

I hated them both for everything. She knew he was mine and didn't care. He'd made his position clear when he'd told me to go away.

He was behind her, one of his favorite positions, jamming his cock into her hard and quick. Still swaddled in invisibility, I crept close. I had to time this just right. If I missed my strike, my undead life would be forfeit. No one raised their hand against the master Vampire without consequences.

He was making the sounds I used to love, the keening cries that said he was nearly there. Beneath him, the slutty bitch cried out, back arching, as she came. It was now or never. I raised my blade and swung hard, severing Mistral's neck from his body when he was so lost in lust he couldn't fight back. It would have been gratifying to make certain he knew it was me, but I'd been a Vampire long enough to understand that was a very bad idea.

Becca was shrieking as blood spurted from Mistral's severed neck vessels. That wouldn't last long. Before his wasted ancient body crumpled to dusty bones, I teleported away from there, leaving the blade where I'd dropped it.

Nothing like fingerprints to give me away back in those days. And the weapons in the armory smelled like all of us since we traded off keeping them shiny and free from rust. Mistral had loved his weapon collection, and now it was his undoing.

I wanted to run as far and as fast as I could, but then everyone would figure out it had been me. I returned to my chamber and sent powerful magic to heal my hands fast. I'd avoided all the blood since I'd struck from behind.

To cut to the chase, I got away with it. I cried as long and loud as anyone once news of Mistral's death raced through the seethe. I must have been convincing because the other women circled the wagons, commiserating with me. I'd been closer to him than anyone, and they assumed his end had devastated me.

The harsh truth was it did. I didn't have to work very hard to present a credible show of grief. Guilt added an unpleasant bitterness to my sorrow, but Mistral hadn't given me a choice. Once I had time to think things over—and believe me, I thought of little else in the weeks afterward—I understood he'd tired of me. He'd tried to tell me, but in an oblique male fashion that left the path to my bed open.

I plotted my leave-taking, although no one knew about it until I vanished about a year later. The seethe had devolved into an internecine war as we fought over who the next master would be. Becca lost her mind and was committed to a local madhouse—after several of us drank liberally from her.

Poor sad little bitch.

I never wasted even a minute feeling sorry for her, and I should have. In her own way, she was as much Mistral's victim as I'd been. Just one more man out to exercise his dick with the youngest, prettiest pussy he could find.

I rolled over in my bed, seeking peace, but it had eluded me ever since I'd decapitated my maker. I still missed Mistral's body and the way he'd touched me and bitten me and loved me. I missed the taste of his blood, hot and sweet and coppery. But it was still better this way. He'd never been mine except in my imagination.

I'd belonged to him and the seethe, so walking away wasn't an option. Once he was gone, I had no master. I'd vowed to keep it that way because it freed me to choose my own course. I'd moved east, through Europe and into the Carpathian Mountains, a journey that took several months because I wasn't in any hurry. Conan had crossed my path then, an abused puppy sparkling with more magic than he could contain.

We'd crossed the Atlantic to the New World toward the close of the nineteenth century, avoiding other Vampires on both sides of the ocean. Scenting Nickolas earlier had been a shock. I'd been convinced I was the only Vampire anywhere around. My lack of a seethe affiliation was how I'd convinced other supernaturals to work at *Ascent*.

They never would have if they'd thought a bunch of my Undead kin were waiting in the wings to strike as the mood suited them.

Like I said, we've never made anyone's hit parade. No one likes Vampires, not even other Vamps. Seethes have outlived their usefulness. They had little place in a world riddled with internal combustion engines and circuit boards that ran everything from cell phones to computers.

Back in the day, we could hide out in a seethe, separated from everything. Modern tracking methods could probably locate most any Vampire nest, so we were better off traveling alone.

Just my opinion. I had no idea if it was shared by other Vampires.

My phone trilled again. This time, I bolted from bed and ran to pick up before it quit ringing. A quick glance at the display told me it was nearly four o'clock. I'd lost most of today in my retreat to my humble roots.

Conan still wasn't back. Damn. I needed to find him.

The display didn't reveal who was calling. The same "private number" notation flashed across it. I tapped the screen and said, "Yes?"

"Glad I got you," Ruby rasped in her deep gravelly voice.

"Were you who called earlier?"

"Aye."

"Why didn't you leave a message?"

She snorted softly. "I don't trust these things. You had problems last night in the alley, huh?"

"Yes." I left it at that, figuring she'd tell me what she was angling at.

"Lotta blood back there," she went on. "The place is crawling with cops. Seems like Roger is dead. He bled out in an ER waiting room in plain sight except no one noticed until he was gone."

"Don't look at me," I muttered. "I've been here since dawn."

"Mmph. Maybe you weren't the only one who had it in for him. Anyway, you should get down here. The cops are asking for you. I've held them off most of the day."

"Be there as soon as I can."

"Does it mean you'll be teleporting?" She lowered her voice to a whisper.

"No. Conan hates traveling that way. I have to get dressed, and then we'll drive in."

"Good enough." She hung up.

I stared at the phone, and then I raised my mind voice. *"Conan. Get back here now."*

As if he'd been skulking around in the yard waiting for my summons, he sauntered through the front door, which obligingly opened to admit him. His head and neck dripped water, but he'd missed a few bloody streaks.

I motioned him into the bathroom and went to work obliterating evidence with hot water and magic.

"Busy night?" I inquired caustically.

"You might say so." He flinched as I scrubbed his muzzle with a washcloth.

We understood one another, but we'd talk later. Maybe in the car. About the time I grabbed a towel to dry his snout, he pulled away. "It's enough." He shook droplets all over the bathroom.

I narrowed my eyes, examining my work. It was, indeed, enough. He'd pass any inspection if it came to that, but my plan was to instruct him to remain out of sight.

"We're going to work," I told him. "You were here with me all day."

"Of course I was." His jaws parted in a wolfish grin, and his tongue lolled to one side, the very embodiment of innocence.

I shouldn't have, but I laughed. It would make censuring him later that much harder. After leaving the bathroom, I ditched the T-shirt, grabbed clothes, and dressed in a hurry. Dressier things than my standard fare. For some reason, I must be feeling optimistic, but I'd always loved the green silk blouse and soft, black linen pants. Perhaps they'd placate the cops milling about in my alley behind the club.

Once we were in the Toyota and bumping down the dirt road, I asked, "The other guy, is he dead too? And how about the third one, who left before the party really got rolling?"

"Maybe."

"Can you expand on that, bud?"

After a pause long enough for us to trade the dirt road for pitted asphalt, Conan started to talk.

CHAPTER SEVEN, ARIANA

"*Y*ou killed all of them," I muttered, still absorbing Conan's tale. Not that he wasn't capable of that level of carnage, but it had been better than fifty years since he'd slipped my control quite that badly. The sun had just set, and I welcomed the coming night. Meant I wouldn't have to meet the cops decked out in veils like Mata Hari.

"They deserved it." The wolf added a snarl to his words. "Sit there and tell me they didn't."

"Not going to do that. They were bad men, but *Ascent* is riddled with cops right now gathering evidence."

"They won't find anything," Conan declared.

"They already did." Breath whistled from between my teeth. How to explain modern forensics to a centuries-old creature?

"How? No bodies."

"Blood. They can match it up and know whose it was."

An annoyed yip told me Conan didn't care for that explanation.

"I understand you were trying to protect us—" I began.

"You. I was protecting you. It's my job." He drowned out my words with his own.

Love and gratitude for him swelled, making it tough to keep driving. I resisted an urge to pull over, crawl into the back area, and hug Conan, breathing in the clean, wolfy smell of him.

Once I had my emotions under control, I picked and chose my words. "I appreciate you looking out for me, but Roger and the other dude wouldn't have come back. They were nothing but bullies, and we scared them good. The third fellow was such a coward, he ran somewhere safe with his tail between his legs."

Conan growled. "Found him in a falling-down building, hiding in a corner." After a longer growl, he said, "I made it quick. For all of them. They should have suffered, but I was worried about being gone too long."

I frowned, only part of my attention on the road. We'd be on the expressway soon, and it would turn into bumper-to-bumper commuter traffic. What exactly had the cops found? Roger's corpse in the ER, for sure. But had they located the other two?

An idea formed and I pulled off the road. If this worked, it wouldn't set me back by more than half an hour or so. Eh, perhaps an hour depending on how far we had to travel and if we had to avoid other people.

"What are we doing?" Conan lifted his big head off his front paws.

I buried the car in a grove of evergreens about a quarter mile from the road we'd been traveling on and got out, opening the hatch for him to jump down. I hunkered in front of him and took his head between my hands. "I want you to show me where the other two bodies are. Not Roger, but the others."

He crinkled his snout. "You aren't going to drink their blood? It's rancid."

I patted a jowl. "No. I most assuredly do not want their blood. What I want is to make certain no one finds those bodies." I sucked in an unneeded breath and blew it out. "You can come with me, or you can send me images of where you left the men."

"I'll come," he said gruffly.

It surprised me, knowing how much he hated the touch of my spells. After I pushed upright, I began piecing a travel spell together, but Conan shook himself and said, "You will come with me this time."

My eyes opened wider. In all our years together, I'd never joined one of his teleport spells. Could I deal with not being the one in control? It left a squirmy, uncomfortable spot in the center of my chest.

Conan was staring at me; knowledge spilled from his amber eyes. "Not so simple, is it?"

If I'd still been human, I'd have turned red from embarrassment to be caught out. I stood straighter. "Not simple at all," I told him, "but I trust you, so let's do this. Bring us out a little ways away so we can see if it's safe."

He made a whuffly noise that might have meant he was

annoyed by my instructions. In his lupine mind, we could fight our way out of anything.

"The idea," I said, "is to be clever and avoid discovery. Low profile, and all that."

"Humans are stupid," he grumbled.

The feel of his magic with its scents of forests and fur and rain-wet rocks folded around me. I didn't fight him, but it was hard to relax. I'd been in charge—of everything—since I raised that blade against Mistral. No one to blame but myself for every mistake, but I wouldn't trade the freedom to make those mistakes for being under anyone's thumb again.

The transition was quick. In less than two minutes, something like a junkyard took shape around us. A sharp woof rang in my ears just before a dog that looked like a German Shepherd mix barreled toward us, fangs bared. Conan snarled, and the junkyard guardian did an about-face.

"He won't bother us again," Conan said, switching to telepathy.

"Was he here before?"

"Yes. Getting rid of him was easy then too. Come on."

My nostrils twitched as I sorted scents. Easy enough to locate a dead human. Vampires are decent trackers; we home right in on blood. I've been lucky and found the occasional almost-dead mortal to drink from. I never counted them as kills since they'd have died anyway, even absent a small push from me.

Automobile carcasses in varying stages of dismantlement surrounded us, along with rusting appliances. Clearly, this was a dumping ground for metal. I hoped they'd made a commitment to recycling and then muffled a snort.

So far, no one but the dog was anywhere near. No one living, anyway.

I followed Conan to a garage-like affair with the roof falling in on one side. Mmph. Was this place even still an active business? The guard dog suggested it was, but it had a deserted feel about it. My wolf wriggled through a hole in one wall. I could have crawled through. Instead, I slithered around the building and located a door with a shiny, new padlock.

Intriguing. What were they hiding inside? Especially, why secure the door when anyone could work their way in through that gaping hole. *"Conan?"*

"Yes?"

"Did you make the hole in the wall?"

Lupine laughter rippled through my mind, telling me he was guilty as charged. I took hold of the padlock and hit it with a shot of Vampiric mind control. The tumblers clicked and clacked, and the mechanism fell open. I unhooked it, lifted it off the hasp, and walked inside.

Conan stood over the corpse of the man whose shoulders I'd dislocated. What I should have done was grab him and go. Instead, curiosity got the better of me, and I glanced around the inside of the humble structure. It was far nicer than I'd have expected from its exterior appearance.

Metal boxes with padlocks of their own lined a couple of shelves. Riding on instinct, I cracked one and stared at stacked and banded twenty and fifty dollar bills. Not a junkyard. A front for hiding cash from something illegal.

Yeah, like skimming liquor crates off the top of customer orders.

Roger hadn't been working alone, damn his black soul. There had to be at least ten grand in this one box, and there were nine more, presumably similarly stuffed.

"What are you waiting for? I thought we were in a hurry." Conan pricked his ears at the dead man, in case I'd missed him.

"We are." I hoisted Thug-Number-Two over one shoulder and held onto the box.

Sensing I was ready, Conan transported us back to the Toyota. "Be right back," I told him and left the cash next to the car. Vampires can move fast when we need to. I bolted through the trees, until I found what I was hoping for, evidence of a cougar den. They'd know what to do with my gift, and I pushed the dead man into their cave after I'd relieved him of his wallet. If anyone found him, they could identify him from DNA and dental records, but I wasn't worried.

I rejoined Conan. He was nosing the metal box. "Why'd you want this?"

"Not certain."

"Then why'd you take it?" he persisted.

"Can I explain later? We still have the other guy to collect."

A small raise in his upper lip told me he wasn't happy with being put off. I unlocked the car and dropped the box inside. My phone screen was full of messages. Yeah. Ruby was probably wondering what in the fuck happened to me, or maybe some of them were from Kirkland's boys in blue.

Conan woofed to hustle me along. He was right. Staring at my phone was a big fat time-waster, so was calling anyone back. His spell caught me up as soon as I hit the clicker to lock the car. This time, our destination was a rundown neighborhood at the outskirts of Kirkland.

Unlike the junkyard, it wasn't deserted, and I wrapped us in an invisibility spell to cross the front yard and unlatch a gate leading to a badly neglected and overgrown backyard.

"Too bad you can't shapeshift," Conan groused.

"What were you when you tracked him here?"

"Many things, but I was myself when I killed him."

I was proud of my wolf. No skulking in shadows when faced with the hard shit. The back door was partway open. I scanned hastily for anyone who might give us problems, but we were alone. Conan had cornered the man in his bedroom. He'd fought back, not that it had bought him much.

He lay on his back, eyes open and unseeing, in a congealing pool of his own blood. The other corpse hadn't been messy like this one. Maybe just seeing Conan had stopped his heart.

No point taking time to look around. Was this man part of the money-laundering ring? I didn't know, but my first guess would be yes. I felt certain the primary cash hoard was in the junkyard, though. A worn leather wallet sat on top of a scarred dresser. Excellent. I'd just leave it there.

Conan nudged the corpse with his nose, getting more blood on himself. Phooey. No way for me to avoid it, either. Unless...

I called up magic and wrapped it around the corpse, making a neat package. It shouldn't leak on me. I hoped. Once I had a decent hold on everything, Conan transported us.

"Find a creek and wash your muzzle," I told him while I moved corpse-number-two to the cougars' cave. They'd returned *en masse* and were already feasting on my first gift. Several surrounded me amid a bevy of snarl and growls until they understood I'd brought them another present.

Once I dropped the man onto the ground and withdrew my spell, the big cats forgot all about me. "Eat well," I murmured and bolted for my car.

Conan was waiting, water dripping off his chin. I loaded him into the car and set my phone on Bluetooth as I started returning calls.

"Where the fuck are you?" Ruby screeched.

"Chill, sweetie. I ran into something I had to take care of, but I'm back on the road. Should be there in maybe twenty minutes."

"Why didn't you call me? Shit. I've left like ten messages. And I loathe leaving messages."

"Didn't have my phone with me. I'll explain everything when I see you..." I let my words hang, knowing her inherent distrust for all things digital.

"You'd better. I have to go," she muttered. "We're getting ready to open."

"But it's not even six, yet. You have a good hour."

"Yeah, well, I've been entertaining cops. It put a crimp in my schedule."

"I owe you, Ruby."

"You damn betcha you do," she retorted and hung up.

I scanned my phone. All the other calls were from the Kirkland PD. I'd deal with them when I showed up. Setting my phone back in its charging cradle, I squinted over a shoulder at Conan stretched out behind the front seats.

"Thanks. For everything."

"Does it mean you're not mad at me for killing them?"

I refocused my attention on the road and thought about his question before I answered. "I was never angry about what you did, but I was worried about potential consequences."

"We should go back across the water."

Suddenly, his insistence on moving made sense. "It's not the same as when we left," I told him.

"Of course, it is."

I shook my head. "No. The world has changed everywhere. We wouldn't recognize that little hamlet in the Carpathians where I found you."

"How can you know?"

"When we get home, I'll find pictures of it on the Internet and show you."

A low growl filled my ears. "How can you be certain they're real?"

"Because no one would waste time taking thousands of fake pictures. Sibiu has over 150,000 people."

A disgruntled yip said he didn't believe me. And why should he. When we'd left, it had barely held 20,000 inhabitants. Traffic was moving along, maybe because we'd missed the worst of rush hour. I pulled up behind *Ascent* at ten minutes past six.

Four officers were prowling about; two more were kneeling scraping the asphalt with some kind of forensic collection devices. "Maybe you should stay in the car," I told Conan.

"I'll teleport inside. No one will notice me."

"Can you bring the box?"

He nosed it. "Maybe."

"Do the best you can," I told him and got out of the car before the cops converged on my door.

I smiled and shook hands and said, "Sorry. I was a bit under the weather most of today. Had no idea you were even here until late afternoon, and then I needed to clean up. What's this all about?"

"Are you ready to make a statement?" a man I didn't recognize asked in a gruff tone. I peered at his badge and read, Detective Bryce.

I adopted my best confused expression. "About what? You haven't told me what the problem is?" I swung my arms to encompass the officers I did know, and went on. "These fellows can tell you I take pride in running a tight ship."

I expected a chorus of assents, but they remained silent. It didn't bode especially well.

"We understand you had an argument with the Northwest Sprits delivery man," Detective Bryce said.

"I did." I nodded. "He's been shorting my deliveries for quite some time. Finally caught him at it three weeks ago, and I'd been waiting for an opportunity to take a stand. I've already called the distributor and alerted them he was cheating me. I got the impression from the gal I spoke with that I wasn't the only unhappy customer."

The detective was scribbling on a tablet with a stylus. "Are you aware Roger Crist is dead?"

"Yeah. Ruby told me." I shrugged. "I'd be lying if I said I was sorry. He's cost me thousands of dollars, and I'm just guessing. It could be more than that."

"Where did you say you were all day?" the detective pressed.

"Home."

"And where exactly is that? I wasn't able to locate an address."

I shuffled through possibilities. I didn't exactly have an address, but I did not want to go there. Everyone rattled off their home addresses as if they were no big deal, but they weren't Vampires with a secret "other life" to conceal.

"Ms. Hawke?" Detective Bryce prodded.

"I don't like to give out my address," I said. At least that part was honest. "Am I under arrest or something here?"

A swirl of Vampire essence almost made me snap my head around, but no one else could scent or see it. What the fuck was Nickolas doing back here?

He strode quickly down the alley, hustled to my side, and draped an arm around my shoulders, offering a knowing male smile to the policemen. "The lady spent her day with me, fellows." He tightened his grip, probably anticipating I'd squirm, trying to duck from beneath his touch.

"No good denying it, sweetheart," he purred and aimed his next words at the cops. "She's been hiding our trysts for months now. She's one of those modern, independent types."

"Is this true, Ms. Hawke?" Officer Ridell, a man I'd gotten to know rather well over the years since I opened *Ascent*, asked gently.

I adopted a hangdog look and wished I could manage a

sheepish flush. "Uh, yeah. Nick and I spend most days together." I twisted to him. Still playing the outraged-to-be-outed card, I hissed, "What the fuck are you doing here?"

"I've told you, sweetheart, I want more. Time to move our commitment to the next phase of—"

"Stop it." I rolled my eyes. "Next thing, you'll be insisting we get married."

"It's a grand idea. I'll take us to Paris. Deck you out in the latest fashions and fly our friends over for the happy event." Vampiric persuasion rolled off him.

The cops sort of shuffled from one foot to the next. Everyone but the detective faded toward their cars. "What's your name?" he barked at Nick.

"Nickolas Giovanni." Nick smiled pleasantly.

"Are you willing to sign a statement Ms. Hawke was with you all day today?"

"Of course. Where would I do that?"

"How can I reach you?"

I wondered how Nick would respond, but he didn't miss a beat. Not bad for an ancient Undead who'd been out of commission for a while. "Call the club. I'll show up wherever you want me."

"You don't have a cell phone?"

"'Fraid I misplaced it." Nick had skewered Bryce with his green-eyed gaze, and he had him in thrall. The detective even took a step closer and tilted his neck at a perfect angle for fangs.

"If it's all right with you," I said to the detective, "I need to go inside and help my staff set up for tonight."

"Sure. That would be fine, Ms. Hawke," he said in a singsong voice.

"Let me know if you need anything more from me," I told him.

This time, it was my turn to grab onto Nickolas. "Come on," I muttered. "We have work to do."

After a longing glance at Bryce's warm, beating jugulars, he let me drag him inside *Ascent*. I slid the back door shut and locked it before I rounded on him. "What in the unholy hell were you going to do? Drink from him?"

"Not in front of everyone." Nickolas adopted an injured tone. "But I was going to mark him to make him easy to find later. How do you eat?"

"Very sparingly, and mostly animals." I dug my nails into his arm and lowered my voice. "I have no idea how long you were in stasis, but if you feed from a mortal and get caught, they'll lock you up forever. Or kill you outright."

"I'm already dead. Or have you forgotten how things work."

"You know exactly what I meant," I shot back. "How long have you been awake?"

He shrugged. "Eh, maybe thirteen nights."

"And how long were you asleep? Scratch that. Were you in stasis for more than fifty years?" At his nod, I went on. "Then you have a lot to learn. I'd take it easy tossing your mesmerizing powers about until you know considerably more."

He yanked away from my grip. "Fine. No thanks yous for providing an alibi? Where were you today, by the way?"

"Thank you," I said stiffly, followed by, "None of your business. Why did you come back here, anyway?"

He dropped his bantering tone. "Because I need answers. You're right I slept for a long time, and I have some decisions to make for me and mine. I've read everything I can find, but—"

Conan chose that moment to glide out of a shadowed alcove with his incisors on display, growling.

Nickolas reached a hand his way. Conan ignored it.

Ruby strode into the back room and immediately began cooing over the wolf. He pressed his head into her hands as she scratched his ears. When her gaze raked over Nickolas, she dispensed with her glamour. Wings in full view, she said, "What are you doing back here?"

"It's okay, Ruby," I said, feeling oddly protective of the Vampire who'd just bailed me out. "I invited him."

She sniffed. "Just so we don't end up with a bunch of you guys."

"Not sure what you consider a bunch," Nickolas said stiffly. "We are three. Me and two associates."

"They're not here," Ruby observed.

"Nay, nor will they be," he countered.

"Suits me fine."

"Aye, we're none too fond of Fae, either," he tossed back at her.

I sucked in a superfluous breath; it whistled through my teeth. "Enough. Both of you." I looked from one to the other. "Humans have declared war on us. It means we're batting for the same side. Got it?"

Crap. I'd just gotten here, and I wanted to teleport to

bumfuck nowhere, corner something, and drink its blood. "So long as you're here," I told Nickolas, "come with Ruby and me. Plenty of work for all of us."

"I brought the box," Conan said out of the blue.

"What box, sweetie?" Ruby asked.

"The money one."

Ruby shot me a "spill-it" look, but I said, "Later. Pretty sure we found where Roger and his buddies were keeping their ill-gotten gains."

"Oooh, gold."

"Nope, paper, but it spends the same."

When she smiled, her wings fluttered, and her golden eyes gleamed with anticipation. I swear, she must have some Leprechaun blood somewhere. I clapped my hands together once and headed into the bar, figuring everyone would follow me.

If I hadn't done something, Ruby would have started nagging for where the "gold" was, and she wouldn't quit until she knew.

"What about my questions?" Nickolas asked as he strode after me.

"Work first," I said. "Questions when we get breaks."

"Good enough," he mumbled, but he sounded disappointed. Too bad. My first priority was getting the club open. Everything else took second place.

I raised my voice as we walked into the main room. "Nick will be helping us tonight. He'll float from station to station, so don't be shy about calling him over if you're shorthanded."

A chorus of "got-its" rose around us, and I settled in to

work. I'd been expecting pushback because of Nickolas being a Vampire, kind of like I'd gotten from Ruby, but no one else said a word. Not because they were more kindly disposed to Vampires than her, but because they didn't want to add to my woes. Today had been a bitch, and they all knew it.

As we hauled booze from the back and got the tables and chairs ready to go, I wondered what Nickolas could possibly want that would have driven him back to *Ascent*. When he'd left the previous night, I'd been certain I'd never see him again.

CHAPTER EIGHT, NICKOLAS

*D*usk had just fallen when I teleported to the alley behind *Ascent*. Damn good thing I was careful and had warded myself because the narrow road was chockful of men in uniforms. A closer look told me they were police. What the hell were they doing behind Ariana's club?

When Clive, Lorenzo, and I had retreated to our cave, this part of the country lacked any sort of law enforcement at all. No need for it since there weren't any regulations to apply. The western sector of North America was wide open. People did what they wanted, and there weren't many of them to worry about.

To say my brief look at what the country had turned into had shocked me would be a vast understatement. Nothing was the same, and I felt ashamed, but I was floundering.

Since I was here—and well hidden—I listened to what the men were saying. Apparently blood in this alley matched blood from some fellow who'd died in a hospital under unusual circumstances. But it wasn't the only blood in this small area. They'd identified blood from another man as well. I resisted rolling my eyes. I could have told them as much.

Plus, a couple of cats had wandered through, along with assorted rats, mice, and birds. One of the cats had killed plenty of mice and left traces of their blood behind a collection of metal bins with labels like "glass," "metal," and "paper." I had no idea why anyone would have gone to the trouble of painting names on those bins, but they appeared to be overflowing with just those items.

Apparently, modern mortals required directions to dispose of their rubbish.

A pushy, talkative policemen seemed convinced Ariana had been behind one man's death. Seemed very odd to me since there wasn't a body to go along with the blood, and Ariana wasn't here.

Ruby, the Fae with many-colored hair, popped out of a door and put her hands on her hips. "Christ on a fucking crutch, you're still here," she said in a strident tone that meant she aimed to get their attention. If she'd been truly intent on accomplishing that, she should have dropped her glamour. Wings would have done the trick.

And then I remembered the supposed war on supernaturals. Displaying what she was might spell major trouble for the Fae.

The man who'd been most vocal about Ariana being guilty stomped to where Ruby stood and glared at her out of bloodshot blue eyes. He looked about forty with cropped black hair, the start of a beer gut, and whiskers dotting his cheeks and chin.

"Yeah, lady. We're still here. You got a problem with that?"

She narrowed her violet eyes. "Yeah, I do, Detective-boy. We're about an hour away from opening, and you being here will make our patrons...uncomfortable."

He offered her a face that said he could care less about *Ascent's* customers. "You told me your boss would be here an hour ago. Where is she?"

"Actually, I said she would probably be here half an hour ago. My guess is she ran into traffic, or stopped to pick up something for the club. Ariana will be here. She always is. I already told you she won't know anything beyond what I already went over—in excruciating detail, mind you. Roger Crist was a rotter. He stiffed us for a whole lot of money, and you should be hunting down where he stashed his loot instead of bothering us."

"Want to join the police force, lady?"

"Pfft. In your dreams, dude."

"Thought so. Until you're wearing a badge"—he tapped his and I noticed it said Detective Bryce—"keep your opinions to yourself."

Damn it. He was annoying. It wouldn't take much for me to jettison my invisibility illusion and yank the cheap tin badge off his chest. Right before I sank my fangs into his stringy neck. What was it with mortals? They'd never had to prance about wearing name tags before.

Were they afraid they'd forget who they were without an instant reminder?

"When will you leave?" Ruby tapped one foot. Anger swirled around her in visible waves, except the man couldn't see them. Fucking with the Fae was a very bad idea for mortals. He could end up dickless or marked in some other way that wouldn't please him at all.

Or turned into a worm or a bat or a crab or a cockroach.

The sound of an approaching car brought my head around. They were another thing I wasn't used to. At all. Not something I wanted to get used to, either. Noisy, smelly, and obnoxious, there were hundreds of them. Nay, probably more like millions.

My nostrils twitched. Ariana was in the car. So was that wolf creature of hers, who was actually a shapeshifter. I'd never known a Vampire to take up with anything like a pet, and I wanted to know the story behind their affiliation. She wasn't drinking from the wolf. I'd checked for telltale markings and not found any.

If he wasn't a food source, what in the hell was the attraction?

I value my clanmates, but it's different from truly liking them. We lose our humanity when we're turned. We still look like mortals, but that's where the similarity begins—and ends. We're nothing like humans. We have totally different needs and motivations.

And they're pretty damned simple. Blood and sex, in that exact order. Some of us lust after power. Those are the ones who create enough minions to start internecine wars within a clan. I never viewed a phalanx of fawning underlings as attractive. Too much responsibility.

Clan Giovanni was unusual, as Vampires go, in that we

were mostly self-governing. We had a few basic rules, like not making new Vampires without first securing permission, not killing for sport, and keeping a low profile so the clerics didn't come after us with silver stakes and iron blades.

I traded my human life for this one toward the close of the 1500s. Mistral had been dead for quite some time then, but my clan was still in an uproar over his abrupt end. When I was newly made, and the bloodlust all I could think about, I slipped my maker's leash many times on the prowl for Mistral's killer. If I could find him, bring him down, I'd be a hero.

Luis always found me—probably wasn't very difficult since my hunger left a track a league wide... Anyway, through a process of sheer longevity and magical strength, I ended up at the helm of Clan Giovanni. It wasn't a post I'd craved, but I understood the concept of duty. I was better suited to the post than anyone else in our clan. I'd only been master for about seventy years when I hatched up what turned into an ill-conceived plan to troll through North America for a few choice additions to our group.

Not one of my better ideas, but everything is clearer when viewed through the lens offered by hindsight.

Ariana had gotten out of the car. My gaze lingered on her. I couldn't help it. No woman—not even a Vampire—had a right to be that striking. Even more remarkable than she'd appeared the previous night, a green silken blouse clung to her full breasts. Her black hair had been drawn back, and it showed off her high graceful cheekbones, full lips, and rounded chin. Dark slacks accentuated her long legs, flat stomach, and flared hips. She nailed the cop who required a badge to remember his own name with her icy blue eyes.

He stared back. He'd asked for her address. I admit I was curious about where she lived too, and I gave myself a brisk mental rebuke. What was I going to do? Show up during the day and talk my way into her bed? It should be simple. Vampires love sex, but I had a feeling she rarely indulged her carnal side.

When she didn't pony up a location right away and stammered something about not wanting to give out her address, I sprang into action. Even hampered by my hundred-year cultural gap, I recognized she needed an alibi. First, I had to put a bit more distance between them and me —so no one would see me bounce out of thin air.

Once I was visible, I laid on the Vampire charm. We're good at being charming. It's what's kept us well-fed all these years. Hustling to Ariana, I adopted a knowing expression, one any male worth his salt would recognize. Oozing a combination of possessiveness and sexual satisfaction, I dropped my arm around Ariana's shoulders and said, "The lady spent her day with me, fellows."

My gambit worked, and eventually the policemen left. What I hadn't counted on was the impact Ariana would have on me once I was actually touching her. If I'd thought her irresistible before, it took everything in me not to sweep her into a teleport spell and take her somewhere to ravish her.

Good thing no one was looking at me—and that it was dark. My cock stood out like a flag, tenting my cheap trousers, and there wasn't a damned thing I could do about it.

By the time we filed into the back of the nightclub, my hard-on had retreated, but not by much. Until the Fae started carping at me, making it clear she didn't trust Vampires. Her brutal assessment was quite the libido-killer.

Well, I didn't trust her, either. Not as far as I could see her, but I didn't throw fuel on the flames. I kept my mouth shut. So far, this entire venture was turning out to be far more taxing than I'd anticipated. From my thwarted desire for Ariana to coming face-to-face with animosity from other supernaturals, I was almost sorry I'd gone to the trouble of showing up here.

Almost.

I'd done Ariana a good turn, and her wolf wasn't nearly as hostile as the Fae had been. I reminded myself not to take Ruby's words personally. It wasn't me she had no use for, but all Vampires.

Except, apparently, Ariana.

Somehow, she'd inveigled her way into everyone's good graces. I spent the first couple of hours watching her covertly as we did everything from hauling crates of liquor to polishing the long, shiny bar to making certain all the glassware was clean.

It was easy to see why the assorted crew of supernaturals worked well together. Ariana made suggestions and followed them up with pitching in until she was satisfied a particular task was well underway. Her instructions didn't come across as orders, and she obviously cared about the Fae and Shifters and Sorcerers.

Tonight, there were two Sorcerers.

I took a chance when I was paired off with Percy. We

were outside, walking the perimeter of the club to make certain the front door was the only way inside. Maybe not a big chance as all that, since he worked the white magic side of the street, but I wasn't certain how much to reveal. He might have known the Sorcerers who'd driven me into stasis.

I tried for a casual tone when I asked, "So, are there many Sorcerers in this area?"

He drew black-and-silver brows into a thick bushy line. "We have a guild house, just like all the other supernaturals."

I must have looked surprised because before I could formulate a follow-up query, he asked, "How long were you asleep?"

I adopted a sheepish expression. It wasn't hard because it mirrored how I was feeling. "Long enough, everything is very strange."

His frown deepened. "Seethes are rather akin to guilds."

I shrugged. "I was never especially fond of them. Too much power vested in one Vampire."

"But you're part of a clan. You said so last evening. Ari was convinced you were its master." We'd nearly finished our transit of the front of the club and were heading along the side toward the rear wall. As we passed decorative slabs of wood, he tapped one. "I wasn't sure how these would work out. They're temporary until the cabinetmaker can create permanent ones. We used to have windows. Until last night. Ariana finally agreed to replace them with something that wouldn't break."

"What happened?" I asked, grateful to move the conversation away from seethes and guilds and clans, particularly my role in Clan Giovanni.

"Someone heaved a boulder through a window. It wasn't the first time by a long shot. Makes sense to have something that won't break." I nodded, but he probably didn't see me because he was in front of me and it was dark. "Why'd you ask about Sorcerers?" he asked.

I could have stumbled around, but he'd have sniffed out a half-truth and thought it odd if I didn't answer at all. "Some of your ilk developed a fancy for Vampire blood. We couldn't evade them, so we dropped out of sight. Appears to have worked because they weren't milling about waiting for us to waken."

Percy whirled so fast it startled me. I thought only Vampires could move that quickly. "Not. My. Ilk," he growled, inserting spaces between the words so there'd be no mistaking them.

I held up a hand. "I assumed they were Sorcerers. They practiced the dark arts, and they weren't Witches or Sidhe or Fae or any other paranormal I've run across."

He growled again, this time without words, and wrapped a hand around my upper arm, squeezing until it hurt. I ignored it. Vampires aren't especially reactive to pain.

"Some Sorcerers lose their way." He paused, maybe considering how to educate me. "They're seduced by black magic. It's quicker, easier to master, and far more destructive. But it eats away at you from within. The bright, shining magical core of you loses its luster until naught is left. If Sorcerers pursued you for your blood, it had to be ones who'd strayed from the path."

I nodded. "I'd assumed as much. Are they still around?"

He cracked a bitter smile, but it was welcome after the

ANN GIMPEL

emotional storm that had passed through him. He couldn't hurt me, but he could break a few bones. They'd take a day or two to heal depending how vicious he was. "If they are," he replied, "they've not crossed paths with me. If they did, I'd make short work of them. They make the rest of us look bad."

"Thank you. I am in your debt, along with Clive and Lorenzo."

"Minions?" He furled a brow.

"Clan Giovanni hasn't exactly had a master Vampire, in the sense you mean, during my lifespan. Ariana was correct that I am the *de facto* leader of the clan, but I don't hold absolute power. In truth, I'm certain they've replaced me by now. The three of us crossed the sea in search of promising humans to freshen our lines. The European tribes suffered from inbreeding—not that we produced children, but almost all new Vampires came from distressingly similar stock. Our magic was growing weaker as a result.

"After discussing it amongst ourselves, I volunteered to come to the Americas. Clive and Lorenzo accompanied me. They are younger and look to me for direction, but they could have refused stasis and struck out on their own."

Percy let go of my arm. I resisted rubbing the divots he'd carved into my undead flesh.

How long ago was that?" Percy rumbled in his deep voice. The moon had risen, and it shone off his bald head.

"We made the journey around 1910, so better than 100 years ago. We'd been here for a relatively short while—much of it spent crossing the country—and were still assessing how to best proceed when the Sorcerers made our decision for us."

"You selected a fortuitous path," Percy said. "If you hadn't vanished, the black Sorcerers would have hounded you until naught was left."

Good to know I'd chosen well. And that Clive and Lorenzo had listened to reason.

We'd completed our transit of the building. *Ascent's* big front door stood open. The night was young, but a few early drinkers had wandered inside and taken up residence on barstools.

"What's next?" I asked.

He squinched his big face into what might have been a smile—or not—and said, "I take up my post by the front door again. See if anyone else needs an extra hand or two."

I stopped, unsure whether to thank him. Vampires aren't big on manners, but I was in a whole new environment. I cleared my throat, as unnecessary as breathing, and said. "Thanks for your candor. I appreciate it."

"Apologies for my corrupt kinsmen." He turned away, scooted a tall stool over with a booted foot, and settled his bulk across the seat.

I was relieved *Ascent* wasn't a hotbed for dark sorcery. From the sounds of things, the Sorcerers' guild had disowned their dark kinsfolk. I looked around the bar to see who I could help next, not that I'd done all that much to assist Percy, but maybe two sets of eyes were better than one when it came to security.

Ariana stood behind the bar with a clipboard, maybe noting inventory before the night got busier.

"Nick, over here," a female voice called. It belonged to Christa, another Fae with dusky skin and milky-white eyes. Her glamour made her appear "normal," but I could see through it to her decidedly non-human eyes and silver wings, dappled in jewel tones. Dressed similarly to her outfit last night, she wore mostly black with lots of jangly earrings and a silver necklace that looked like a seer's torc to me.

I didn't care for the silver jewelry, but I strode over to where she stood unpacking glasses from cartons. "You do this part," she said. "I'll wash them."

For the next hour or more, I extracted glasses—big ones, little ones, tumblers, shot glasses—from an endless parade of boxes. I could see where having two of us was a timesaver, though. By the time we were done, the club had filled with a noisy crowd.

"Thanks," she said.

"My pleasure." I smiled, forgetting I didn't need to wow her with my Vampiric charm.

She rolled her milk-white eyes. "Save it for the mortals," she muttered and hastened to add, "but not here. Last thing we need is someone sporting fang marks."

"I know better." More words burbled at the back of my throat, but I kept them penned up before I launched into a lecture that she was treating me like I'd just been turned.

She scanned me with magic; I felt its sting as it tracked from my head to my feet. "Maybe you do," she said.

Ariana made her way to where we stood, wiping her hands on an apron she'd tied around her waist. "Thanks for all the help tonight." She nodded my way. "If you want to talk, now is as good a time as any. We'll do nothing but get busier as the night wears on." She turned and walked toward the doorway leading to the back room.

I started to follow her, but Christa grabbed my arm. I turned toward her and met her implacable blind stare. "If you hurt her," she said softly, "or drag her into some seethe or something, all of us won't rest until we've hunted you down and extracted retribution." She lowered her voice still more. "Ariana is precisely where she needs to be. She is a key element in our defense against mortals. Do not think for even one moment she would be better off among your kind."

I bristled. "My kind is also hers. Have you told her about this 'key element' theory?"

"Not yet, and neither will you. It's far more than a 'theory.'"

Something hot settled around my head. Prickly and uncomfortable, it carved a swathe through my mind before it became part of me. Christa wasn't taking any chances about me revealing anything about key elements to Ariana.

"You didn't have to do that." I yanked out of her grip.

"Better safe than sorry." She offered me a too-sweet smile and turned to serve a customer who'd walked up to the bar.

"Nick?" Ariana called, sounding irritated I hadn't been right behind her.

I hustled through the door, shutting it to mute the din from the teeming club. "Sorry," I said. "Christa wanted to, erm, talk with me."

"Anything I should know about?" She zeroed in on me with those amazing eyes of hers.

"Nope. Nothing at all. Thank you for making time to talk with me." I kept my tone formal.

"You're welcome. It was a reasonable request, and you lied to help me earlier. Seemed like the least I could do. I can't promise we'll get through everything on your agenda. If something goes south out there"—she jerked her chin at the door I'd just closed—"I'll have to deal with it."

"I understand." No reason to waste time pointing out that Vampires lying to humans is normal for us—or telling her I'd have done anything to ensure her freedom—so I dove right in. "Are we the only Vampires here?"

"Depends. How far does 'here' encompass?"

"Can we look at a map?"

"Sure." She dug one of those infernal phone things out of a pocket and tapped the glass front several times. When she was done an outline of North America flared across the device.

I hesitated to touch it, but she had, so I scribed my fingers in an arc over its surface.

"Far as I know"—she tapped another few things and drew an oblong in red on the thing—"at least this region has no others like us. Why is it important? Aren't you planning to go home? While I'm at it, is home still northern Italy?"

"Yes, the Tyrol, but I'm not sure about returning," I replied, trying for honesty.

She offered me a sympathetic look, an unusual expression on any Vampire. "Yeah. Hard to know what you'll find after all this time."

Conan materialized out of nowhere and said, "I want to go home, but Ariana says there's nothing to go back to."

I looked from her to the wolf, expecting her to correct her

creature. Instead, tenderness and caring carved lines into her forehead as she murmured, "I know you do, sweetie."

"You said you'd prove it with pictures," the wolf went on.

Ariana nodded. "It's a good idea. I can find photos of both places, where we came from and Nick's region as well."

Confusion swept through me. I must not have heard her correctly. "What do you mean pictures?"

"You'll see. Come back here to my desk where I have a real monitor. It's tough to see stuff on the phone."

CHAPTER NINE, ARIANA

*I*t only took me a few moments to settle into my desk chair and bring up photographs of Sibiu. Conan stood by my side. A disbelieving whine was followed by a series of whuffly barks. "It's not the same place," he declared in between making wolf noises.

"Yes, dear, it is. Look there." I tapped the screen. "It's the mountains we used to live in. And here's our river."

Meanwhile, a sharp intake of unneeded breath told me Nickolas was rattled as well. "That's Sibiu?" he asked in a strangled tone.

"Modern Sibiu, yes," I said. "It's huge and progressive and busy. Just like Seattle, the city we live near. It didn't look anything like this when you went into stasis."

"Quite the understatement," Nick muttered. "And it runs far deeper than sheer numbers of mortals."

Maybe because I'd lived through the time he'd been asleep, the shift had been more palatable, but the discovery and mass production of the internal combustion engine had changed a whole lot. Once people were no longer stuck in the towns they'd been born in and education more readily available to everyone—

Conan swiped his nose over the glass. "Make it move," he demanded.

I understood and dialed up a video of Sibiu for him to watch. I'd been prepared to zero in on our old hamlet with Google Earth, but it wasn't looking as if I'd have to go that far.

The wolf leaned his head against my upper arm and whined as some travel tour company's video representation of a dream vacation scrolled past. Once he got past his resistance, Conan was bound to recognize landmarks. At least they didn't change, no matter how many homes and businesses had sprung up.

I let the video run for a few minutes before I asked, "Seen enough?"

He growled. I took it as an invitation to hit the escape key and give him time to process what was surely the destruction of his memories of our former home. My fingers flew over the keys as I prepared to give northern Italy a similar treatment.

"You said the Tyrol." I glanced at Nickolas, who stood off to one side. "Can you narrow it down?"

"Castelrotto," he said. "Literally translated, it means knights' village. It's in the Dolomites."

Soon, I had another collection of still photographs marching across my monitor. Nickolas leaned so close I felt his muted warmth. Our heat feels very different from mortals', and it had been a long while since a Vampire had been this close to me. Once I got past the oddness of it, I rather liked the sensation.

Until I realized it reminded me of my years with Mistral.

Damn it, anyway. What was up with Mistral? I hadn't thought about him for a very long while, but he kept popping into my thoughts like a jack-in-the-box on speed.

"Can you make that one bigger?" Nickolas tapped one of the photos of what might have been a medieval monastery.

"Sure." I showed him the key combination that made photos larger—and then smaller again. Once I was certain he understood, I got up, offering him my seat. While he was poring over what was probably a mini-death of his hopes and dreams, I edged closer to where Conan had holed up in his favorite spot. A break in the shelves led to something not unlike a cave. I'd done a better job angling them to make certain Conan fit in the space. It gave him a retreat from the craziness *Ascent* turned into most nights.

Not wanting to crowd him, I squatted and asked, "You okay?"

"No. Why would I be?"

"Would you rather not have known?" I let the question hover in the space between us. After a few moments, he scrunched forward enough to lay his head in my lap. I dug my fingers into his fur, soothing him.

Nickolas hunkered next to us. "I know exactly how you feel," he told Conan.

The wolf picked up his head and snarled.

A bitter noise—part laugh, part grunt—emerged from the Vampire.

I smothered a laugh tickling the back of my throat. Now wasn't a good time to mention they were bonding over feeling sorry for themselves. Besides, I'd never knowingly have hurt Conan's feelings. Nick was another story. He was just a ship passing through. He'd never become a permanent part of my life.

Keep telling yourself that, an inner voice piped up. I shushed it.

"Did you want to look at anything else?" I asked Nickolas.

"No reason to. If Clan Giovanni is still intact, we—er, they—have gone elsewhere. Our erstwhile village is far too crowded; nowhere for a group of Vampires to hide themselves. We could never bring anyone new into the clan. One slip, and the mortals would hunt us relentlessly."

I knew precisely what he meant by a "slip." New Vampires have one hell of a time keeping their fangs to themselves. "Just a sip," we tell ourselves. "What could it hurt?" But once the blood is flowing, the sip turns into this runaway hunger that doesn't let up until nothing is left.

"One big difference beyond all those new buildings," I said, "is now everyone knows our weaknesses. Ask the average joe on the street, and he'll be quick to tell you about salt and silver and holy water and beheading. From time to time, men have fancied themselves Vampire hunters and packed up to hunt us."

Nickolas turned his green eyes on me. The touch of his gaze ignited something deep within my essence, something that had died the day I'd ended Mistral. Alarm bells tolled; I moved Conan's head off my lap and stood.

"How long have things been...like this?" Nickolas asked as he got to his feet.

I shrugged. "Certainly the last fifty years, but the seeds for today began about the time you chose stasis." I slitted my eyes. "Why?"

"Why what?"

"You're hedging. You knew precisely what I was asking," I muttered.

He looked away, which was a relief. The pressure from his unrelenting gaze made me long for things that would never be mine again. It wasn't as if I had a full complement of human emotions.

I didn't. When my human veneer had been stripped away, only a few things remained. Blood lust, anger, possessiveness—as in *mine*—and sex.

Mistral had reminded me my days of being his were over, and he'd done it in a blunt, in-my-face way. Look where it had gotten him. And me. He'd assumed his role as master would protect him from my fury, but he didn't know me at all. He probably wouldn't read it this way, but he was the lucky one since I had to live with what I'd done. It would never go away, and I was worse than an idiot if I thought time would erase my fall from grace.

I wasn't looking at Nickolas, but I felt the weight of his gaze as he sought me again. "I already told Percy why we chose stasis," he said. "Black Sorcerers trapped us for our blood. They believed it would feed their power. We couldn't teleport away, so we sank beyond their reach. It was the only option, other than giving the Sorcerers what they wanted."

It made sense except for the length of time. "Why so long?"

"You know how it is. I had to select a rough timeline. We'd be weak emerging from stasis, so I wanted to make damn good and sure the bastards would have given up and left by then."

"Have they?" I raised a brow.

He nodded. "It seems so." He stopped for a moment before adding. "One good thing balanced against many not-so-good ones. Tell me about this war with mortals. Is it widespread or only here?"

I looked for Conan but couldn't see him. He'd either slunk deeper into his corner or teleported elsewhere. Hunting fixed a whole lot, and I wished him the bounty of bunnies and deer.

Reaching over, I put my computer into sleep mode and considered where to begin. Nickolas didn't require excruciating levels of detail. I sank into my desk chair and swiveled it to face him. He hefted a liquor crate from a nearby shelf and sat across from me. I liked that he didn't feel the need to fill the silence between us. He'd asked a question and was content to wait until I answered him.

"About fifty years back, or perhaps it was only forty, the Sidhe and Fae decided humans had evolved enough to coexist with magic wielders. If they'd put it up for a vote, they'd have lost the argument, but those like us have always segregated ourselves into covens or guilds or seethes."

Nickolas nodded. "There's certainly never been much in the way of sharing between them and us. They've always made it abundantly clear they think we're scum."

I winced. While I knew it was true, hearing it spoken rankled. I'd gone a long way toward bridging the breach when I made a conscious decision to staff *Ascent* with supernaturals. At first, I'd been hard-pressed to get even one to sign on, but after a few months everything shifted, and a variety of magic-wielders showed up when I posted openings. By being fair and open-minded, I'd gone from someone to be shunned to a viable source of income for paranormals, who'd become virtually unemployable—unless they hid what they were.

"Ariana?"

"Sorry. I was just thinking. Been doing too much of that lately. Anyway, the Fae and Druids held a big coming-out party. It might not have been so bad, but they named most of the rest of us."

A corner of Nick's well-formed mouth twitched. "Am I correct assuming most didn't include Vampires?"

I nodded. "They did finger point at the Sidhe, Shifters, Witches, and Sorcerers, though. For a while—maybe half a dozen years—it appeared things were progressing if not speedily, at least in a forward direction."

"Let me guess." Nick's tone was laced with sarcasm. "Someone got frisky throwing power around."

"Exactly. A bunch of teenaged boys had been baiting a Fae family. One fine day, the kids roared up on motorcycles and took up their taunting. The Fae decided they'd had enough and scared the fuck out of the boys by dropping their glamour." I stopped long enough to decide whether to tell him the rest.

"And?" he prodded, clearly intuiting I'd left something out.

"The women fucked the boys and then let them go."

Nick groaned. He understood those boys would lust after Fae forevermore, that nothing else would satisfy them. "That's all it took for mortals to declare war on us?"

"No, but it was the beginning. Each time humans had their noses rubbed in our superior power, it riled them further. They view themselves as top-dog, and they didn't take kindly to having their shortcomings highlighted."

"They've always been a bunch of bigots," Nickolas said matter-of-factly. "They get off on searching for scapegoats, someone to look down on."

A smile made it past my defenses. Damn it was good to talk with someone who shared some of my memories, or maybe it was more shared interpretation of events.

"Anyway, about two years ago," I went on, "there was this big showdown. A bunch of mostly humans, who called themselves Witches, but weren't, hired the real deal to do some fortunetelling. Obviously, I wasn't there, but I heard the mortals didn't care much for the soothsaying. It pissed off the lead Witch, and she flung enough magic around to turn three of the phony Witches into toads."

Nickolas chuckled. I could tell he was trying to hold back, but he ended up laughing uproariously. When he got hold of himself, he made a snorting sound. "I shouldn't have done that, but they got precisely what they deserved."

"Erm, they didn't see it that way," I pointed out. "The ones who were still in their human bodies dragged the toads to the local police shouting for blood, for retribution. It was the beginning of proclamations requiring everyone with magic to register with local authorities.

"None of us fell for it. We knew the next thing would be removing our freedom. And so, the war began. It's not exactly, 'shoot 'em on sight,' but it's not far from it, either. I've adopted a don't ask, don't tell policy for *Ascent*. I know who's human in my club. And who isn't, but everyone is welcome so long as they don't create a scene or make any of the other patrons uncomfortable. So far, it's worked. One of Percy's fellow Sorcerers is a skilled forger, and he's made documents for many of us who lacked them because we were born hundreds of years ago."

"What kind of documents?" Nick frowned.

I rolled my eyes. "Driver's license. ID card. Passport. Social Security card."

"You may as well be speaking Old Gaelic," Nick groused.

"Yeah. I know, but if you're going to stay here, you'll need a basic complement of identification papers too. Kind of like earlier when the detective asked for your cell phone number. You can't get one of those without identification." I waited for all the information to sink in before I asked, "So?"

Vampires are an arrogant crew, and I waited for him to brush everything into a corner and state it didn't apply to him. He didn't. It astonished me when he said, "I honestly don't know. I'm more confused than I was when I began. Returning to the Dolomites doesn't appear to be viable. Besides, I couldn't get there without these identification documents."

"True enough," I agreed. "It's too far to teleport."

"This Sorcerer associate of Percy's, what type of payment would he require?"

It was a solid question, and I thought about it before I said, "You'd have to ask him, or have Percy ask on your behalf. So far, his price has been tailored to the type of magic-wielder... You know. Charms. Spells." I stopped there. No reason to explain there wasn't much Vampire magic that would tempt a Sorcerer to do anything.

Fae could spin white magic, provide jewels or prophecies. Sidhe were masters at coming up with gold. Witches could craft charms. About all we traded in was blood.

"Say no more," Nickolas said. "I'll talk with Percy. It wouldn't be only for me."

I hadn't exactly forgotten about the other Vampires, but neither were they at the forefront of my mind. "Where are they?" No reason to beat around the bush.

"I'm not certain. I saw Clive earlier today. He and Lorenzo and I decided we'd be better off splitting up."

"Good call. Do they know to keep a low profile?"

"No lower than we were used to in Italy." He skewered me with his beautiful eyes. Up close like this, the irises were rimmed in gold with little golden flecks throughout. "None of us have been awake long enough to do much beyond getting our strength back."

"Tell them," I said, my tone sharper than I'd meant. "Do it now before they do something stupid and bring the wrath of everyone watching for us down on our heads."

His gaze turned hard around the edges. Clearly, it had been a very long time since anyone had told him what to do.

I flirted with apologizing, but it might dilute my message, and I couldn't afford to do that.

I did gentle my voice when I added, "If mortals had their way, they'd imprison every one of us, killing those they can and surrounding the rest of us with iron to weaken our power. All the major nations have signed agreements to work together in that regard."

Nick's copper eyebrows shot up. "All of them?"

"All the ones that count," I said. "Everyone big enough to have a militia and jails to hold us. It's not pretty. Peace talks broke down permanently about six months ago. Before that, I hung onto a slender hope reason would prevail. It never did. Humans don't trust what they don't understand. They don't want to coexist with us. They want us dead, and they've made it profusely clear they have zero interest in meeting us halfway."

"Surely there must have been a few dissenters."

I shrugged. "Nothing is ever a hundred percent with humans, but the peaceful faction didn't win. And now they're running scared because one of the recent proclamations states any mortal engaging in dealings with us is also subject to punishment, up to and including lifetime imprisonment."

Nick's pleasant expression faded; he balled his hands into fists. "What if we cut a swathe through them, murdered them like the rats they are? Or"—he grinned nastily —"turned them? I wouldn't wish new Vampirehood on my worst enemy."

"We've discussed similar approaches," I replied, "but what it comes down to is this. There are millions of them and only a few thousand of us. We might gain the upper hand at first, but we would make things worse, and eventually they'd prevail by dint of sheer numbers. If we went on an out-and-out slash-and-burn, they'd develop some kind of system to test for magic. Everyone would be forced to go through scanners, and we'd be apprehended at the grocery store, or—"

"We don't eat that kind of food," he broke in.

I rolled my eyes and exhaled noisily for emphasis. "It was an example. All of us want to go balls-out and kill those sanctimonious fuckers preaching from every news outlet. But it would be an empty victory because they'd just keep coming. Eventually, we'd fold."

"I see," he said at last. "Besides, being engaged in warfare from now until forever has no appeal. Even thinking about it makes me tired."

"Did you raise your minions?" I circled back to ensuring the two Vampires didn't get themselves beheaded by being too visible.

"Nag. Nag. Nag. They're not minions in the sense you mean, but lower-ranking clan members. I'll notify them right now. And then I'll go find Percy."

I grinned at the nag commentary. Mistral had accused me of much the same, and with good cause. I can be relentless when I want something. It was why *Ascent* had succeeded against long odds.

Christa dashed into the back room, a drawn look on her face and her glamour slipping. "Trouble, boss."

I jumped from my chair. "What?"

"Those bloody cops from earlier are back. Someone told them you're a Vampire."

I swathed myself in magic to make myself irresistible to mortals and bolted from the back room as if jettisoned from a slingshot. I'd make those bastards sorry they ever questioned me.

"Right behind you." Nickolas sounded determined—and pissed.

I liked it that he had my back, and I bit my tongue before a long list of instructions rolled from my mouth. Either I trusted his good sense, or I should order him to remain in the stockroom.

Not that he'd obey any command from me. I had no authority over what he did or didn't do.

Sometimes fate ponies up what you need. I hoped to hell I hadn't guessed wrong, and this was one of those times.

CHAPTER TEN, NICKOLAS

$\mathcal{I}$ hadn't been joking when I told Conan I knew how he felt when Ariana showed him his former home. It shouldn't have been quite as big a shock to the shapeshifter as it was to me. He'd watched as the world changed around him, but perhaps he'd nurtured the illusion only this part of things had altered. Animals held a unique view of their environment, one I hadn't considered for a long while.

And then I reminded myself Conan was far from a pet. He might look like a wolf, but he was as magical as creatures came. Did he have a human form? I'd have to ask Ariana. If I asked Conan, all I'd get would be a mouthful of teeth aimed in my direction.

I felt certain he knew Vampires only tolerated pets as a potential food source, but he'd come to terms with Ariana and her feeding habits. In truth, we far prefer humans, which would have put Conan and Ariana squarely on the same side. When I was careful, I could keep my living menus alive for a long time. Some even developed loyalty to me. I wouldn't go so far as to say they were proud to contribute to my strength, but not far from it.

Buildings, roads, cars, and sheer numbers of mortals were the least of the changes I struggled to absorb. From my limited exposure to "now," I'd sensed an irreverence, a lack of respect for anything. Mortals appeared to have set themselves up as gods, and I wondered how they lived with the consequences.

Too many kings and queens never worked out. Someone had to pick up the reins and take responsibility. When everyone did, clashes were inevitable. Serious ones where people killed each other over imagined slights.

I'd been ruminating on where to go from here since returning to Castelrotto would probably be a waste of time. I'd been gone long enough, Clan Giovanni must have reorganized around a new power structure—if they even still existed. From the series of images on Ariana's contraption, I wouldn't have taken bets either way.

I was getting ready to have a quick, terse conversation with Clive and Lorenzo when Christa interrupted with something even more urgent. I was beginning to regret waking at all. Perhaps if we'd slept another fifty years, much of the current unrest would have resolved itself.

Not very fucking likely.

Conan had left while Ariana and I were talking. I could have remained in the back room with the liquor and raised Clive and Lorenzo, but I'd be damned if I'd abandon Ariana.

She probably didn't need me, but I'd help if I could. What I'd done earlier had defused things.

It wasn't as if I'd get lucky two times running, but it wasn't a reason to remain out of sight and let the chips fall where they might. For some reason, I expected to see the same uniformed men who'd been in the street behind the nightclub, but the two men standing by Percy's stool wore dark-colored wool suits, not uniforms. Their garments were cheaply made, barely a step up from what I'd stolen from the used-clothing store.

One had close-cropped fair hair; the other was mostly bald. They oozed a slimy unctuousness that put me on edge. I paid out a subtle thread of seeking magic to pin down if they were truly human. They didn't smell quite right to me, but I admit I'm out of practice.

Eh, not that out of practice. When a Vampire can't sniff out human blood, we're finished.

Percy wore a stone-faced expression that said he'd as soon pound the men into dust as talk with them. The air around him shimmered with menace that should have sent the duo screaming for cover. Meanwhile, the bar was emptying out fast, which couldn't be good for Ariana's profits for tonight. Good thing Conan had left. His wolf form was unsettling enough, the men might draw the weapons peeking from holsters beneath their jackets and shoot him. When he didn't die—or even whimper—they'd try to capture him in their ongoing efforts to purge the world of everything magical, and the whole place would erupt in conflict.

I had a feeling the men could summon aid. Hell, for all I know, ten more just like them were waiting outside. Now that was something I could check, and I pushed my experimental seeking thread beyond *Ascent's* walls.

Ariana sashayed in front of the men, dripping Vampiric charm. "Evening, boys. What can I do for you?"

Jealousy speared me. I knew what she was doing, and I resented the hell out of it. She was directing come-fuck-me vibes at the men, bathing them in a spell that would have them salivating for time alone with her. If she turned up the heat a bit more, they'd come to blows over who got to accompany her to a dark, secluded spot.

In the era I was familiar with, as soon as she got the winner somewhere private, she'd sink her fangs into his neck and feed. He wouldn't remember much of anything, but he'd be stuck with telltale marks in his neck. Did the current crop of humans even recognize Vampire bites?

I had a feeling they might not.

The baldish man, who looked to be around fifty with deep lines in his face, cleared his throat and tugged something shiny from a pocket. Once it was free, he swung a clear crystal with runic markings in front of him. "Ms. Hawke. We have it on good authority you are one of the Undead. How do you plead?"

The shiny thing radiated a primitive version of a truth casting, but its maker hadn't been especially skilled. Good thing. Witchy charms could be incredibly efficient, but whoever had sold the men this one had hoodwinked them. One step up from painted glass, the charm was worthless.

Ariana adopted a stunned look that shaded to anger. I silently applauded her superb acting skills. "You're flat fucking nuts," she gritted through clenched teeth. "You ran all my customers off for this tripe? Get out of my bar."

The man sung the charm faster. "You're a Vampire. Make things easy for all of us and admit it."

"For fuck's sake, I'll admit no such thing. It's not true. Tomorrow, when your administrative offices open, I'll be filing complaints against both of you. I might take you to small claims court for lost revenue for this evening. Where are your badges? What are your names?"

Nervous tension sheeted off the men. I smelled their fear as they exchanged glances that said this was not the outcome they'd been expecting. A long, rolling howl told me Conan had returned. He bounded across the empty bar and planted himself next to Ariana, fangs bared and growling. Almost as an afterthought, hackles bloomed along the length of his back.

She dropped a hand onto his shoulder and said, "Behave."

He growled louder.

"What is that?" the fair-haired man blurted.

"My dog," she said sweetly. "He helps keep order around here."

Conan woofed once, playing at being a pet.

Ariana turned her attention back to the men. "Who told you I was a Vampire?" she demanded. "I want to know?"

The one who'd asked about Conan opened his mouth. Before he could say anything, the other one dragged him through the door.

"Wait!" Ariana shouted and bolted after them. "Your names."

Percy stopped her with a hand across her chest. "I've got this. I'll be right on their asses." He pushed through the door, turning to smoke before it shut behind him.

Neat trick, but it would never be part of my repertoire.

"Damn it." Ariana made a fist and drove it into a wall. Wood splintered, and plaster flaked to the floor. The only ones left in the club were her, me, Conan, and assorted staff. Every patron had made a run for it. If I knew anything about human nature, they wouldn't return tonight. And maybe not for many nights to come. Everyone had secrets, things they'd done wrong that they feared would come to light. Keeping your head down was second nature.

"Something wasn't on the up-and-up with them," Ruby mumbled. "Even before they hauled out that phony charm, they seemed edgy, not like other cops I've run into."

"My take too," I said. "I don't know how your current crop of those who enforce laws are supposed to act, but they didn't smell right. If I'd known they were going to run away, I'd have tried harder to figure things out."

"Where do you suppose they got that bogus charm?" Ariana asked.

"Looked Witch-made to me," Christa said. "But not by any Witches in the guild. They're all traditionally trained and would never pass off such sloppy products."

Ariana knitted her brows into a single, black line. "That argues there's been a resurgence of black witchcraft."

If I'd been the breathing type, I'd have exhaled long and loud. As it was, I settled for asking, "Are they related to black Sorcerers?"

"Not exactly," Ruby said and held up her index finger.

"Witches come in three iterations. Mortals who call themselves Witches but who have zero magic. They sit around and light candles and chant and dance in graveyards, but they're just enjoying themselves."

Christa jumped in and said, "And then there are white Witches. They have true power—and they could dabble in black magic—but they've settled for the trade-off of having less power that works on the side of good."

"Rather than a whole lot of magic that destroys things," Ruby muttered.

Ariana made a disgusted hissing noise. "Any of them could do a better job crafting a charm than that piece of shit the man had. How could he have assumed prancing in here and dangling that worthless bauble around would do anything but piss me off?"

"Someone must have assured him it would work," I said slowly still assessing the wrongness I'd glommed onto. Human, but not completely. What could it mean? Damn it. Despite all the hours I'd spent in the local library, I wasn't any nearer to understanding how things worked here than I'd been before I'd cracked my first book.

"I agree," Ariana muttered. "Which means they're both stupid and desperate. But why? Is there some time crunch we're not privy to? Did someone tell them they have to come up with a scapegoat by high noon tomorrow? If so, who's behind it?"

"Will Percy figure out who they are?" I asked.

"Depends," Ruby replied.

"Of all of us, his magic has the best chance," Christa said.

Ariana glanced at a clock mounted over the bar. It wasn't

even midnight yet. "May as well shut her down for the evening," she said.

Selene, a coyote shifter patted her arm. "We'll pack 'em in tomorrow."

"I'm not so certain of that, but thanks, honey." Ariana made a wry face.

A thin, spare woman with ropy muscles, midnight-dark hair, and high cheekbones emerged from a shadowed corner. Medium height, she'd been here last night. When I searched for her name, I came up with Dee. Witchiness spilled from her, and her appearance was timely. We needed someone who actually was a Witch to shine some light on the weird charm.

She squared her thin shoulders. "That charm was not Witch made."

"Not to put you on the spot, but how do you know?" Ariana asked.

"No one in the guild would do such slipshod work."

"Are there Witches working independently?" I asked.

She slitted her eyes my way. "Watch it, Vampire. I'm a necromancer."

"Nice to meet you too." My fangs started to drop; it's a reflex when I'm annoyed. How far could her enchantment reach? I'm dead, so at least in theory, it should offer her power over me. Necromancers had a long and storied history in the Old Country. Vampires always gave them a very wide berth, but they'd never actually bothered any of us.

"Do you know who might have made the charm?" Ariana pressed.

Before Dee could answer, a column of misty gray-white

smoke formed, swirling down from the ceiling. Percy was back. I hoped to hell he had something we could use. Ariana had floated good arguments for not fanning the flames of mortals' fear, but I can kill quietly, discreetly, and I wanted those two men dead.

They'd threatened Ariana. Worse than threatened. They'd marched in here full of intent to imprison her. Or worse. It was unconscionable. If Percy had anything to go on, anything at all, I'd run with it.

Strike now and be done with things. I've always worked best alone, and I'd take care of this problem by myself too. Surely, their deaths would send a message to whomever they worked with to back off. Maybe while I was at it, I'd figure out who was hawking phony charms and kill them too.

A clean sweep.

I liked it—from every angle. I'd be useful again. I'd be ridding the world of garbage, and I'd be easing Ariana's burdens. She'd been generous and done her best to help me by inviting me to *Ascent*. It was the least I could do in return. I needed to focus on that aspect, not the possessiveness that was sending shoots out at every angle.

I used to joke about Vampires being loosely related to dragonkind. We don't breathe fire, but we are collectors at heart. I've been in seethes sporting art that would make the curator of the Louvre salivate. I wanted Ariana because she wasn't mine, pure and simple, and I had to forget about my growing hunger to mark her.

Back in the old days, sure. Then I'd have found a way to entice her into my clan. Once she shared blood with us, she'd be ours, lost to Clan Hawke forever. Interestingly, we didn't enforce the rules quite the same way for males. None of it mattered a whit. Ariana was her own Vampire without a clan affiliation, and she wasn't looking to alter that.

The smoke whirled and puffed, gradually turning into the burly Sorcerer. Ariana was already firing questions at him, and maybe he was answering her in telepathy.

Once Percy was corporeal, I saw the charm pinched between two fingertips as if he wanted to limit his contact with it. Some magic has a perverted aspect. Creepy and wrong, its touch is like someone running their fingernails down a chalkboard.

Dee snatched the magical bit out of his hand, yelped, and immediately dropped it onto the wooden floor where it started to smoke. "Thing has a bite," she sputtered.

Power arced from Percy's ham-sized hand, forming a clear, domelike keep-safe around the charm. No longer green, it was turning black. What the hell was it? I stretched my own magic, probing, sensing, but the only thing that bounced back at me was Percy's sorcery, probably because he had the thing under his control.

"Those fellows were not cops," Percy growled, "but then we'd pretty much figured that part out." He shook himself much like Conan might have. Maybe it was a way to sort out what he'd seen.

"How'd you get the charm from them?" Dee tilted her head to one side.

Percy nodded. "You'd know about that, huh?" When she didn't say anything, he went on, "Catching up with them was easy. Found 'em in a fancy house not far from here. They about pissed themselves when I showed up in their living room. When I got pushy about culling through their minds—after they refused to talk with me—different magic rolled through. Before I got a bead on who else was there, both men started clawing at their throats.

"I made a token effort to save the younger one—better chance of him talking with me—but it was hopeless. I did figure out black witchcraft killed them. It has a certain stink about it."

"Figured they had to be dead," Dee muttered. "No one hands over charms like that. They're keyed to whomever they were made for."

"Did they exercise those guns of theirs?" Ariana asked.

Percy shook his head. "I kept expecting one of them to shoot me, but it never happened."

The dead part sank in loud and clear. I was glad they'd breathed their last even though it would make it harder to determine who was behind this. "Did you search the house?" I asked Percy.

"Nope. Wanted to get out of there before whoever turned black magic against the men decided I was a liability. House had an emptiness to it, like it was only used as a staging area. Figured I could feed the address into the city database and see what pops up."

Ariana snorted. "Still hacking on the side?"

Percy shot her an enigmatic look, and I wondered what the hell hacking meant in this context. I understood the word well enough—it meant to chop something up. The librarian had alluded to a database when I was hunting for reading material, but I hadn't understood her meaning until she'd brought up a long list on a screen not unlike the one in Ariana's back room.

Rather than slow things down with questions—once I began asking them, I might never shut up—I listened carefully to what came next.

"I'm grateful for any information," Ariana continued, "but be careful."

"I'll cover my intrusion with magic," Percy assured her.

Meanwhile the charm had caught fire. Dee crouched next to it, hands extended, chanting in a language I wasn't familiar with. "Fuck," she sputtered. "Can't even slow it down."

"If it was keyed to the one with the bald head," Ruby said slowly, "wouldn't him being dead mean the charm would die too?"

"Sure, but not immediately." Dee flicked a glance at the Fae.

I caught a spark of magic between Ariana and Conan and assumed they were conversing. Sure enough, she said, "Conan and I agree the charm is a dead end. What we have to do is figure out who—or what—is behind those men showing up here tonight."

She twisted her mouth into a determined pucker. "Too much has happened in too short a time to be accidental."

"I agree," Percy rumbled. "Unfortunately, Vampires have a lot of enemies in every camp from mortals to other supernaturals."

"Tell me something I don't know." A fang dropped, peeking out of her mouth. I found it fetching and adorable; I buttoned up my thoughts fast in case anyone was helping themselves. Plenty of mage-power in this room. I was the new guy, and I'd do well to watch myself.

"You found money," Ruby spoke up. "I say we go collect it before the cops divvy it up amongst themselves."

"But then they'll never pin Roger's thievery on him," Ariana protested.

Ruby shrugged. "He's dead. What difference does it make?"

"The difference is the cops will believe he was stealing from me—and others," Ariana shot back. "Right now, it's mostly he-said, she-said."

"So, we won't take it all." Ruby hesitated a beat. "You already lifted one box. How many were there?"

"A lot," Conan said.

Ruby turned her golden eyes with their vertical pupils on the shapeshifter. "That's right," she purred. "You could lead me right to it. What do you say, honey?"

The charm finished burning in a burst of noxious greasy smoke that smelled like rotten cabbages. One of the advantages of not having to breathe is I could pick and choose my moments.

Side conversations were starting up including one between Ariana and Conan where she was telling him he would not be escorting Ruby to the boxes of cash.

"We have several tasks," I said loudly enough to get everyone's attention. Worst case, they'd chase me out of here. No one told me to fuck off, so I plowed forward. "Makes sense to split our forces. Percy has the hacking thing to do. Maybe Dee could locate other Witches. One of them might know something about black magic charms."

"I'll get hold of the good detective first thing tomorrow," Ariana said, "and let him know about our visitors here. We caught them on our surveillance vids, so I'll have something to show him."

"Caught them on the what?" I broke in.

Percy started to laugh. "Bet you had no idea what you were saying when you told me to go hack something."

I could have covered up with bluster and bravado like a good Vampire. Instead, I nodded agreement. "Truer words were never spoken."

He clapped me on the back. "I like you Vampire; you're only the second one to move the needle on my Undead sympathy meter."

"Uh, thanks, I think. What's a vid?"

"Short for video," Ariana said. "Cameras are mounted in strategic spots all around *Ascent*. Mostly so we can have hard evidence if someone commits a crime."

I put two and two together. "You have moving pictures of the men, kind of like the images on your, erm, machine back there." I jerked my chin at the storeroom.

"Exactly. We have a few extra hours tonight. Dee could get started rustling up the coven leader."

"She's a guild mistress," Dee said frostily.

"I stand corrected." Ariana adopted a formal tone. "Would you be so kind as to talk with her on my behalf?"

I winced. I'd been tossing orders about like these mages reported to me. Before Dee answered, I said, "Apologies if my suggestions came off as orders. I did not mean them to. I have lots of excuses, but I won't bother you with them. I'm still getting my bearings, and I'll support however you choose to proceed."

"How about the other Vampires you were in stasis with?" Percy asked.

"They'll help if you wish it," I replied.

"How can you speak for them?" Ruby furled a dark brow.

"Technically, I can't, but they have good hearts—for our kind. I can't see them turning their backs on me. So long as I ask pretty." I smiled to lighten the mood and to forestall someone calling them my minions and me correcting them. It would deflect attention away from our real problems.

Clive and Lorenzo were bit players at best in this drama.

"I will do my best to alert the guild," Dee was saying. "This is a problem that could impact us all. No one but journey level Witches are allowed to create charms, and each one bears the stamp of its maker. It was what I was hunting for when I snatched it from Percy, but that charm lacked aught in the way of identifying marks."

"I'll put in some screen time," Percy said.

"Ruby and I will do what we can to gather information. Won't we?" Christa hooked a hand beneath Ruby's elbow. "And I'll cast the runestones seeking a relevant prophecy."

"I'll alert my Shifter kin," Selene said, not sounding happy at the turn of events.

I didn't blame her. If magic wielders' freedom hung by a slender thread, maintaining invisibility was critical. If a bunch of us got riled up, someone was sure to notice.

"Thanks, everyone," Ariana murmured. "This doesn't have to be your problem."

"Wrong," Percy said. "Tough for us to find work these days. *Ascent* has been goddess-sent."

A ringing chorus of yesses filled the room.

"What happened to the other Sorcerer?" Ariana asked Percy. "The one who came to work with you tonight?"

"I had him teleport out of here at the first whiff of trouble. He's young, and I didn't want to risk his magic getting out of hand."

I almost choked on surprise. I'd thought young Vamps were the only ones requiring tight supervision.

"Unless you hear different," Ariana said, "come in at your regular time tomorrow."

"Will do, boss," Ruby said. Everyone echoed her words. The large room emptied out until only Ariana, Conan, and I remained.

I waited, not wanting to make assumptions or push my own agenda. Ariana had enough problems without me creating another.

She drew her dark brows together and asked, "What do you want to do?"

She wasn't going to chase me off. A very un-Vampire-like thrill pushed through my body. "Whatever you need me to."

After a long, intense look that scoured me to bedrock, she nodded once sharply. "Fine. Be back here tomorrow night around five. Try to at least have a cell phone by then."

I groaned. With everything that had transpired, I'd forgotten about the whole identification thing. "Never got a chance to ask Percy about the forger."

She held up a hand; I took it to mean I should shut up.

Moments later, Percy shimmered into being. "Come with me, Vampire," he said gruffly. "I'll get you set with Rob."

"I have no way to pay him." I needed to make that clear.

"We'll come up with something." He grinned. "A few years of indentured servitude, perhaps."

I did my damnedest not to react, but my fangs dropped anyway. Others with magic might view us as scum, but we see ourselves as king of the heap, not as servants of any kind.

"He was joking," Ariana observed. She kept a straight face but seemed to be working at it.

Embarrassed by my hair-trigger reactiveness, I pulled my teeth in and trusted myself to Percy's travel spell. I'd made enough of an ass of myself for one night. No reason to compound my sins by insisting on controlling the teleport casting.

CHAPTER ELEVEN, ARIANA

I managed to wait until the men were gone before erupting in laughter. Nick was so typical of male Vampires—all bluster and bravado and a shorter-than-fuck fuse—it amused me. He'd wanted to lunge at Percy after the indentured servant comment. That he hadn't spoke to admirable restraint, not something Vampires are known for.

I've lived mostly among mortals for long enough to have put distance between me and my Vampire roots, but there'd been a time when I'd have torn into anyone who so much as breathed the possibility of taking away my freedom.

"We should get moving." Conan head-butted me.

"We should," I agreed, "except I'm not sure where to go first."

"I liked Ruby's idea about collecting some of that money. Not all of it, but a few more boxes."

"Why you greedy little thing, you." I ruffled his fur.

"Not greedy. Practical. War requires resources. Everything we have is tied up in this nightclub."

A long, low whistle blew past my lips. Conan had been paying attention after all during those hours I spent with my spreadsheets. "I should put you in charge of accounting," I murmured.

He flexed a paw in front of him as if to say if it weren't for his lack of fingers, he'd be all over it.

"You could take human form," I suggested softly.

He reared back and barked in my face before saying, "Never."

I waited. Through all our years together, this was one topic we'd never broached. I'd tiptoed around it, but he'd always put me off. When he didn't say anything else, I pushed a bit. "I've seen you take insect forms, small rodents, big rodents, cats, snakes, bears. The only shape I've never seen you in is human. Why?"

He pushed himself tall on his long legs, dignity sheeting from every pore. "I refuse to become something I don't respect."

"Admirable, except you don't turn into those other creatures. You're still you," I murmured as I shuffled through my memories of finding him as a scrawny pup. The bite of his magic poked my forehead as he helped himself to my thoughts.

"I may not become them, but I could be tainted by their views. We will not talk of this," he said.

I put out a hand, but he didn't push his snout into my palm. "Whatever happened before I found you wasn't your doing. You were a puppy."

He drew his upper lip into a snarl. "Men are evil."

"Not all of them."

He tossed his head. "Not worth my time—or my magic—to sort through the dregs looking for the unlikely."

I crouched until my butt was nearly on the floor, so I was lower than him, a sign of respect in wolf packs. "They hurt you, misused your trust. If I could find them, I'd kill them for you, truly I would. Except they're all long since dead."

Conan growled. "This is leading up to something I will not like."

I grinned ruefully. "You know me too well. Probably better than anyone. Yeah, you won't like this, but difficult times lie ahead. We will gather allies where we find them. Some may be mortal. In truth, we would be well-served if some humans joined our cause against their fellows. The level of brainwashing runs deep; it's grown harder to locate any human who doesn't believe that the only good supernatural is a dead one."

Another growl vibrated against my breastbone.

"Mostly," I went on, "I wanted to float the idea and get you used to it. I could be dead wrong, and this might end up a clean sweep where no humans find us worthy of so much as a second thought."

"You don't like them," Conan insisted.

I set my mouth in a tight line. "Not in the way I like mages," I agreed, "but I've learned to get along with humans so long as they don't cross me."

"If they knew what you were, the getting along part would go up like so much smoke."

"Only because they don't understand Vampires," I

retorted. "We're really quite the bon vivants. Charming. Witty. Cultured."

Conan barked what sounded like lupine laughter, and I was grateful he'd moved beyond the funk of his memories. "Before mortals retracted the welcome mat, I wasn't exactly mowing through human jugulars," I reminded him and strode into the back room, flipping out lights as I went. The front door was already locked and the neon open sign off.

I'd given more thought to the boxes bursting with cash and decided Ruby and Conan were right. "First stop is the shack with the money," I said. "We're going to take maybe four more boxes."

"And then, what?"

"Leave them at home, and then we're going hunting."

Excited yips suggested hunting was right up Conan's alley, but it was because he'd taken me literally. "We're hunting clues, not victims," I told the wolf. "No more killing unless we're cornered and have no choice."

The yips shaded to a disappointed whine. If he'd been a kid, I could just see him saying, "Boring."

"You don't have to come," I said. "You really can go hunting if you'd rather. Not for people, but for anything else."

I let him think about it while I constructed a journey spell to return us to where we'd retrieved one of the bodies. This time, I aimed for the interior of the building. It seemed unlikely a forensic crew would have located the place, and even if they did, no one paid out triple-time wages for middle-of-the-night work that would go faster and easier by the light of day.

For them. Not for me. Nighttime was my time, and I gloried in the darkness.

It didn't take long before we were home with the loot. No one knew about my house—at least I didn't think they did. Even so, I schlepped the boxes through a trap door leading beneath my kitchen and left them in the cellar. Conan and I had settled on taking half plus one of the remaining boxes, so we now had six counting the original one. He picked them up with his teeth and handed them down to me.

When I was done, I climbed the ladder, replaced the floor panel, and covered it handily with a hooked rug. A patina of light magic cast a don't-look-here spell over everything.

"That space finally came in handy," Conan said.

"Told you." I smirked. When I'd been building the place, I insisted on a partially finished full basement. Much like with the lack of windows, the contractor had thought I was nuts. I'd come up with a story about needing a cool, dark place for all the canned goods I planned on producing. It had shut him up.

For a while.

When he'd started nagging about what a poor choice so few windows were, I'd fucked him into malleability. If nothing else, the last half century had improved human males. They were less pushy and listened better.

Some of them, anyway. Roger and his two compatriots were definitely "old school" macho where women should smile pretty and shuttle between the bedroom and kitchen.

Conan swatted my side with his head. "Why'd you want that underground place?"

I furled my brows his way. "In case you came home with a mate, and she produced puppies?"

I thought he'd joke back. Instead, he whined plaintively. I felt terrible. I'd just reminded him how alone both of us were. Until Nickolas showed up, there hadn't been any Vampires around, and I'd never come across another dire wolf shapeshifter. Wolves were pack animals, so I felt certain Conan felt the lack of others like himself keenly.

On my side, it was a relief not creeping between warring factions of Vampires. We don't get along with anyone. Besides, if anyone ever found out I'd been the instrument of Mistral's demise, they'd be out for my hide. No one raised their fangs against their master. It was the highest crime of all.

If you were a Vampire.

I wanted to ask Conan about his people. Where they were. How he'd ended up separated from them. Probably most important, why I'd never seen another wolf like him. But he was unhappy enough. So I settled for saying, "Shit happens. I thought I might slip up and have bodies to hide."

"Could still happen," Conan said.

I nodded. Locating the mountain lion den had been a godsend, but I couldn't always count on local predators to cover up my missteps—or, in this case, Conan's.

"I'm leaving," I told him. "What do you want to do?"

"Where are we going?" His ears pricked forward with an expectant tilt to them.

"I want to start with the house where Percy found the

false cops. We'll have to be careful. It wouldn't surprise me if someone was there clearing the place of bodies—and evidence."

"How would they have found out so fast?"

"Someone killed those men. They didn't just drop dead. If fate smiles our way, we might get there soon enough to nose about and determine just what they were." I crafted a spell as I was talking.

"Human, mostly," Conan mumbled around a whuffly snarl.

"Yeah. It's the mostly part that bothers me," I said and set a travel spell in motion. My first stop was the dark alley behind *Ascent* to pick up the men's trail—and to make certain my club was intact. Everything was quiet, as it should be in the middle of the night.

From there, I latched onto the feel of the men and set out on foot with Conan running along next to me. I'm quick, so the wolf and I made good time. Percy hadn't been kidding when he said the house was close. Many swanky neighborhoods are adjacent to Lake Washington. The house was located in one of them. When we got closer, I wrapped us in invisibility and slowed our pace considerably.

"Has to be that one, right there." Conan switched to telepathy.

I agreed. Far from smiling, fate had done a good job fucking us. One of the big, fancy homes was lit up like a Christmas tree. Now, if they'd had my imminent good sense —and build the place with fewer windows—it wouldn't have been such an obvious contrast with the sleeping neighborhood.

Why hadn't they pulled the drapes or dropped the blinds?

"Only two inside," Conan said. *"We can take them."*

The Vampire in me thought it was a hell of a grand idea. Before my fangs dropped and we teleported inside and started kicking some serious ass, I asked, *"Two what?"*

"Does it matter?"

"Um, yup. It does."

He turned his amber gaze full on me. Moonlight reflected off his luminous eyes. *"Why?"*

Instead of answering, I said, *"Let's get closer. Maybe we'll figure out what's inside."*

I didn't wait for the wolf to launch arguments. He was really good at stonewalling when he didn't agree with something. Moving as stealthily as I could, I deepened the warding around us and crept up the neighboring house's driveway. A six-foot fence separated their property from the one I was interested in. I cleared it handily; Conan landed next to me, head swiveling from side to side as he took in a neatly manicured yard with dead grass, flowering shrubbery, patios, and expensive outdoor furniture.

While he was casing the joint, I slithered up to a window, reminding myself no one could see me. I was warded. It was dark. All good points, unless whatever was inside had strong magic. If they did, they could sense my presence—if they were looking for it. That was the kicker. No reason for them to expect Vampires or dire wolves playing Peeping Tom at a back window.

What was Nickolas up to? Had he made certain to pass the word about flying beneath the radar to his non-minions?

Of course, he wouldn't have put it in those terms. He wouldn't understand the allusion, and neither would the other two Vampires. I wrenched my full attention back to the window. Why was I thinking about Nick? I hadn't wanted other Undead around me since I left the clan house.

Being alone had obvious advantages. My self-enforced solitude had been more of a blessing than anything. For one thing, it saved a lot of explanations, like who was I? Which clan? Had I been around when Mistral was beheaded?

Easier not to deal with any of it.

Movement caught the corner of my eye. I groaned but muffled it fast and held my nonexistent breath. A crone, complete with a long, black cape and tangled gray curls was bent over carrying something. She had to be a Witch. Another woman carted the other end of the burden. On closer inspection, a body hung suspended between them. Bitch-number-two was a hell of a big faery. Mostly, they're around three feet tall, but this one stood at least five. Silver-and-rust hair hit her at knee level, and she was dressed in formfitting leather with a bow slung across her back next to a quiver filled with gleaming, silver arrows.

Yeah. I knew all about the Sidhe and their fucking arrows. Metal doesn't bother them, which gives them an advantage over the Fae.

"Since when do Witches even talk with Sidhe?" Conan was back by my side, nose pressed against the triple-pane glass.

"It's a black Witch and one of the dark Sidhe," I murmured, leaving out they had another point of commonality: their antipathy for Vampires.

The women dropped the body they'd been carting. Why they hadn't used magic to transport it remained to be seen. Did it mean their reservoirs were low? That they were husbanding their strength?

The Witch straightened and turned, probably going back for the other dead faux cop. She'd been worried enough about the men talking out of turn, she'd dealt them the death card. I wasn't certain how I knew she was in charge, but I'd have bet my next meal on it. Vampires don't barter in blood unless we're certain we'll win. The Sidhe followed her out of the room.

Conan growled low into my mind. I understood what he was angling for, and I was coming around to his way of seeing things. It was only the Witch and the Sidhe. We could slice-and-dice them handily.

No better chance to sneak inside.

"You got it, bud," I told the wolf and used a shot of magic to pry the window open. Big windows are simple affairs to slither through. Especially compared with how they were constructed in the Old Country. Humans in that era were well aware they shared breathing space with immortals, and they developed tricks to keep us out, like iron bars set into plaster. Silver gewgaws and the well-positioned bucket of holy water were plenty to keep me away. I've never been into fighting for my food.

I managed to quietly lower the window once we were through. So far, no one had come racing back to see who'd violated their space.

I kept us hidden in an alcove at the far end of the room until the women huffed and puffed their way back with the second body. When the Witch extracted a charm from her robe and began to chant, I understood her game plan. She was going to set the corpses on fire and hadn't wanted the flames to be too visible until the men were well and truly immolated.

It was why she'd moved them to the back of the house.

So long as the bodies were here, I wanted a chance to examine them, and that opportunity would literally go up in smoke if I didn't move fast.

"One. Two. Three," I breathed the words and dropped the wards concealing us.

The Witch cursed in a perversion of Gaelic. The Sidhe did her damnedest to teleport out of there.

They were both too late.

Vampires aren't just fast. We're fucking fast. Superhuman strength and speed are our métier. Conan isn't much more than a blur once he sets his sights on something. He leapt on the Sidhe, knocking her flat before she got a chance to nock one of her arrows. Normally, something like that wouldn't bother him—except these had been crafted with faery dust shimmering on top of the silvery tips.

I was fairly certain I could have neutralized it, but I didn't have to.

I jumped on the Witch. The old bat was stronger than she looked, but it was still no contest at all. I got her on the carpet with her hissing and spitting at me. "Die, Vampire," she growled.

"Dream on, sweetie," I said almost cheerfully. Witchy-gal was deader than dead, but should I feed first? Or just kill her and be done with it?

Conan stuck his blood-and-gore-streaked muzzle in my face. "Finish it," he said sharply.

The Witch's eyes widened. "He's more than he looks."

"You have no idea."

Beneath me, the Witch writhed, bucked, and heaved. If she'd been able to change forms, she'd have turned into a snake or scorpion, but I'm immune to virtually all poisons. Tired of playing with her, I ripped one of her jugulars open with the nail on my right index finger that I keep long and sharp for just such occasions.

The scent of her blood, rich and heady, made up my mind for me. I wouldn't drink much. We had too much work to do, but I'd be an idiot to ignore the windfall pumping onto acres of thick, beige carpet.

I'm quick—and efficient. Not five minutes later, the Witch breathed her last, and I'd had enough sustenance to hold me. The crunch of teeth on bone told me Conan hadn't let the opportunity pass, either. Faery blood held an eerie sweetness. Did their flesh taste as enticing?

I swiped the back of my hand across my mouth and stood. The Witch still clutched a charm in one hand. I pried it out of her fingers and dropped it into a pocket. Maybe Dee could give it to the guild mistress, and it would help identify whomever I'd just killed.

I hadn't had any choice. Once we revealed ourselves—Conan and I—the next part was a foregone conclusion. He'd left off feeding and was nosing the men, snuffling like a mushroom-hunting hog.

"I'm going to give the house a quick once over," I told the wolf.

He lifted his muzzle. "Mostly human," he reported. "Someone tried to make them more than they were, probably so their cop charade would be convincing."

"Mmph. That would probably be the charm Percy lifted off them. The one that self-destructed."

Conan went back to snuffling. I activated my magical antennae and let them guide me through all three levels of the huge house. A Witch—probably the dead one—had set up a workshop on the top floor. It stank of black magic so wicked my eyes watered, and I rarely have a physical reaction to anything.

I'd love to have cordoned off the place—kind of like police do with a crime scene. Best I could hope for would be to send Dee or one of her Witch-buddies by to take a look before someone dismantled and sanitized it.

If they knew about me, what else had they figured out? Had they targeted mortals too? Or were they only interested in fucking with Vampires? If it was true, what a shortsighted tactic. Were they thinking they'd curry favor with mortals by waving Vampire scalps about?

Pretty lame approach since until very recently, I'd been the only Vamp in the area. Except maybe they didn't know that. They'd found me, but they could still be looking for more of my Undead kin.

I should warn Nickolas, and I would as soon as I got out of this hellhole of a mansion.

The whole thing pissed me off and made me tired. I wasn't the least bit sorry I'd killed the Witch. She had it coming. Her own kinswomen would have done her in for practicing black magic. I did them a favor by finishing their dirty work for them. Would they thank me or chide me for overstepping my authority?

Or cluck at me with their inscrutable witchy expressions?

Eh. It didn't matter. I hustled back to where I'd left Conan, except he wasn't there. I found him in the kitchen. "They killed in here," he said. "And more than once." After a pause, he added, "people," in case I'd thought he meant chickens or black cats.

Running on instinct, I tugged open a huge refrigerator/freezer combo and started undoing neatly wrapped packages. The first two were human remains, butchered into meal-sized portions. Made me assume the rest were too.

"Ewww. What the fuck were they up to?" I mused and stuffed the packages back into the freezer, shutting the door of the macabre butcher shop. I'm not squeamish, but the surgical precision of those seal-a-meal packets gave me the creeps.

"As long as the paper is undone, I want what's inside." Conan tried hooking a paw around the freezer latch, but his claws were too big.

"We need to get out of here," I told him. "If we hang around eating, someone will show up."

He flicked his tail. "We'll kill them too."

The corners of my mouth twitched as I tried not to laugh. I settled for telling Conan how much I loved him and teleported us the fuck out of there. Next stop was *Ascent*; we'd figure things out from there. I had to get hold of Dee, and I needed to splice shit together from the surveillance cameras, so I'd have something to email to the precinct in the morning.

This was one day I wouldn't be going home. Hopefully it would be overcast, or even better, pouring down rain.

"You have blood on you," Conan said once we stood in *Ascent's* back room.

"So do you," I countered as I walked to the sink and flipped on the taps.

Once I was done scrubbing away the evidence, I turned around washcloth in hand to clean the wolf, but he was gone.

"Smart boy."

I laughed. He'd hated me washing his face when he was a fraction of his current size. He was probably cleaning himself in a creek somewhere.

I started in on the video compilation and shot Dee a text.

CHAPTER TWELVE, ARIANA

*I*n less time that I would have expected, Dee burst through a bluish portal accompanied by two other Witches. The trio wore hatchet-faced expressions reminiscent of the trio of Witches in Macbeth. I was alive when Shakespeare wrote it, so I knew the Witches he patterned his make believe ones after.

Not that these women looked anything like the small, gray-headed crones in Macbeth. No one was bothering with introductions—presumably they knew who I was. Perhaps their names were on a need-to-know basis. One woman was extremely tall and gaunt. The only thing exuberant about her was her clouds of spiky, red hair. Her tresses stuck out at all angles and hung to the middle of her back. She had eyes the shade of polished emeralds and a sharp face that was all planes and angles. My bet was she was the guild mistress Dee had alluded to earlier. Tattered jeans hugged her long legs, and a worn green cable-knit sweater hung to hip level.

Scuffed boots hit her mid-calf. On a shorter woman, they'd have reached her knees.

The other woman was medium height and rounded. Her skin was the deep mahogany brown typical of the Caribbean islands. Sculpted bone structure highlighted eyes an unusual shade of light blue. Her hair was braided in tight rows against her shapely head. A colorful skirt hung from her hips topped by a fuzzy white jacket. Despite it being winter, she wore rope sandals.

"What'd you find, exactly?" Dee bit off each word. She wore the same jeans and red T-shirt she'd had on earlier. Her black hair was mussed, and circles etched beneath her eyes.

I hadn't wanted to go into too much detail in my text since those kinds of communications can be easily intercepted. After rattling off an address, I fished the charm out of my pants pocket and handed it over. "A Witch was practicing deep black magic. Her studio is on the top floor of the house. It was so thick with evil, it made me choke."

Before they could pepper me with questions, I added. "She was working with a Sidhe from their dark court. They were who sent the phony cops here earlier tonight, and presumably who killed them when Percy dropped in unexpectedly. They were about to burn the evidence when Conan and I stepped in."

Dee narrowed her eyes to slits. "Where are all of them now?"

I turned my hands palms up. "The men were already dead. Conan and I killed the Witch and the faery. They're still there—all four of them."

I let my gaze settle on each Witch in turn, trying to read

them—and waiting for them to light into me. One of the reasons other supernatural beings dislike Vampires is our proclivity to settle things permanently.

Doesn't get much more permanent than death.

The Witch with all the red hair adopted a thoughtful expression that sent creases spiraling out from the sides of her eyes. "I'd have liked to question the Witch, before *I* killed her"—she stressed the I part—"but it's difficult to choreograph these types of things. You were already there. If you'd waited and summoned us, the Witch might have been gone before we arrived."

"There's more," I said.

"Out with it," the Witch ordered.

I wanted to sputter I did not answer to her. Instead, I said, "The kitchen freezer is full of meat. Human meat in nice neat little portion-sized packets."

Eyebrows shot up all around me. Mouths gaped. "I take it you opened one of these...packages?" Dee choked out.

"Two, actually. It was all I could do to hold Conan back. He hates mortals for what they did to him when he was young."

"We may return," the guild mistress informed me.

"If we don't, I'll be in at my normal time," Dee said.

I considered mentioning I'd be here if they needed me, but they seemed quite self-sufficient. Besides, Witches aren't in the habit of coming to Vampires for help with anything.

Ha! Neither are any other supernatural creatures. Or humans, so long as I'm on a roll here.

Once they teleported away from the storeroom, I returned my attention to splicing the vid feed together. All in all, the meeting with the Witches hadn't gone badly. They weren't shy or into wasting energy on manners or being polite. If they'd been furious with me, I'd have known.

They didn't rebuke me for killing one of theirs.

Conan leapt through a portal, landed a foot from me, and shook droplets all over the place. He loved grand entrances, and this one made me laugh. The water smelled dank, like a creek where water had been sitting for long enough to grow a hefty collection of bacteria.

"Where exactly were you?"

"I found something. You should come."

I raised my eyebrows. "That's it? You're not going to give me a hint, something to tantalize me?"

"I'm going back there. Are you coming?"

"Sure. Hang on a moment." I finished splicing the video into an abbreviated version that hit the high points of the phony policemen's visit to *Ascent*.

The scents of Conan's magic, all soft fur, rain-wet rocks, and wild things, surrounded me as he transported us. Ceding power to him was easier this time than it had been when we'd been obliterating evidence of his kills. As soon as we emerged, the rancid water smell intensified. Conan must have neutralized the worst of it clinging to his coat. I felt certain he hadn't chosen this particular fetid swamp to clean blood off his fur.

He trotted lightly across a boggy field. I had no idea where we were, but I didn't sense humans close by. Not alive, anyway. Lots of dead bodies lay all around us. "What is this place?" I asked Conan, keeping my voice quiet. The dead wouldn't waken, but what if I was wrong about no one else being here? Magical beings could have shielded themselves.

He dropped back until he was even with me. "The rest of the bodies are here."

"Huh? The rest of what bodies?"

"The ones from that house." Conan's tone took on a patronizing note at the proof of how inferior my nose was compared with his.

Damn. I felt stupid. Of course there had to have been leavings from all those hermetically sealed freezer packages. Like bones and organs. Normally, death and dead things don't give me the creeps, but there was something so wrong about this I suppressed a shudder.

Get over it! I gave myself a good swift kick in the backside. If I could, I'd have lived on human blood, but I could stop myself before I killed my dinner. Whoever was behind this had killed methodically.

Had they tortured their victims? Or had their ends been swift?

Conan had started dragging bones out of the swamp. Whoever had butchered them had done a shit job. Muscle and sinew still clung to every bone, and they smelled horrible. The skulls still contained brains. Apparently, the person behind this didn't consider them a delicacy. Because Conan was better-suited to locating remains, I arranged what he rescued into sloppy piles. My sniffer was plenty good enough to determine which remains went where. Once he stopped dropping bits and pieces on a place the ground wasn't submerged, I asked, "Is this all?"

"All the bones. What's left isn't worth going after."

I nodded and glanced at five stacks that had once been people. All female judging from the spread of their hipbones. Fuck. Had we stumbled across a modern-day Jack the Ripper? Cautious to shield my message, I tried to raise Dee with telepathy.

"Can you hear me?"

After a minute or so ticked past, an equally cautious, *"Yeah,"* zinged back my way.

"We found the rest of the packages."

"Where?" This time, her response was immediate.

I was reluctant to disclose exactly where we were—in case someone was listening in. *"Meet me back where we started."*

"Stay put. We'll find you."

I closed off the channel and focused on Conan. "How'd you locate this place?"

"How else? I tracked the scent from the house."

"Smart of you. Can you tell if the Witch and Fae were responsible for these murders?"

He shook his big head. "I smell them here, but there were many smells in that house. They weren't the only magical creatures who passed through there." He woofed softly. "I was wrong before, about this batch being killed in the house. Other people were, but the women were killed here."

I sent directional vectors spinning outward to determine precisely where "here" was. We were north of Kirkland in the middle of what appeared to be a deserted tidal flat fed by several healthy creeks. Land along Puget Sound is generally very expensive, so why the hell was this stretch empty?

When I extended my hunt, I felt the prickle of magical barriers. They'd do the trick keeping the place deserted. Humans stumbling into the area would sense the wrongness and hightail it the other way. Which argued the victims had been dragged here against their will. Poor gals. They'd been scared. Vestiges of their terror hung all around me now that I was looking for it.

Dee and the other two Witches shimmered into view a couple of feet away. I didn't bother to ask how they'd found us. Probably the same way Conan had located this spot, but my bet was he'd come on foot.

The one I assumed was the guild mistress walked around the five piles of remains. Grim-faced, she clucked her disapproval before falling into a soft chant. I didn't recognize it, but my bet was she was praying over the souls of the dead and wishing them safe passage to the afterlife.

It was something I should have done, except my power doesn't work that way. No one welcomes Vampire magic. Whoever was guarding the gates to the realm of the dead wouldn't appreciate anyone I sent their way.

They'd let them in, but they'd be shunted to some back corner of Hell.

Dee sidled next to me. "Did you figure anything out?" I asked softly.

"Not really. It seems the Witch and the Fae were hired help. We were tracing all the other magical footprints in the house when you reached out to me. Oh yeah, and we emptied out the freezer. Ick. Cannibalism is just wrong."

Done with her incantation, the guild mistress picked her

way through standing puddles to where Dee, Conan, and I stood. "Excellent work locating the bodies," she said.

"It wasn't me, but Conan," I told her.

She offered what I felt certain was a rare smile at the wolf. "Good boy."

He woofed once to acknowledge the compliment, but I knew him well enough to understand her calling him "boy" rankled.

"Dee said you cleared out the freezer."

"Couldn't leave it there. We're burning it in batches back at the guild house," the Witch said.

I picked my way through what felt like a minefield. "Erm, whoever killed these women did it to turn them into meals. Any idea why?"

The tall, thin Witch shut her eyes for a moment. When she opened them, she said, "Those who travel dark paths require an additional psychic boost. They get it from absorbing energy from living things. The higher up the food chain their prey is, the stronger it makes them."

"That's the case for dark witches, black mages, all of them," Dee tossed out.

Great. Fucking great. Dark magic was running loose and targeting humans. The fallout was certain to hit the rest of us broadside. Remaining hidden wasn't going to work much longer if many more incidents like this one occurred.

"What happens next?" I asked, unsure whether to boot the bones back into the swamp or alert the authorities. Before mortals decided to kick us to the curb, it would have been a non-decision. We were all playing on the same team, and this was definitely a crime scene.

"Not sure," the guild mistress said. "By the way, I'm Dahlia."

"Ariana." I held out my hand. After a brief hesitation, the Witch shook it. I took it as a positive sign.

The other Witch muttered, "Cerys, here."

I shook her hand too. So long as I was on a roll, I didn't think she'd refuse me since the head of her coven hadn't.

Dahlia sank into a crouch. "Those poor women," she murmured. "They suffered before they died. Their pain lingers even now."

"And their fear," I agreed. "If it wasn't the Witch and the Fae, then who killed them?"

"Not sure," Cerys answered. "We were working on it."

Dahlia drew her thick russet brows together. "That house sits on a nexus of ley-lines. I'm certain it offers entrance to at least one other world."

While I was digesting exactly what that meant, she asked me, "Do, um, your kind exist on other worlds?"

I felt like telling her she could say the word, "Vampire," and not have her tongue fall out, but I restrained myself. "I didn't know other worlds existed beyond this one."

Her frown deepened. "Don't take this wrong, but do you go to some kind of school after you're, um..."

"Turned," I inserted into the blank spot. "Yes, we learn about the Vampire clans, the history of our clan, and how to not give in to blood hunger. It's pervasive at first. Some of us choose to study more widely."

"You have clans?" Cerys looked surprised.

"We do." I nodded. "Each approaches Vampirism differently. I'm part of clan Hawke. It's also my last name, but that was a purposeful decision on my part. I could have maintained my original surname once I was turned, but I chose not to because I'd fallen in love with—"

I shut my mouth with an audible *clack* once I understood Cerys had spelled me to talk. "Stop that," I told her. One of my hands had formed a fist. I relaxed my fingers. "Until you feel I'm hiding something critical, how about if you don't practice witchcraft on me?"

Conan had laid next to me, and he growled. Nothing loud, but he made his feelings clear. I was his, and he wouldn't stand by while anything or anyone took advantage of me.

"Sorry." She stopped there, which made me wonder how sorry she truly was.

I glanced from one Witch to the next. "Dee knows me. She's worked at *Ascent* for a couple of years now. I assume she's found me honest and forthcoming, or she'd have quit."

"True enough," Dee said.

I could have hugged her for even that small crumb of support. "For now," I suggested, "the rest of you need to decide if I'm trustworthy or not. If you can't work with me, I respect that. Conan and I will go home, and we'll piecemeal what we can together."

I took a breath to make myself appear less alien and continued. "I believe that's the wrong approach, though. Each of us has certain skills. If we pool our resources, we should get to the endgame faster."

"Agreed," Dahlia said. "Dee tells me there's another Vampire?"

"Actually, three," I replied. "Conan and I came across

Nickolas the other evening while we were out hunting. He'd just awakened. He and two min— er associates entered stasis over a century ago to escape persecution by a group of black Sorcerers."

"Hunting what?" Cerys asked in a choked voice.

My fangs wanted out in the worst way. I rode herd on them and ground out, "I don't have to answer you, but I will in an honest attempt to put you at your ease. That night I drained a few small rodents. Conan found a feral hog, but it had already been emptied of blood. It was how I found Nick."

"Do you only hunt animals?" Cerys probed.

"Usually, but when the Witch was bleeding all over that house, I helped myself to her blood." I shrugged. "No apologies. I am what I am."

"Focus." Dahlia's command was sharp.

"Yes, Mistress," Cerys muttered.

"So there are four Vampires nearby?" Dahlia sought clarification.

"That I know of," I told her. "I haven't met Nick's two companions, but they're from Clan Giovanni. I believe it's a more traditional Vampire clan than mine, but I could be wrong. Anyway, it doesn't matter since our clan structure has fallen apart."

Cerys opened her mouth, but shut it before anything emerged. My bet was she wanted to know what I meant by more traditional.

"My hunch is this," Dahlia said. "Something is using that house as a portal from wherever they live. I have no idea how long they've been visiting Earth, but the current breakdown between supernaturals and mortals could be playing right into their plans."

"To do what?" I asked.

"Not certain, but they must have offered inducements to get a Witch and a Sidhe to play nice together."

"Or to play together at all," Dee inserted.

"That too," Dahlia agreed.

"Do you suppose there are other bodies in this area?" Dee asked.

"No," Conan spoke up.

I hunkered next to him and dug my fingers into his thick, rough coat. "Why?"

"There might be more dead, but the remains here match up with what was in the freezer."

"I'm not doubting you, but I didn't have the freezer open all that long."

"I went back to the house. Might have figured out how to get it open."

The corners of my mouth twitched. I didn't ask for details. The wolf was quite resourceful when he was motivated.

"Do you have a way of transiting the barrier or boundary or whatever sits at the nexus of the ley-lines?" I asked.

Dahlia nodded. "There are many other worlds. Locating the proper one will be the problem. Showing up in a different place can be extremely dangerous."

It made sense to me. I thought about the men posing as police officers. "Any clues on the dead men?"

Dee made a sour face. "There's so much magic in that house it trips over itself. But we couldn't find the men."

Shock rustled through me. "What do you mean, couldn't find them? They were right in the middle of the large room facing the rear of the house."

Conan's hackles rose beneath my hand. "Were they gone when you went back there?" I asked him.

"Don't know. Didn't look," he replied in a tone that told me he was kicking himself for not exploring the rest of the house. But he'd been focused on one thing and had unearthed a significant find in this swampy tidepool.

"It's okay," I murmured. "You did good."

"Dead things that don't belong to Earth don't remain here," Dahlia said.

"What? So the men were from this other dimension?" At Dee's nod, I continued, half talking to myself. "It might be why they weren't turned into food like the women."

"Possibly," Dee agreed.

"No wonder they didn't feel quite right," I went on. "I assumed they'd received an infusion of magic from whomever, but it could explain why they never drew their guns. They didn't view them as anything beyond props."

"We'll never know for certain," Dahlia said.

"Of course we will," Conan said around a whuffly snarl. "More just like them will come through."

Something about his tone and his comment suggested he knew more than he was telling us, but that was a conversation for a more private locale.

"We're going back to our guild house," Dahlia said. "I wish to confer with a few other Witches."

I pushed upright and looked right at her, employing my own brand of enchantment because I wanted a straight answer. "Are we working together on this? Or are Conan and I on our own?"

"I like you," Dahlia said. "You're direct. I'll get pushback from some of the others, but yes, we are working together."

Conan growled.

"What was that about?" Dahlia asked.

"He doesn't like you any better than you like Vampires," Dee said, "but only because you haven't totally accepted Ariana."

It was as good an opportunity as I was likely to get, so I jumped in with both feet. "We have to get over this us/them shit," I said. "Mortals are out for our blood. They're not going to forget about us or quietly go away. They're mounting defenses around the world to rid Earth of supernatural creatures. You know. Us. We can fight them individually, but we'll lose. Our only chance—"

"I get it," Dahlia spoke over me. "It's the same message I've been preaching since mortals declared war on us. I'll be in touch once we've figured out which way to go next."

"Shouldn't Conan and I be part of that discussion?"

"Probably, but the initial parts will go quicker if they happen within the guild," Dahlia said.

I nodded, not liking the message but understanding Dahlia had a practical streak not unlike my own. "I'm returning to *Ascent*. Not planning to go home today. I'll alert the detective fucker who jacked me up last night and give him digital evidence from my camera system. Once I've done that, I'm going to hunt Nickolas down and see what he and his associates are going to do."

"I thought you had to be underground, like in a coffin or

something, during the day," Cerys said. To her slender credit, she held up a hand and said, "Sorry."

I rounded on her. "You should be. I never claimed to know zip squat about being a Witch. Clearly, your knowledge of Vampires is lacking as well. We'd do well to educate ourselves."

Dahlia wrapped a long-fingered hand around Cerys's upper arm and said, "We're leaving before you sink us further."

"It's all right," I spoke up. "It's good for her to know old Vampires aren't nearly as sun-sensitive as the legends suggest. I don't volunteer to go outside during daylight, but neither do I melt into a puddle of goo when I do."

Dee dropped a hand on my shoulder. "See you this afternoon," she said.

"Good." Dahlia nodded once. "You can relay what happens at the guild without risking telepathy."

"Before we leave, we'll kick the bones back into the swamp," I told the Witches. "No reason to have the local cops decide a paranormal crime happened here and use it to fan the flames. Humans are scared enough as it is, and frightened people make very poor decisions."

"I can help with that." Dahlia extended both hands. White light arced from her fingertips, and the piles of bones sank beneath the wet ground, as neatly buried as if she'd had a shovel. By the time the bones had vanished, so had the Witches.

The sky was beginning to lighten. It was time to hustle back to the nightclub, but before we left, I turned to Conan and trusted my instincts when I said, "You came from one of those other worlds, didn't you? It would explain so much. Like why there are no others like you here."

He got to his feet, shook himself from snout to tail tip, and summoned magic to move us away from the burial ground. He might choose not to answer me, but my bet was he would.

Maybe not tonight, but eventually.

CHAPTER THIRTEEN, ARIANA

*T*he day marched along. I did some of the prep work to get the club ready to open this evening—assuming our usual complement of customers didn't boycott us because of the previous night's excitement. No one likes cops, me included. Detective Bryce had grudgingly agreed to look at the recording from my surveillance cameras after telling me that type of evidence wouldn't hold up in court. I was certain he was wrong about that, but perhaps I've watched too many crime procedurals on television.

Anyway, the whole question was moot since the bodies had vanished. I'd been hoping maybe someone at the precinct would recognize the men, but if the Witches were correct and the men weren't from Earth, chances of them showing up in a police blotter were slim.

Conan hadn't said two words to me. As soon as we returned to *Ascent*, he retreated to the lair I'd made for him behind a few storage shelves. I assumed he was still back there but hadn't checked. I was hungry and crabby and tired. Not much I could do about the hungry part—unless I teleported home to my freezer or into the woods to hunt after it got dark.

My eyes felt gritty. I kept getting up to rearrange the heavy curtain over the single storeroom window, but no matter how I draped the fabric, an arrow of sunlight wormed its way through. Why the fuck couldn't it be raining today?

Back at my desk, I folded my arms and laid my head on top of them. Shutting my eyes was blissful. Too bad I couldn't close off my thoughts as easily. I kept imagining those five women, immersing myself in their pain. It was a nowhere path, but I couldn't snip the tape loop that repeated endlessly. Since I couldn't escape, I took a hard look at why their plight had gotten to me.

If they'd just died, their fates would have fallen into the too-bad-but-acceptable camp. Their suffering added a whole new layer. Some Vampires enjoy terrorizing their prey. I've heard quiet chatter about how fear adds spice to the blood. From a physiological perspective, it makes some sense. Adrenalized blood does have a different taste. More piquant. I squeezed my eyes tighter shut, disturbed I'd nosedived down a rabbit hole of trivia.

Had surviving on bags of sanitized, pasteurized crap provided by the government in an attempt to corral those like me, and then on animal blood, diluted my Vampiric edges?

Of course, USDA blood had only been available in places like New Orleans where there are sizeable Vampire groups. I'd been curious and made a special trip down there. The commercially available blood I'd sampled hadn't impressed me. Neither had the Vampires. Everyone in that region had been affiliated with the Ravnos clan. They'd made in clear if I remained, I'd have to eschew my clan affiliation and sign up with them.

All good reasons to beat a path back to the Pacific Northwest. Plus, the other Vampires had cast a whole lot of sidelong glances at Conan. They saw him as food, but they'd have been in for a surprise if any of them had tried to drink from him. The wolf can rip out throats with the best of them. Vampires have exceptional healing ability, but not if all four neck vessels are spewing ichor. It's why beheading is one of the few effective ways of doing away with us.

On that cheery note, I lifted my head off my folded arms. An errant beam of sunlight stabbed the back of one of my hands. I moved it fast. A glance at my phone told me it was pushing three. Going home made zero sense at this point, but sitting here had grown old. It would be another hour, and then some, before I could venture outside without layering myself in garments.

Unless I rode Conan. My full-face helmet did double duty covering everything from the neck up. I was just about to ask him if he was up for a ride when I caught a sweet, musky whiff of Vampire.

Nick strode through a portal, neatly evading the bit of sunlight. He nodded curtly. "Hoped you'd be here." He frowned at me. "You look like hell. Rough night?"

I shrugged. "You might say so. How'd the ID project go?"

"It's why I'm here." His green-eyed gaze skittered sideways, and he came as close to looking embarrassed as a Vampire can. It's not an emotion that comes easy to us.

"Percy's friend made me what I need," Nick continued, "but it will cost me a thousand dollars. How much did I earn working last night?"

I tried for a straight face, truly I did, but I started to laugh as I murmured, "Nowhere near a thousand bucks."

"I fail to see what's so funny." He tried for dignity, but at least he didn't launch into a litany about how he had no idea how much anything was worth in today's world.

"Don't mind me. I'm sleep-deprived and hungry. How about this? I'll loan you the money, and you can work it off."

He slitted his eyes. "Too open-ended. Roughly how much would I have earned working so far?"

It was a fair question. "I pay fifteen bucks an hour to new hires. After six months, you get a raise to twenty. Staff splits the tip jar each night. Depending on the crowd, that could put an extra hundred in your pocket."

"So a bit less than seventy hours. I could do that in ten days easily."

"Wouldn't even take that long with tips," I agreed and walked to a wall safe. I spun the dials and once the reinforced door clicked open, I extracted the cash box, counted out ten hundred-dollar bills, and handed them to him.

"Thank you," he said solemnly. "I will return by five with the ID."

"There's a Verizon store at the end of this block," I told him. "Once it's dark, stop by there and get a cell phone."

"Something else requiring money?" He furled a copper brow.

"Is part of this identification package a credit card?"

He turned his hands palms up. "I have no idea what such a thing even is."

"New plan." I smiled, hoping for supportive, but in my current state I wouldn't have made bets on anything. "Come back here, and we'll go to the phone store together. You are planning on remaining in this region, right? Did you talk with your minions?"

A corner of his mouth twisted downward. "Not my minions. But yes, I did speak with them. None of us want to remain here, but neither do we see a simple way to leave. Even if we teleported in spurts and ended up on the eastern coastline of the continent, we still wouldn't be able to cross the ocean absent a ship."

"Or an airplane," I tossed out.

"The silver things in the air," he mumbled. "Trusting one would be a challenging first step. And I suppose they cost money as well."

"You suppose correctly. Where are they?" I persisted. "The non-minions."

"In a sheltered cavern waiting out the day. They're on the younger side and more sun sensitive than me." He paused for a beat. "It isn't as if we're attached at the hip. They may leave, hunting for others like us."

"They won't get far without any form of identification."

Nickolas nodded. "I told them as much, but neither seemed particularly interested. They know where to find me if they need assistance."

I perched on a corner of my desk, avoiding the sunbeam. "You said I looked trashed. A lot has happened since you left..." In as few words as possible I filled him in on the night's events—and the human lives sacrificed on the altar of dark magic. "Now that you have some background," I went on, "what do you know about other worlds?"

"Probably about the same as you," he said. His attention had sharpened through my tale. He leaned slightly toward me, eyes alight with interest. I tried to ignore how fetching he looked, how desirable with strands of copper hair framing his face and muscles bunching across his shoulders. It didn't work very well. When I progressed to imagining the press of his chiseled lips against my own, I tossed the coldest mental water I could find over my misplaced lust.

If I wasn't careful, he'd scent my arousal, and then I'd have a different type of problem on my hands. Denying my interest would be pointless, and I didn't have time to waste arguing about why sex would be a very bad idea.

It took me a moment to resurrect his last comment before I said, "If your knowledge matches mine, it means you know nothing. I had no idea such things existed."

He tilted his head to one side. "Apparently, I misspoke. Yes, I am aware there are many other worlds. I've never traveled to any, but some of my kinsmen have. I believe it can be as simple as finding a location where the veils separating worlds are thin and walking through them."

"Mmph. Your thinning veils and the Witches' ley-lines probably mean the same thing."

"Want to go have a look?"

"Don't you have to pay the Sorcerer?"

"That won't take long. We could have a look about as soon as I'm back." Nick didn't wait for an answer from me; the air around him took on a glistening aspect and he vanished, leaving the clean scent of Vampire in his wake. I inhaled hungrily and reminded myself his scent was all of him I was ever going to experience.

I pushed off the edge of the desk and walked around the shelving to where Conan should be. His head was up, and he regarded me somberly. "Do you think it's wise?"

"Which thing? Trusting Nickolas or taking a field trip to another world?" I shook my head, thinking I'd entered some psychic twilight zone.

"The other Vampire is all right. I'd have taken him out if he was a threat."

My eyes might have widened. Conan had a casual approach to carnage, but his assertion had been so matter-of-fact, he believed it to his lupine bones. "Talk with me," I urged, hoping the wolf would shed light on the question I'd asked before we left the tidepool with its burial ground.

Conan got to his feet and pushed past me and into the storeroom. "If you go, I'm coming." He ducked his snout into the pail I'd turned into a water bucket and lapped noisily.

"Like I could stop you if I tried," I mumbled. "Conan. Did you recognize that those men weren't from here?"

He kept right on drinking.

"Fine." I slapped my palm down hard on my desk. "If you don't trust me after all this time, I've misjudged our entire relationship."

He did lift his head then and regarded me. Water sheeted off his snout and spattered on the floor. "No. You haven't. Some items aren't important. Mortals are bad news no matter where they come from."

I started to chime in with my usual, "not all of them," but

kept quiet, hoping Conan would keep talking. Much to my relief, he did.

"You are correct my existence began in another place, but the Sorcerer you found, the man who shaped my magic, had as much influence over what I became as my origins."

"So you know how to transit the barrier or veil or whatever?"

He lifted his shoulders in an approximation of a shrug. "When I crossed as a pup, I was terrified. I have no memory of how I managed it, but I escaped my tormentors and ended up not far from where you found me."

"How soon after did I come along?"

"Not long at all."

I closed the distance between us and cradled his head between my hands. "Not that any goddess watches over Vampires, but someone was watching out for you that day. A scrawny, frightened puppy with power spilling from him wouldn't have fared well without protection."

He leaned into my touch, perhaps in wordless acknowledgement.

Nickolas popped back into the storeroom. "We can leave now," he said before he was fully corporeal. "Our best bet is returning to that house where the Witches believe the veils are thin."

"Not until dusk," I countered. "That place has a whole lot of windows."

"We don't have to go inside. A storm is blowing in. Sun's gone, and it's pretty dark out there."

"All right, but we need a game plan. What exactly are we looking for?"

"I'm viewing it as a reconnaissance," he said. "It might take a few tries to find the proper world. I remember what the men smelled like, and I bet you and Conan do too."

The wolf barked, maybe because he appreciated being credited for his sharp nose.

"Before we go, show me what you got for that thousand bucks," I said.

Reaching into his coat, Nickolas pulled out a creased leather billfold and handed it over. Within, I found an ID card, a social security card, a driver's license, and two credit cards. The address listed for everything was *Ascent's*.

"He also gave me these things." Nick dragged out a folded manila envelope. Inside was a birth certificate that said he was thirty-seven years old and had been born in Seattle, a high school diploma, and a passport.

I handed everything back, and Nick asked, "Did I get my money's worth?"

"You did, indeed. There's enough here to get you started. The credit cards spend like money, but you'll have to pay the bills when they show up every month."

"Rob made that part clear." Nickolas smiled wryly. "He also set me up with numeric codes that make the cards work."

Damn. He was so flipping gorgeous, he stole my breath. "Did you write them down somewhere?"

He shook his head and tapped his forehead. "Steel-trap memory."

Conan woofed, his way of saying if we were going to go, we should get moving. As usual, the wolf was right. It was not quite four thirty. We could afford to spend an hour mucking around, but then we had to get back to make certain all the "t's" were crossed and "i's" dotted for opening tonight. Maybe we'd put out the sign for happy hour special pricing.

Cheap booze was always an inducement.

"I'm ready," I told Nick and added, "Conan's coming with us." I didn't reveal the wolf's secret about his origins. He'd been right when he'd told me some things didn't matter.

I brought us out behind the house and well-warded. Good thing. The place wasn't empty any longer. Nick switched to telepathy. *"I count nine inside."*

It matched my impressions. "I'd feel better if I knew what all of them were," I mumbled. No way they could hear us out here.

"Ha. Looks like the reconnaissance came to us." Nick's eyes glittered with anticipation; he looked stoked. About the only thing he didn't do was rub his hands together.

I wrapped my fingers around his arm. He felt good. Tantalizing. Alluring. Mortals are too warm. He was just right, and the ripple of muscle beneath skin excited me. "We are not going in there," I said.

He turned an incredulous glance my way and shelved the telepathy. "Why not? Those numbers aren't anything we can't handle."

"Depends what they are. Two feel like Witches to me. One is a Fae."

"One is a Sorcerer," Conan said into my mind. *"The other five could be anything."*

It was his way of telling me to use mind speech. Some magical creatures have preternaturally sharp ears. *"It's not so much the nine we sense,"* I went on, *"but what if the gateway to the other place is open and they summon reinforcements?"*

"I could call Clive and Lorenzo," Nick suggested. *"It would even up the odds. They like a good scrap."*

The specter of a fight was appealing. I'm just like the next Vampire. Conflict is where I live, but I've learned to tone down that part of myself. Otherwise, I'd have hammered the first drunk who grabbed my ass, and *Ascent* would have been doomed soon after it opened for business.

"Let's see if we can eavesdrop," I said. *"Maybe we'll learn what they're up to, why they're here, and what they have planned. If we go in, guns blazing, and fuck it up, whoever these bastards are will move their base of operations. Right now, knowing where to find them is our only advantage."*

Nick laid a hand over mine where it still gripped his arm. *"All excellent points. The other world aspect adds an extra wrinkle. They could dive through the portal, shut it, and show up anywhere next time."*

Conan growled. His vote was to fight, and it might come to that.

We stood near the back fence. A grove of evergreens halfway to the house would be a better vantage point for listening. I pointed at it and tightened the warding around us. We should be invisible, but a mage with exceptional magic could drill right through my shrouding.

If I'd been the breathing type, I'd have held my breath until we repositioned ourselves. We scuttled across the expanse of dead lawn. So far, so good. It didn't appear we'd been discovered. Nickolas and I huddled shoulder to shoulder. The press of his body against my side was captivating, provocative...

And I had shit for brains. With firm instructions to focus on whatever was happening inside the house—not inside me —I redirected my attention. Conan sat in front of us, ears pricked forward, nostrils flaring. Words caught at me, but not in coherent sentences. More like one here, one there.

Fuck. I needed to move closer.

I was getting ready to suggest a lush thicket that bordered the back wall of the house when Conan growled low. Before I could shush him, he leapt straight into the air, twisted, and hit the ground running flat out for the back fence.

What the hell?

Nick sprinted after the wolf.

I gave up on the ward. We had to be next to each other for it to be effective. Conan fought with something I couldn't see. Power jetted from Nick's hands as he cycled through various magics quicker than I could follow what he was doing. He hit on the right combination because the shielding around a pack of demons went up in smoke.

Literally. Smoke billowed upward. We'd be lucky if some do-gooder neighbor didn't sic the fire department on us. Conan finished off the demon he'd been grappling with by biting halfway through its neck. Nick had already killed one, slashing through its femoral artery with a short blade I didn't know he'd been carrying.

Green blood spewed, a garish contrast to the demons' red hides.

The urge to jump in feet first and join the bloodbath was nigh onto irresistible, but I held back.

Any hopes for stealth had evaporated, right along with the smoke from the demons' warding. About five feet tall, they were naked with red skin, horns, forked tails, and hoofs instead of feet. They were so picture perfect, I had a hard time believing they were real and not someone's illusion meant to distract us.

The thought had no sooner hit than I understood we had to leave before the second act crashed down on us. *"Nick. Conan,"* I screamed in telepathy. *"We have to get out of here now."*

Without waiting for them to agree with me, I wove a teleport spell, added their energy to it, and pulled us back to *Ascent.*

The sulfur stench of demon clung to us as we popped out in the alley. Damn it to fuck. I'd been aiming for inside, but no harm done. No one was back here. If this had happened last night, we'd have been so screwed.

"Why'd you do that?" Conan demanded. Green streaks coated his snout and flanks.

"I'd ask the same thing. We were winning," Nickolas said. It didn't seem possible, but he was even more alluring with bloodlust in his eyes and demon debris peppering his hands and face.

I hustled us all inside before I said, "Don't you see? They were too perfect. Hell doesn't produce clones like that. Someone wanted us distracted. Waiting around to see what would show up next wasn't in our best interest."

"I still say we should have killed all of them," Nickolas grumbled.

A corner of my mouth twitched. "Killing becomes us," I reminded him. "Never easy to walk away from enemies who are still on their feet."

"Eh. Maybe so," Nick grudgingly agreed. "We stink. Do you have a shower here?"

"We smell like warriors," Conan corrected him.

My next move wasn't wise or well thought-out. "Closest shower is at my house," I said. "Only thing here is a sink."

"Does it mean you're going to take us there?" Nick eyed me expectantly. "Can't very well wait on customers like this."

"I'll take us," Conan said, and the clean, wolfish smell of his power wafted around me.

Words crowded against the back of my throat. A need to swear Nick to secrecy about where I lived, to not tell Clive or Lorenzo or anyone else, but that ship had sailed. I'd opened my fat yap, and if there were consequences, it was no one's fault but my own.

Before we left, I sent a quick text to Dee. Since they're as easily hacked as telepathy, I skimped on details.

Be very careful. You and the others. See you soon.

CHAPTER FOURTEEN, NICKOLAS

A few minutes before
Joy spilled through me as I leapt and twisted and chopped through demonspawn. They needed to die, and I was here and poised to take them down. Green blood wasn't for drinking, but I didn't give a shit. The simple task of meeting an enemy head-on and being the instrument of their destruction fed something primitive in me. A core element of what made me a Vampire kindled and burned fiercely.

Every cell came alive. Every muscle. Every bone. I hadn't been able to kill like this since well before leaving Italy. Savagery swept me into its maw, and as I gutted the demons, I played with doing the same to those arrogant pricks of humans who had the audacity to set themselves up as my enemies.

Or the instrument of my destruction.

No bloody way would I roll over. Mortals would suffer

for their disrespect. I'd become better when I was turned. Stronger. Faster. Magical. Ha. Let them try to match me on any front.

The wolf was in the thick of things, ripping, tearing, and as high on killing as I was. Ariana hadn't joined us. Why? Surely, she was hanging onto control by a thread. When she yelled at us and dragged us back to *Ascent*, I was fuming. How dare she yank me away from the best time I'd had in centuries.

Turning my ire on her was a very bad idea, but I'd be buggered if I'd let a woman dictate my fortunes. While the occasional female Vampire controlled a clan, usually it was men. We were the ruthless ones, the ones who took crazy chances...

Finally, the haze parted enough for Ariana's words to sink in. She had a good point about a portal being open, and with it the possibility of reinforcements from a separate world. She was also damn good looking. Not that I hadn't been drawn to her masses of dark hair, stunning face with its deep-blue eyes, perfect cheekbones, and sculpted lips, but when we hadn't grappled with one another immediately, I'd written her off.

With Vampires, sex either happened or it didn't. Maybe Clan Hawke forbade coupling outside its ranks. None of the clans knew which rules governed the others.

My control was thin because I'd thrown myself into the demon fight, but the vista of breasts pressing against fabric, flared hips, and long legs got to me. My cock thickened, rising in a column against my belly.

Vampires don't pair bond like mortals. We fuck. A lot.

But our loyalties are to our clan and ourselves. I remembered Clive bounding into the cave. His first question had been, "Where's the woman?" When I'd said she wasn't there, his interest vanished immediately, snuffed out like a candle.

Indeed. We might look human, but the similarities began and ended there.

When I asked about cleaning up, I'd assumed there were facilities here. Instead, we were heading to Ariana's home, her lair. If my cock had been hard before, it expanded a few more notches. Arguing with my appendage was pointless. I hadn't come since before entering stasis. I'd have to bring myself off in the shower, which should take less than a minute given my current state.

Our clan house hosted giant orgies most days. Going outside wasn't on the agenda, so we fucked the time away. You'd think it would have had a modulating effect, but it didn't. Special gathering places had begun to form before I left Italy. Mortals were fascinated by us—and horrified. It added spice to their forbidden lust. I met women in out-of-the-way roadhouses, human women who wanted a taste of my cock.

Some I fed from. Some I didn't, but the feel of their bodies was sweet as they writhed beneath me.

The direction of my thoughts wasn't helping at all. Pheromones must be pouring off me. Ariana would be certain to pick up on them, and there wasn't fuck all I could do about it.

A cozy home formed around us, but beyond noticing the bare basics—walls, furniture, bookshelves—I was too sunk in heat to pay attention.

"The bathroom is at the far end of this big room. It's the door on the left," Ariana told me in a strained voice.

Damn it. My pathetic arousal was bleeding all over the place, and I'd put her in a tough spot. Rather than doing things the Vampire way, and dragging me to bed for a quick fuck, she'd taken some kind of mortal-spewed high ground and chosen to ignore the obvious. I sped off in the indicated direction and placed a door between her and me as fast as I could. I'd stolen a shower at the Salvation Army the night we'd pilfered the clothing. Were it not for that, it would have taken me longer to figure out the hot and cold taps.

In the world I remembered, hot water came from heating it over a fire in kettles and carting it to a bathtub. There was a lovely copper tub in Ariana's bathroom, but I opted for expediency.

I left my boots and clothing in a pile on the floor and immersed myself in jets of hot water. Steam filled the bathroom, and I wrapped a hand around my jutting member. My estimate of a minute had been generous. It only took a few swift strokes before semen shot from me in long, delicious waves. Far from diluting my desire for Ariana, coming intensified it.

I ached for her in a very un-Vampirelike way.

I'd have to get over it damned fast.

By the time I'd washed myself, my heart rate was back to normal and my cock somewhat deflated. As if it were telling me it could jump back to attention at a moment's notice.

I picked up my clothes, examining them. They still stank of sulfur and brimstone from the demon pack. I hated to put them back on. Resorting to telepathy—leaving the bathroom with a towel draped around me was a very risky idea—I said, *"Teleporting to my cave for clothes. I'll meet you at Ascent as soon as I'm decent."*

If I'd expected her to argue, I'd have been disappointed. "Good plan. See you soon," she called through the bathroom door. "If you leave the clothes, I'll dump them in the washing machine."

Had she been right outside the whole time?

The thought excited me all over again. Before I opened the door—another very bad idea—I removed the leather wallet and tan envelope from my jacket. Leaving the stinky garments, I grabbed my boots and my socks, and left.

I'd no sooner landed in my impromptu home when Clive rushed toward me. "Been waiting for you, mate. Why are you naked?"

"It's a long story." I dropped what I was holding so I could dress. He'd tell me what was on his mind without prodding.

I was mostly garbed in items quite similar to what I'd left at Ariana's when Clive said, "They got Lorenzo."

Shock shot through me like a high voltage charge. I stopped what I was doing and faced Clive. "Who got Lorenzo?"

"I told him not to fuck the mortals. That this place wasn't the same as the one we left. He didn't listen." A muscle danced beneath one eye, certain evidence of how upset Clive was.

"Go on," I urged.

"He got this circle thing going where he had three of them. Three women. He told me about it telepathically, and

I'd just shown up when he rolled over and casually sank his fangs into the neck of a gal. The other ones started screaming and ran out of there buck naked.

"I tried as hard as I could to get Lorenzo to leave off. We could still get out of there, but he didn't let go. I slapped his ass. Screamed at him. Even bit him. No dice. He was as buried in draining the girl as I've ever seen any of our kind. Probably, it didn't start like that, but you know how it goes."

Yes. I did know how it went. That was the problem. Except Lorenzo was well past the young-Vampire-lack-of-control stage of his life.

"What happened?" I pressed for details, aware I had to show up at *Ascent*. I owed Ariana a debt for the funds she'd loaned me, and I wouldn't welch on it.

"When I couldn't make him quit, I warded myself. Just in time, it turned out. A pack of men wearing uniforms and masks blasted inside. One told the others to stand back. He had some kind of gun-thing and he fired darts into Lorenzo's back. I knew immediately they were silver stakes. The stink of silver permeated the place until I felt so ill keeping my ward in place was tough."

He shook his head and sank to one knee in front of me. "I failed our clan. I stood by and did nothing while mortals killed one of ours. I am ready to accept whatever punishment you deem necessary."

"Get up." After he shot me a disbelieving look, I repeated my command. "Get up. Now. Nothing you could have done. If you'd revealed yourself, they'd have killed you too."

Clive got his feet under him, but he was moving like a

sleepwalker. When he looked at me, I felt his guilt. "If I'd attacked the mortal squad, there would have been honor in my passing. I took the craven's path and hid."

I dropped a hand onto his shoulder. "I fail to see how sacrificing yourself would have helped anything beyond your guilty conscience. I have to go somewhere. I won't be back till daylight. If you wish, you can remain here."

"I should go back for Lorenzo, so we can burn his remains."

"The body won't be there. Mortals will have taken it."

"But they used to fear touching us," Clive muttered.

"Many things have changed. If you're here when I get back, we can talk further." I let go of him, slid my feet into socks and boots, and summoned enchantment to return me to *Ascent*.

"Can I come with you?"

His question surprised me. Vampires aren't especially gregarious. "Only if you're willing to work. This is a public house, and there is much to do, but it serves mortals—and supernaturals. You have to maintain the guise of being human."

He furled his brows. "Why are you working there?"

"Because the proprietress loaned me money for identification papers. I owe her."

His brows edged higher. "The papers I said I didn't want?"

"The same. Decide, Clive. I'm late as it is."

"I'll come. It beats sitting here watching Lorenzo die over and over in my head. Maybe I need to earn money so I can get my own papers."

I gathered the tattered edges of my teleport spell. "The woman who owns the nightclub is a Vampire, but she's not like the ones we remember. Once she was part of Clan Hawke, but she walked away from them long ago."

Clive cracked a weak smile. "I won't try to fuck her, if that's what you're getting at. After watching Lorenzo's rutting be the death of him, I'm not feeling especially amorous."

"Eh, you'll get over it." I launched my spell, and the now-familiar walls of *Ascent's* storeroom took shape around us.

Conan bounded in front of us, upper lip drawn over his teeth, snarling.

"Bloody fuck. What is he?" Clive took a step back.

Rather than answering Clive, I told the wolf, "It's all right. This is my associate. There were two, but mortals killed the other one earlier today."

"What?" Ariana bolted from some back corner of the storeroom to where we stood. "Humans killed a Vampire?" She patted Conan's head, and he stopped growling.

Clive nodded sadly. I hastened to say, "It's complicated, but it was his own fault. He engaged in very public feeding after equally public fucking. Some kind of squad wearing masks showed up with a gun that shot silver stakes."

Ariana made a clucking sound. "Sounds like one of the riot squads. Usually, they come armed with tear gas. I'd heard rumors about them carrying silver stakes but didn't believe them, mostly because Vampires have never been a problem here."

I had no idea what tear gas was, but this wasn't the time

to ask. "Clive's willing to work," I told Ariana. "He knows he has to pass as human."

Dee hustled into the back room. "Wahoo! The cheap drinks sandwich board worked. We're starting to pack 'em in." She stopped dead, staring at Clive. "Aw fuck. Another of you."

"Stop that." Ariana's tone was sharp. "Remember the let's-all-gather-at-the-river-kumbaya discussion from earlier?"

"I do," she said soberly. "We have an enemy, and it's not other supernaturals." She focused on Clive. "Apologies."

"None needed," he said gallantly, adding, "My name is Clive, Madame Witch."

"I'm Dee," she said, still sounding sullen.

"Did Ariana tell you about the house?" I asked her.

"Yeah. And I alerted Dahlia and the others. It was timely since we were preparing to return there later tonight. We still will, but more as a stealth operation to see if we can't figure out who the fuck they are—and how we can get rid of them."

"What in the bloody hell are you talking about?" Clive blurted.

"I'll tell you later," I said. I agreed with the necessity of ridding ourselves of magical beings from another world. Our first priority should be mortals. If we split our attention among too many fronts, we wouldn't do well anywhere.

Ariana clapped her hands smartly together. "Get to work, everyone. Dee, take Clive and get him started washing glasses."

"You got it." She offered a jaunty salute and beckoned for Clive to follow her.

"I'm sorry about your clansman," Ariana said softly once they'd left.

"Me as well." After a brief inner struggle, I said, "Feels like I failed Lorenzo."

"You warned him," she reminded me. "About things being different here."

"Yes, I did, but apparently I wasn't specific enough. Clive was there and had the good sense to conceal himself."

"So that's how you knew what happened. I wondered about that." She gripped my lower arm. "Sorry if my hospitality earlier was...lacking." Her sea-blue eyes latched onto my gaze and held it. "I'm attracted to you, but us getting together is a very bad idea. We have many battles ahead of us. Diversions aren't wise."

I'd stopped listening after she admitted being attracted to me. Delight coursed through me, kindling every nerve ending. My errant cock heard someone singing his song and sprang to attention.

She tightened her hold on my arm. "Nickolas. I did not say yes. What I explained was why you and I are a no."

"Got it," I told her. Except I didn't, not really. At some point, we'd clear a path to one another. In a retreat to my pre-Vampire roots when I'd been a knight, I raised her free hand to my lips.

Conan growled.

Ariana grinned. "It's okay," she told the shapeshifting wolf. To me, she said, "My. How old-fashioned. Are you planning to court me despite my nay-saying?"

"Until you chase me away." I smiled back. "On a more

somber note, could we have a farewell ceremony for Lorenzo?"

"Without his body?"

"It would have been mostly bones. He was young by our standards, but still over two hundred years."

"Sure." She nodded. "We can do that tomorrow morning before dawn."

"Thank you. It would mean a lot to Clive. Are we going back to the ley-line house after the club closes?"

Ariana nodded. "We are. The Witches will already be there along with several Sorcerers and some Fae."

"We're planning a battle."

"We are, indeed. Got to nip this problem in the bud so we can get back to the primary one."

I curved two fingers into the sigil against evil. Mortals use it on us, but in this case, I was cursing them. "No reason we can't win," I muttered.

"Um yeah. There are a whole lot of reasons why an all-out war with mortals will eventually be the end of us."

I didn't see it that way. "We're stronger. We have magic."

"They have sheer mass. It's unfortunate the Fae and Druids outed us, but it's not the kind of cat you can stuff back into a bag."

I placed a hand over the one she still had curled around my arm. She didn't shake me off. I considered it a good sign. "We've coexisted with mortals since the beginnings of time," I argued. "No reason we can't retreat to invisibility. It's not as if they didn't know we existed before whatever the Fae and Druids did."

"It was a different time. Humans stopped recognizing

the existence of magic. A few continued being superstitious, but it was more out of ritual and habit than actually believing putting milk out for goblins did anything. Or carving turnips on All Hallows Eve to honor your dead. Or any of the small concessions humans engaged in to recognize they weren't the only inhabitants on Earth."

After a small pause, Ariana kept talking. "The change was gradual, but sometime around 1900 or so, men made a full commitment to science. We'd have been better served to remain in the shadows. Out of sight. Out of mind. But the Fae—and a few others—were convinced enlightened minds could absorb our reality.

"Didn't work for very long. Not many years passed before humans needed a scapegoat."

I nodded my understanding. "We were convenient, huh?"

A corner of her mouth twisted into a frown. "Too convenient. We argued we deserved at least the same rights as humans accused of wrongdoing, but no one was in an especially generous mood.

"And so, we hid ourselves once again. The big difference was humans couldn't pretend they didn't know about us. They ditzed around the point and finally settled on tossing us into iron-lined prisons. Forever."

"Blasted bunch of cowards," I muttered. "What? Was murdering us too brutal for them?"

"Something like that. They fancy themselves a few steps better than us." She shook her head. Conan snarled.

I felt like snarling too. Instead, I said, "I need to go to work. I'm not addressing my debt at all standing here."

"Help Percy man the front door," she suggested. "I've got a few things to do, and then I'll be along."

As I was untangling myself from her, I kissed her hand one more time. The feel of her skin beneath my lips was incredible. Letting go was hard.

"Next you'll be asking for my scarf for a jousting tournament," she joked.

"I'm guessing they don't still have those."

She made a snorting sound. "Nope. Replaced by rodeos, and a piss poor substitute if you ask me."

"Can you show me pictures?" I was curious.

"Sure, but it's mostly a bunch of men on horseback roping cows and riding around barrels."

"Eh. Don't bother. If they're not killing each other, it's not worth much."

Ariana offered me an enigmatic smile, but without any explanation. On that note, I hustled into *Ascent's* main room. It was comfortably full. After waving at Clive, I trotted to where Percy stood next to the door.

"Trouble's brewing," he said quietly. "I feel it in my bones, and I'm almost never wrong."

CHAPTER FIFTEEN, ARIANA

*W*hen Nickolas made an offhand comment about rodeos being boring as fuck because men weren't engaged in mortal combat, it reminded me how differently Vampires view the world. I agreed with him. Any event that didn't feature death was, indeed, dull as dishwater. We may be different from humans, but we're also in a class by ourselves on the supernatural front. None of them embrace killing quite the way we do.

Or sex.

Earlier, at my home, I'd been painfully aware of Nickolas's arousal. It had taken all my self-control not to storm into the bathroom and join him in the shower I heard running. The results would have been explosive. No such thing as bad sex for Vampires.

But it wouldn't have stopped there. Or with the next time or the next. I wasn't put together like others of my kind. I'd unabashedly fallen in love with Mistral. It was far more than idle infatuation. Not only had I never gotten over it, I'd become increasingly more jealous and possessive as the years clipped past. Unlike others in Clan Hawke, I never took part in casual couplings, preferring to wait until Mistral took me to his bed.

It was always his desire, not mine, dictating our trysts. That part annoyed me, but I accepted it—until he made it clear he was done. I hadn't believed he was serious. I'd been certain he'd get over himself and come running back to me.

Until he hadn't.

Bringing that simpering bitch home had been the last straw. Even now, anger rose as I recalled that horrid day. My temper had ended Mistral, but it had branded me as well, taught me it wasn't prudent for me to get attached—to another Vampire.

Conan was safe.

Humans were too, since they were temporary sources of entertainment. The day I'd hid out in my room after leaving my master's headless pile of bones, I vowed I'd never, never take up with another Vampire. What had happened that day could happen again, and I might not be so lucky.

Crimes against our own weren't tolerated. My Undead existence would be forfeit, and I'd be damned if I'd give it up for a philandering dick who didn't appreciate me enough to be faithful...

I slammed the flats of my hands against the nearest wall. Time to push everything aside. Vampires weren't built to be monogamous. Only me, apparently. I wasn't going to change Nickolas. I sure as hell hadn't changed Mistral.

If Nickolas and I got together, I'd just be one more fuck

to him, but I'd probably do the same thing I'd done before and decide he was mine and mine alone. And I could never tell him about Mistral. It would always be a squishy, uncomfortable secret between us.

How could I even begin to consider a relationship that wasn't based on absolute trust?

I'd been wise to hang onto shreds of distance when Nick was in my shower. No reason to plop myself back into an untenable position. It wasn't as if I thought much about sex—or I hadn't until now. If my overheated libido didn't settle down, I could take care of myself. It was less messy than setting my sights on one of the bar patrons. Even the married ones would be so entranced by a quickie with me, they'd turn into pests. It wasn't me so much as a mesmerism unique to all Vampires. Once upon a time, it had ensured we'd never go hungry.

Conan nudged my side with his head. He must have sensed my unrest. He didn't know about Mistral. No one did, and I aimed to keep it that way. An old saying about the only way two people can keep a secret is if one of them is dead flitted through my mind. The sheer black humor of it made me smile.

"I'm okay," I told the wolf, more to reassure myself than him.

After a quick check of the liquor stocks, I headed into the bar. The noise level had offered a clue about how busy we were, but it was gratifying to see crowds milling through the place. Too bad we'd had to offer cut-rate drinks to make it happen, but booze has a pretty comfortable markup.

Maybe I could talk Ruby and Dee into playing their

instruments, a guitar and a lute. If I worked the bar, it would take up the slack. I let myself into the space behind the bar. "Might be a good evening for a spot of entertainment," I said.

Dee shot a haggard glance my way. My bet was she was worried about later tonight. Or maybe about the other Witches. They're not immortal like the rest of us. Long-lived, but not immortal.

"We're doing all right," Ruby said as she slapped a couple of gin and tonics on a bar tray along with two bottles of Mexican beer. One of the waitresses snatched up the bounty and vanished into the crowd.

Drink orders rolled in via an electronic order system I'd had installed the previous year. Like everything digital, it had a few bugs but worked smoothly for the most part. I pitched in filling orders; tray after tray of everything from shots to fancy custom drinks flew off the bar.

The crowd thickened still more until I figured we were close to our stated maximum per fire department regulations. While I was considering if I wanted to ask Percy or Nick to do an actual head count, a vague feeling of unease buffeted me. A wrongness, but so obscure I might have imagined it.

At first, I chalked it up to being edgy. After everything that had happened, anyone would be skittish. Ruby sidled next to me. "Sweetie, did you feel that?" she hissed near my ear.

Fuck.

"Maybe," I said carefully. "What exactly are you referring to?"

"A hitch in the warp and weft holding Earth separate

from other places," Dee muttered, proving she'd overheard us.

"You felt it too?" I connected with the necromancer's dark eyes. Her pupils were so dilated, it was tough to tell where the iris began.

"Yeah. I—"

Her words were drowned out by the fire alarm blaring. Someone had pulled it. Patrons stampeded for the door. I'm tall, but not tall enough, so I jumped on top of the bar. Percy and Nick and Clive did a masterful job making certain no one was trampled.

Ascent emptied in record time. The alarm fell silent.

"I don't get it," Dee yelled. "There's no smoke. No fire. What the fuck?"

What the fuck, indeed. I cracked the power within me open and sent it spinning outward. Conan leapt onto the bar next to me, barking. Hackles raised the full length of his back.

Percy shut the front doors and dropped a heavy length of wood into place to lock them. I saw him on his cell phone. When I focused power his way, I heard him explaining to someone it was a false alarm.

Probably the fire department. The alarm was set up to alert the nearest station house. I had a feeling Percy was behind activating it. In one fluid jump, I left the bar and crossed to where he stood.

He dropped his phone into a pocket. "Sorry, Ariana. We have to get out of here. It was the fastest way to clear the place."

"Why?" I didn't doubt his assessment, but I needed to know.

"A swat team will be here soon. Someone, maybe that detective who wanted to pin Roger's death on you, decided we're suspicious. Those women the Vampire had sex with kicked the whole supernatural hunt into high gear. They're all over the news."

A staunch cracking brought my head whipping around in time to see gateways open in three places. Weird shit poured through. At least I'd recognized the demons. No one had bothered to turn these monsters into something palatable. Wasps as big as eagles with stingers a foot long flew past, reeking of poison. Pig-like things with sharp, shiny tusks thundered through, their hooves making clopping sounds on the wooden floor.

Conan started forward. "No." My command probably startled him because I never ordered him to do anything. Thank fuck he stopped. I could just see the hogs playing bait and switch and one of them goring him.

The last portal disgorged two men whose magic felt something like Percy's. Tattered black robes swathed their tall, robust bodies. Matted gray hair fell to their shoulders, and they surveyed the bar with keen, yellowish eyes. My money was they were some perversion of Sorcerer. They barked words in an unfamiliar language, and the pigs and wasps circled them.

"We're here for the Vampires," one of the men said.

"Aye, quite the chase you led us on, but we've found you now. One is missing, but there's a new one, so everything adds up."

Nickolas and Clive snarled, fangs dropping.

One of the warped Sorcerers spied Conan. "You're quite the find, wolf. Haven't seen one like you in a long while. You'll fetch a high price at auction."

"Like hell he will," I growled.

"Kill them all," Conan shouted into my mind.

"Grand idea, but do nothing," I told him.

"Why?"

"You'll see. My way is better." I didn't bother to point out by the time we cut our way through the pigs and wasps, we'd sustain major injuries. Both reeked of toxins that were probably lethal to supernaturals. Otherwise, why bring them along?

The noise of distant sirens blared. I remembered Percy's warning about a supernatural task force *en route* to jack us up. An idea formed. I snatched my phone and dialed 911. After the tinny little voice asked what my emergency was, I yelled, "My bar is under attack. Send help." For good measure, I took a picture of the intruders and sent it to the dispatcher. Her steady stream of chatter broke off abruptly after that.

"What are you doing?" Ruby asked.

"Back room, everyone," I ordered and pocketed the phone.

"Fine, darling, so long as you and the other two stay out here." One of the Sorcerers leered my way.

I poured on Vampire mesmerism, layering it thick. He was probably immune to my magic, but let him think I was saving my staff. The portals still pulsed, alternating nacre with gray. Sure proof the men assumed they'd seize us and leave.

A wasp broke from the circle and flew after Christa. Percy focused a beam of power at it, and it exploded midair, showering everything around it with noxious fumes that smelled like a charnel pit, putrid and stagnant.

The sirens were getting closer.

"Your fangs," I hissed at Nick and Clive. Meanwhile a hog scuttled across the floor, intent on spilled food. One of the dark Sorcerers yelled at it, but it ignored his command. A jagged spike of black lightning forked from the dark mage's mouth, and the pig stopped cold—right before it caught fire. Tortured squeals pounded me until I felt sorry for the animal.

I stifled a gasp. Shit. They were killing their own?

Luckily, the blaze was confined to the hog. Once it was gone, nothing else—like my wooden floor—caught fire.

My phone rang. I didn't answer it. If anyone asked me later, I'd tell them I was too busy. Ruby handed over a rifle we keep behind the bar before hustling into the back room. Mostly, the gun was for show, but I needed to look as if we were fumbling through on our own. I'd have fired a shot or two—to keep things real—except I wasn't up for putting holes in my walls, and the bullets wouldn't hurt the Sorcerers.

Calling the cops was a desperate gambit on my part. Convenient they were already on their way. Still, we had to play our parts and play them well to make this believable. The only ones left in *Ascent's* main room were Conan, Percy, Nickolas, Clive, and me.

The sirens had reached a deafening level. I figured the first rush of the swat team was toast, but they'd figure shit out soon enough. Their job was to protect me—and my property.

I wasn't about to let them off the hook.

Percy sent a jolt of power across the room; the drop bar that locked *Ascent*'s main door unlatched. Just in the nick of time too. Half a dozen men outfitted in full battle regalia à la twenty-first century RoboCop slammed into the bar. The Sorcerers laughed; power forked from their hands and mouths as they sent lethal magic designed to stop hearts— and minds.

Swat suits and helmets might be impervious to bullets and fire, but they were no match for magic. The cops cursed and squealed before crumpling to the floor, either dead or not far from it. Radios crackled orders like, "Report, goddammit." Someone outside had heard their buddies yelling, but they weren't worried enough to risk coming inside themselves.

What a bunch of cowardly losers.

"I could maybe save a couple of them," Percy said into my mind.

"No. Not without revealing what you are," I cautioned.

While I appreciated his altruism, I didn't trust the downed cops for one second. They wouldn't be so grateful to Percy they'd give two fucks about keeping him free. Nope. They'd look at it as his job to save them since magic had been their downfall. Once they were on the mend, they'd spare no quarter hunting Percy down.

My phone rang again. This time I answered it and did

my best to sound terrified. "For Christ's sake, do something. They're still here."

"Ms. Hawke," a rattled male voice said. "Are any enforcement personnel still on their feet?"

"No. They look pretty dead to me. Get in here." I inserted hysteria—and compulsion—into my words.

"Where are you located inside?"

"Middle of the room," I squeaked.

"How many of you are there?"

"Three of my staff and my dog. And me. Everyone else made it to the back room."

"Can you get to safety?"

My turn to laugh. "If I could, why would I have called you?"

"Remain on the line," the man instructed.

A bullhorn crackled. "Come outside. Now. If you surrender, it will go easier for you," another man commanded.

One of the Sorcerers tapped two pigs. Ever obedient, they trotted toward the still-open door, followed by three wasps. I debated the wisdom of my next move, but I snatched up the phone. "Watch out. The things coming through the door are poison."

The cop was smart enough not to question my assessment. The muted boom of gunfire sounded, hopefully killing the lethal emissaries. I might have felt sorry for the first pig, but I was over it.

One of the dark Sorcerers started toward me. "Why you bitch," he ground out.

I narrowed my eyes, barked, "Get in here," into the

phone, and shut it off. The police didn't have to hear what came next.

"Compliments will get you everywhere," I purred at the Sorcerer.

Percy raised a hand; power crackled, and the Sorcerer stopped where he stood.

"You can't win," I said sweetly. "Haven't you heard? Mortals are done with those like you. They've declared war on everyone who isn't human."

"Seems like it would include you," the Sorcerer pointed out, equally sweetly.

"You're mistaken." I smiled and tapped my teeth. "Nothing wrong with me."

The other Sorcerer had herded the wasps and pigs into two rows with a wasp flying above each pig. The bizarre army marched through the open door, picking their way around the fallen swat team. While he was busy mind-controlling his troops and Percy had the other Sorcerer trapped, I called a quick teleport spell and moved the five of us to the back room, but I didn't stop there.

"Come on," I told everyone. Leaving the rifle lying across my desk, I marched out the back door and around to the front, careful to stay out of the line of fire. Pigs and wasps were thundering out of the bar. The cops were picking them off one by one.

The stench—a cross between boiled cabbage and rotten onions—made my eyes water.

I led the way to a uniformed officer standing off to one side and ginned up tears before I threw myself into his arms.

"We got out," I sobbed. "Do something. Get those horrid things out of *Ascent*. That bar is all I have."

After a lengthy pause, he closed one arm around me and awkwardly patted my shoulder. "Now. Now. Ms. Hawke. We're doing our best. Who else is in there?"

"All my people are safe," I wailed and repeated, "Get those horrible things out of my bar."

He let go of me and pulled back, making a point to grip my upper arm hard. Maybe it's how they train police to deal with hysterical females. "I understand your staff is safe. Good work."

"W-we made a run for the back room. By then, everyone but me and Percy and Ruby and Nick my dog were already there. I kept expecting those abominations to do that thing they did to your men and drop us in our tracks, but they didn't."

"Ms. Hawke." He shook my arm. "Who is they?"

"I don't know them. Never seen them before."

"Could you pick them out of a lineup?"

Yeah, right.

"Maybe." I kept a quiver in my voice. Meanwhile, someone had managed to drag one of the downed cops outside. Maybe he'd used the march of the pigs and wasps as cover. The man wasn't quite dead yet, and I heard him describe the Sorcerers as blood bubbled from his mouth.

Blood. Beautiful, red, coppery. Delicious. Such a shame to waste it. He was all but gone anyway, and—

I refocused fast, told myself it was points for our side that the dude wasn't dead. What he said would match up with what I told them and the photos I'd sent dispatch. I felt certain *Ascent* would be empty the next time anyone went inside.

The bullhorn sounded again. No one answered its call to surrender.

"I tell you, the place is empty," a man in a swat outfit insisted. "When I rescued Dawson, here, there wasn't anyone else inside. Except the rest of our A team."

Rescued appeared to be a relative term; the last of the man's lifeblood oozed from him. Other duded-up cops peered inside. When they emerged, they carried the rest of their downed companions.

"Aren't you supposed to be doing something about shit like this?" Percy demanded.

"Yeah," Dee chimed in. "Those poor women who had a run in with a Vampire have been all over the news. And now this."

An unmarked black sedan screeched to a halt. Two more men got out. Christ. Didn't the police department ever hire women in other than clerical positions? Once the newcomers reached us, one—Lieutenant Hernandez—said, "We head up the paranormal task force. Want to tell us what happened here tonight?"

"One of those wasps shot through a hole in the air. It came out of nowhere, I tell you." Percy managed to sound horrified. "I was worried about the customers, so I pulled the fire alarm. Nick and Clive and I hustled them outside before things got really bad."

"What wasp things?" The second dude—Lieutenant Riteway—demanded.

Percy pointed to a dead one, and I heard a die-hard gasp

as both men put two and two together. They might be part of a supernatural task force, but I'd bet my fangs they hadn't seen too many actual supernatural critters. It was a good reminder for me to mime breathing.

When it became apparent Hernandez and Riteway were determined to hear the same tale from all of us, I hustled us inside. May as well use the time to clean up. *Ascent* wasn't as bad as it had been when someone chucked a boulder through the window, but neither could we use magic to aid our cleanup efforts.

Conan was nowhere in sight. I figured he'd had a bellyful of my playacting when his preference would have been to rip out a few throats. Good to have him gone, though. It avoided awkward questions about what kind of dog he was and why was he so big.

"What if those things come back?" I demanded shrilly when it was clear the two lieutenants were preparing to leave. The remnants of the swat team were long gone.

"It's rare for this type of occurrence to happen twice in one spot," Riteway assured me.

"How can you be certain?" I laid it on thick, mostly because I wanted him to bury himself six feet under and have to eat his words. Words I'd be sure to remind him of the next time our paths crossed.

"I've studied the paranormal realm extensively." He offered up the patronizing look males adopt when talking down to women.

I felt like telling him he knew shit all about anything. We'd been targeted by the same dark Sorcerers Nick had gone into stasis to avoid. They knew where we were, and they wouldn't rest until they had the Vampire blood they craved.

And Conan.

Hernandez glanced around at the damp, freshly mopped floor. "No property damage. None of your patrons were injured. I'd say you got off cheap, Ms. Hawke."

What he didn't add, but I heard anyway, was my losses paled in comparison to his. "Sorry about your officers," I murmured. "Truly I am."

"Thanks for that. We'll be on our way. Not much to go on, but if you have any other problems, be sure to call us directly." He pressed a card into my hand.

Once they left and I heard their car drive away, I looked around the circle of worried faces. We still had plenty of time to make our rendezvous at the house sitting atop the ley-lines.

"What do you think?" I asked Percy.

"About?"

"Where'd they come from? Will this problem go away if we close off the portal sitting over those ley-lines? How would we even go about that?"

He exchanged glances with Ruby. Clearly, they'd talked about it. "Probably. I give it maybe 90 percent. Not that many spots the veils are thin enough to accommodate gateways, and those Sorcerers were not from here."

Nickolas cleared his throat. "This is my fault. We're who they're after. Clive and I will leave. That way, it will move their attention away from the rest of you."

Clive nodded. "Aye. We're sorry. Never meant to cause you any trouble."

"You will not go anywhere." The words burst from me before I could stop them. "We're all in this together. It may have been about you, but they know about me now. And Conan. Apparently, he's some kind of delicacy where they come from."

The wolf sauntered to my side, amber eyes glittering with ire. "I will never let them take me back," he announced. "Never."

"Were those the men you were running from as a pup?" I asked.

He shook his head emphatically. "No, but others just like them."

Interesting. I'd assumed Conan's tormentors had been mortals, but Sorcerers had targeted him. Maybe before this was over, I'd find out why.

Ascent was locked. The only thing left was to go to the house balanced over those ley-lines. It was just past midnight; we had most of the evening ahead of us. "I like 90 percent odds," I said. "Let's go give them all we have."

Dee laughed bitterly. "Those cops were like a sick joke. We never see things like this twice in the same spot," she quoted in a singsong voice.

"Yeah, well, we'll deal with them next," I said. "One war at a time. The house isn't far. We should conserve our magic and walk there."

Magic flared around Conan, and the Harley took shape. Nickolas whistled long and low.

I got the picture and grabbed my helmet from a peg. Once I had it in place, Percy got the door for us, and my wolf and I rode off into the night. Lieutenant Hernandez might have zero understanding of supernaturals, but he did get one thing right. I had gotten off cheap tonight. If we managed to blow up the breach, we could buy ourselves enough time to figure out how to rid ourselves of the black Sorcerers permanently.

"At least we know who's behind this," Conan observed.

"I was just thinking the same thing," I told him.

CHAPTER SIXTEEN, NICKOLAS

*W*atching Conan shift into a mechanical object was quite a shock. I'd always associated shapeshifters with a human form coupled to one animal. Kind of like Selene, the coyote shifter who worked in the bar. No wonder the Sorcerers were so interested in the dire wolf. His magic was unique, special. Perhaps it augmented their ability in much the same way as Vampire blood.

Clive ran along beside me. We were fast, but not quite as quick as Ariana and Conan. They were easy enough to follow. "What the bloody hell?" Clive sputtered. "Never seen a shapeshifter do that."

"He's one of a kind," I agreed. "Not certain he's actually a shapeshifter in the same way we recognize them. He can alter his appearance, but there's more to his magic."

"Interesting. We should leave." Clive mirrored my thoughts from a few minutes before. "I failed Lorenzo, and my carelessness has brought troubles down on everyone at the pub."

"We will leave," I told him. "After this battle. The others could use our help."

"Maybe," Clive said. The single word held caution. "When that Witch first saw me, her lack of, shall we say, enthusiasm was obvious."

"If our presence creates dissention, and we cannot lessen it, we will go." Easy to say, harder to accomplish. I wasn't at all sure I could walk away from Ariana. I certainly didn't want to. Once I'd understood her strategy back at *Ascent*, my estimation of her—already high—had soared. She was banking on playing the victim card in order to keep the police from looking too closely at her and everyone who worked at the nightclub.

It had been apparent listening to the last two men who'd shown up that they knew less than nothing about supernatural beings. Were all the mortals assigned to capture us as clueless? If so, fooling them might be simpler than I'd imagined. In my mind, I'd assumed they'd be as savvy—and as tenacious—as the Sorcerers who'd painted a target on my back.

We covered the distance to our destination quickly and joined Ariana and Conan on a hillock overlooking our objective. The wolf was back in his usual form, and Ariana's helmet lay on the ground. As soon as we got close to the house, I felt wrongness emanating from it. Others were with Ariana and Conan. Witches. Fae. Sorcerers. Shifters. Maybe forty people. Introductions would be a waste. I'd never remember all their names.

And it got me out from under announcing myself. Not that they wouldn't know Clive and I were Vampires, but sometimes keeping a low profile is useful.

A tall, thin Witch with gobs of curly red hair ran lightly to Ariana's side. "Dee told me what happened via telepathy. What you did was brilliant. Absolutely inspired."

"Not sure about that." Ariana shrugged. "It did get them off our backs for the moment. They're far stupider than I thought."

"Pah. Mortals are only mental giants in their own estimation. We've been here for a couple of hours. No one's come outside, but the complement within has ebbed and flowed. When we got here, there were seven—all Sorcerers. Two more showed up, but then they left."

A raven cawed and dropped out of the sky, perching on the Witch's shoulder and squawking. The Witch nodded. "More Than Never says the ones in the house are furious. Something happened to the Sorcerers who left."

I'm rarely surprised, but confirmation the bird was not only sentient but a spy for the Witch was thought-provoking. Lots of first here. I'd always suspected being part of a community of magic wielders would be useful, except they've never accepted Vamps.

Probably for the best. We're not exactly team players, even within our clans. Mistral's untimely ending flitted across my mind, and I cringed. The ultimate endgame, it still bothered me because it underscored our lack of ability to sit and talk out the rough places.

Clive might be onto something about us quietly slipping away—before we did more damage.

But then I considered Ariana. She'd done a fine job integrating herself with other supernaturals—and humans. Perhaps she'd paved the way for the rest of us. Except from what I could tell, she and I and Clive were the only Vampires for leagues. That we were so few might make it simpler for the others to accept us.

Christa's assertion—and warning—resurfaced. According to her future seeing, or however she leveraged her seer ability, Ariana had a key role to play in the mortals' war against us. According to the Fae, Ariana was precisely where she needed to be.

Ariana made a snorting noise and addressed the Witch's comment. "Something did happen to the black Sorcerers. Cops killed their poison pets and stormed the bar."

"Wait a minute. I missed that part of this story." The Witch held up a hand. "The Sorcerers went to *Ascent*? Why?"

"They consider Vampire blood a delicacy," I spoke up. "They were after Clive and me."

"Fascinating," the Witch murmured.

"Not so much," Ariana growled. "Once they got a look at Conan, they staked a claim to him too. That will never happen."

The wolf snarled agreement. In a show of what had to be sympathy, the raven fluttered to his back and rubbed its beak along a shoulder.

The others from *Ascent* caught up and joined the group. I wanted to know if we had a plan, but it wasn't wise to come off too strong. Hell, I itched to ask if any of the rest of them had any experience plotting military strategy. My days as a knight were long past, but some types of training never go away.

"Any idea how we're going to approach this?" Percy asked.

I nodded his way, pleased someone was holding us on task. So far, we hadn't been discovered. Our best bet was to hatch a plan and institute it.

"Maybe." The Witch beckoned to two others. Dee and a woman with beautiful black skin and pronounced cheekbones hastened to where we stood.

Dee raked a hand through her black hair. "I still think our best bet is to approach the junction of ley-lines. They're beneath the house but not precisely part of Earth's domain."

I leaned closer, intrigued. "Say more."

She nodded once tersely. "My thought is a few of us will enter the realm of the dead. It will be simple for you, Clive, and Ariana to accompany me because..." Her voice faltered.

"We get it, sweetie," Ariana said. "We fully understand we're already dead."

Dee's olive skin developed warmer tones. She cleared her throat. "Anyway, I'd open the gates, and we'd leave this plane. Once we're with the dead, we'll work our way to one of the ley-lines and follow it to the junction."

"What then?" I asked. "Do we block it somehow? Obliterate it?"

The red-haired Witch turned her hands palms up. "When Dee and Cerys and I kicked this around, we weren't certain how to deal with the ley-lines. You may find them impervious to any magic you can levy their way."

"In that case, we'd work to block the energy they carry," Dee said.

"I'll join you," Percy said in his deep voice. "And the other Sorcerers here. We understand how to part the veils and enter the realms of the departed."

"I'm coming," Conan said.

Ariana frowned and sent a worried look skittering his way. I absorbed how different she was from any Vampire I'd ever known, In the first place, we don't keep pets. In the second, we don't develop attachments, yet she clearly loved the dire wolf. He was part child, part beloved companion.

I hoped that was all it was, and he wasn't some kind of secret lover on the side after he adopted human form. For some reason, my earlier jealousy had faded. Conan's possessiveness toward Ariana lacked a sexual component.

I wanted her to feel the same way about me—not that I was a child, but that I was special to her. I chided myself for being foolish. If Ariana had wished to surround herself with other Vampires, she'd never have left her clan house. Had she known Mistral? If so, had the unpleasantness around his undoing been what had driven her away?

I'd never know. Nor could I ask. It was none of my business. I returned my attention to the red-haired Witch.

"I count nine," she was saying. "Three Vampires, Dee, four Sorcerers. And the wolf."

Conan growled. Perhaps being tacked on as an afterthought offended him.

"Odd numbers are auspicious," the third Witch—Cerys? —murmured. "I shall pray to the goddess for your success."

"You'll be doing more than that," the redheaded Witch

informed her. "Those of us who remain will bind the house to keep its inhabitants inside. Once the ley-lines are disposed of, we shall kill whoever is within."

No one raised any objections. Interesting. Maybe I'd been wrong about Vampires being the only ones to embrace slaughtering our enemies. I'd been asleep for a long while, though. If this was the new world order for supernatural beings, I approved. No more namby-pamby Druids preaching about the sacredness of all life.

"Ready?" Dee moved off to one side. Our contingent formed a circle around her. More Than Never squawked and returned to his mistress's shoulder.

"Will this be safe for Conan?" Ariana asked Dee.

A deep, vibrating snarl emerged from the wolf. He clearly cared more about sticking next to Ariana than about his own safety. I respected him for it. Dee crouched in front of him. "Remain close to me."

He didn't argue, and he quit growling when it became apparent no one was about to order him to remain here. Not that it would do any good. I had a feeling the wolf would figure out how to follow us no matter what.

Dee straightened and faced us. "Ignore the shades. There will be many, and they are lonely. They crave companionship. If they can engage you, they will, but we cannot allow ourselves to be diverted. They only appear to have bodies. If they grab you, their hands and mouths will go right through you. It's rather unsettling at first, but you'll get used to it.

"I will build a gateway, and I will hold it while all of you pass through. Wait for me on the other side." She drew her brows together. "If something unexpected happens, you can probably teleport out of there on your own—so long as you can free yourself of shades. Your magic won't work if they're clinging to you because them leaving the realm of the dead is forbidden."

After a final glance at us, one by one, she raised her hands and began a soft chant. A silvery portal formed immediately, and she gestured us through. Ariana went first, followed by the wolf, Clive, and me. The Sorcerers passed the liminal space last, and the portal winked out behind us.

I hadn't had any idea what to expect, but it wasn't the unending vista of black I'd imagined. Pale gray illumination seemed to be a product of some type of exotic lichen lining the walls of the place. After Dee's warning, I'd assumed shades would mob us, but the rounded corridor stretching in both directions was empty save for us. It was tall enough for me to stand up. Percy had to hunch a bit. Prickles jabbed me from all sides, unpleasant but not unbearable.

They retreated as quickly as they'd arrived.

"What was that?" Ariana asked.

"The guardians are checking who entered their domain," Dee said. "If they didn't approve of any of us, you'd either be dead or back where you began."

"What makes the difference?" Clive asked, his British accent more pronounced than usual, which told me he was nervous.

"Never figured it out," Dee replied. "Maybe they have bad days just like the rest of us." She took off at a fast trot along the corridor to our right. The lichen anticipated us, and the track ahead lit before we arrived. When I glanced over a shoulder, where we'd been was dark.

"Geez. Paranormal motion sensors," Ariana muttered.

"Something like that," Dee replied.

I wasn't certain what a motion sensor was, but I bet it had something to do with the rise of electricity that seemed to power everything.

"Where are the ghosts?" I asked Dee.

She slowed and tossed a quick look my way. "I don't know, and it's bothering me. Something scared them enough to keep them away. Or maybe the guardians curtailed their free run of the place to protect them."

"Black sorcery feeds off the souls of the dead," Percy said. "It's not their first choice. They prefer fresh corpses, but they're not overly picky."

"Mmph. Well, that explains it," Dee mumbled. This might be her place, but she sounded rattled as she led us around twists and turns. In a couple of places, she hesitated. Power spilled from her as she assessed which way to go.

A low humming caught my attention. At first, it was pleasant, but as it grew louder, it grated, separating into discordant notes.

"We're near a ley-line," Percy said.

Conan whined. I could only imagine what the buzzing did to his sensitive hearing. He pinned his ears back, and the feel of his magic told me he was doing what he could to mute the noise.

A golden glow joined the hum. When I glanced at the walls, the colonies of lichen had vanished. One more corner, and what had to be a ley-line came into view. Nothing looked like I thought it should. Far from a large cylindrical object, it was a shimmering gold rope wrapped in coppery streamers. Thick as my forearm, it vibrated along with the sound it made. And was the source of the illumination lighting our way.

Dee gave it a wide berth as she walked along its path. "The corridor will grow narrow in spots," she cautioned us. "Whatever you do, do not touch the ley-line. It's excited by how close we are, and it's only a matter of time before it decides it wants our magic."

I stared at the length of magical rope, not feeling anything like hunger from it, but perhaps Vampires were immune. We wrote the book on lust. Takes one to know one, and all that rot. Being this near wasn't comfortable, but dealing with it appeared manageable. Back when I figured we'd be facing a huge tube, I hadn't been as optimistic. Surely, we could snip through something this fragile when we got to its junction with other lines.

We weren't moving as quickly. Dee still had plenty of space between her and the glowing rope. Was the line sapping her energy? Ariana must have had the same concern because she slipped in next to Dee and wrapped an arm around the Witch's shoulders.

"Thanks," Dee murmured, but I heard her. "This will become harder as we get closer to the nexus. The ley-lines protect themselves."

I lost all sense of time. The line extended seemingly forever as we traced its path through the realm of the dead. Idle thoughts crowed, like why ley-lines would be here and not in some other non-Earth locale. Did the guardians keep an eye on them? If so, maybe we could talk them into barring entry from whatever world the dark magicians had come from.

A jolt was the only warning I got that I'd strayed far too close to the ley-line. By the time I recovered, I'd come within a fingernail's breadth of touching the damned thing. "It's insidious," I said loud enough to get everyone's attention.

"Aye. Sneaky and deadly," Percy said. "I saw you edging near it and was about to grab you."

"Thanks. I was lost in my thoughts. Not heeding where my body was."

"That's its favorite trick," another of the Sorcerers said. This one was an old man wearing ragged denim pants and a faded green shirt. His hair was white and cropped close to his head. A white beard fell to mid-chest.

"Good to know," Clive mumbled. Far more guarded than me, he hugged the outer wall. I could see it from his perspective. He'd already fucked up once, and he didn't aim to do it again.

The air thickened with scents, some appealing, some unpleasant. I smelled sulfur and brimstone, no doubt from the demonspawn we'd fought the other day. The pulsing glow intensified until I hooded my eyes.

"Almost there." Dee's voice held strain.

Sure enough. One last corner ejected us into a large cavern. Plenty of room for everyone to stand straight here. The line we'd been following joined with four others, making an eerie star formation. "Are we right beneath the house?" I asked.

Percy nodded and walked nearer the junction, hands

extended. The other Sorcerers flanked him. My simple-minded solution of snipping the rope didn't appear viable. Not that the ropes were any thicker here, but their junction pulsed with tongues of flame. The hum that had damn near hypnotized me vibrated off the walls, building on itself.

Ariana and Conan joined Percy and the Sorcerers. So did Clive and I. Dee sagged against a wall. As I passed her, I stopped long enough to ask, "Are you all right?"

"No. Not exactly, but we won't be here long."

"We'll manage. Leading us here was an enormous help. You can leave if you need to."

She shook her head. "Only reason the guardians allowed you inside is because they like me. Go. Sooner you figure this out, the sooner we can return to Earth."

"You've met these guardians?" I was curious what kind of being maintained this place.

"Not exactly. They've spoken with me a time or two but always arranged things so I couldn't see them. Go and help the others."

I patted her arm and walked next to Clive and Ariana. She cast a worried look my way. "The lines are alive. We can't harm them, or the world might unravel."

Fresh off my own near brush with disaster, I said, "That's what they want you to think."

Conan raised his muzzle and howled. "Ssht." Ariana dropped a hand onto his head. He howled louder, punctuating it with strident barks. She sank to her knees. "You have to stop that," she said. "Something bad might hear you."

The wolf shook her off. His howls took on a rhythm and

a cadence that cut through the insidious humming. More howls sounded. At first, I thought it was Conan's vocalizations echoing off the rounded walls.

His yowls became more strident.

The next time I heard extra wolf sounds, I was certain they weren't echoes after all.

Percy fist-pumped the air. "Yes!" he shouted.

"Yes, what?" I asked.

"The guardians are coming. I'd heard rumors about them being wolves, but none of us have ever seen one," the Sorcerer with white hair said. His mouth stretched into a smile.

I grabbed Ariana's arm. "Do you know what he's talking about?" She shook her head.

Another wolf came into view. In contrast to Conan, this one was silver, and he danced along a glowing ley-line, having clearly followed it to us. Dee had warned us to stay away from the lines, but the power flowing from the wolf to the line and back felt reciprocal. As if they'd been designed to work in tandem.

Three more wolves ran behind the silver one. Another silver, one white, and one black-and-silver like Conan. With all five of them baying, I couldn't hear the ley-lines any longer. The lead wolf jumped off the ley-line and right on top of Conan. The two of them rolled around on the floor, tussling with each other.

Wonder lit Dee's tired features. "No wonder I love Conan," she said. "He's a guardian. Who would have guessed?"

"Who would have guessed, indeed?" Ariana extended her

hands. Power arced between them. She was worried about her wolf, concerned the others meant him ill. By now the other wolves had piled on. From the licking and whining, it looked like a family reunion to me. "It will be all right," I told Ariana.

"I hope you're correct," she said.

Slowly, she lowered her hands as the wolves cavorted around us. Conan shook free. Standing tall, he said, "This is a ridiculous indulgence. We have work."

"Tell us," a silver wolf said.

Dee stumbled to him and fell to her knees. "Guardian. Evil magic has crossed the ley-lines."

The wolf dipped his head until it rested on her shoulder. Power—just like Conan's magic—flickered and flared around the Witch. "Thank you," she murmured. "I'm stronger now."

"Those such as you were never meant to remain near the lines for long," the wolf chided her.

"I know, but our need was great. It superseded my comfort," she replied.

"Can you interrupt the energy of the ley-lines at this junction?" I asked.

The other silver wolf planted himself in front of me and snarled. "Vampire. How did you slip through? We don't allow your kind in our domain."

Conan jumped between us, his upper teeth displayed. "A Vampire rescued me. Raised me. Cared for me. This man is her friend."

The silver wolf woofed once. "You are full of surprises, Brother."

Hackles rose along Conan's back. "If you were truly

brother to me, you'd have tried harder to save me, but the past has no place here. We need you to alter the lines' energy in this spot. Evil truly has snuck past and is wreaking havoc on Earth."

"We can do that." The silver stood taller, his shoulders in a determined stance.

The four wolves stood in a rough circle with the glowing junction between them. After a pause, Conan took up a vigil in an empty place. Power spilled from one of the silver wolves. The others augmented it until a shimmery white banner wound around the spot the ley-lines joined.

I felt their lupine enchantment, full of the scent of fur and forests and wet rocks, intensify. The banner tightened, and tightened once again. In a flurry of light so bright I turned my head to one side, the lines broke apart and reformed in the blink of an eye. Except instead of forming a star, they were once again individual lines extending along five different paths.

One of the silver wolves took on a liquid aspect. When the air around him settled, a man with flowing silver hair stood in his stead. Naked except for a gold circlet around his forehead, he regarded us out of amber eyes.

And then, his gaze shifted to Conan. "Moonwraith. Long have I wondered and worried about your fate. I give thanks to Anubis you are returned to take your rightful spot alongside us."

Conan shook himself from head to tail tip. "My place is with Ariana. I shall never return."

Ariana squatted next to him, her eyes liquid with tears.

I'd never seen a Vampire cry before. "Are you certain, Conan? These are your people. Your pack."

He turned to her and solemnly licked her face. "Pack runs deeper than blood. Pack is who loves you. Cares for you. You are my pack. And I am yours."

Ariana wrapped an arm around Conan's neck. I thought I heard a muted sob.

"But Moonwraith—" the mage began.

Conan barked once, quick and sharp. "My name is Conan. It is what you shall call me."

The man inclined his head. "Conan, then. Your place is with us."

"We have a difference of opinion, Fairclaw. One that will not be resolved." Conan shook Ariana off and stood tall. "Thank you for your assistance this day."

The white wolf morphed into a woman. Knee-length white hair framed her stark, unlined face. A blue stone sat in the hollow of her neck. Tears formed in the corners of her blue eyes and marched down her face. "I am so grateful you are alive." Turning to Ariana, she said. "I am in your debt for saving my son. Name any boon and, if it is within my power, I shall give it to you."

Ariana got to her feet, her face wet with tears. "You've already given me the best gift ever. Conan is..." She hesitated. "He's everything. My closest friend. My only ally. I trust him in a world that loathes my kind."

I wanted to be all those things to Ariana—friend, ally, trusted companion—but I was smart enough to hold silence. This moment wasn't about me at all. We'd finally figured out what Conan was. Where he'd come from. It explained why the dark mages wanted him. He was power incarnate.

The woman nodded. "Conan. My son. I had no hand in raising you, but I couldn't be prouder of who you've become. We are here if you need us."

"Or if you change your mind about coming home," Fairclaw added.

Ariana's mouth rounded into an O. "Home. The others need us. Our job here is done."

"We shall return you to your starting place," Fairclaw said.

"I felt your magic when we entered this place. Did you know I was here?" Conan asked.

The woman—his mother—smiled softly. "Not until I heard your cry. Or I'd have moved all the magic in the heavens to run to your side."

"Once our intruder alert located the Witch, we didn't look deeper," Fairclaw said, adding, "We've come to trust her."

Power eddied, surrounding our small group. In the space between two heartbeats the cavern with the ley-lines dropped away, and the hillock formed around us. Below, the house pulsed with expended magic. "Not too late to get a few blows in," Percy boomed and pounded down the hill.

The rest of us ran after him. There'd be plenty of time later to sort out everything that had happened in the realm of the dead. Now was the time for battle. Anticipation zinged along every sinew. Vampires were born to fight.

I was no exception.

CHAPTER SEVENTEEN, ARIANA

*C*ut off from the magic linking them to their world—
and their exit—dispatching the Sorcerers inside the
house was so easy it was disappointing. We even ended the
two who'd stormed *Ascent* with their wasps and pigs. It gave
me time to think about Conan. Guess I wasn't the only one
hanging onto secrets. Except I wasn't who he thought I was,
either. Not exactly.

Now that he had options, choices—a family who clearly
wanted him—I owed it to him to fess up about Mistral.

A low whirring was the only warning I got. Quick
reflexes pushed me into a twisting leap, but I'm not a bird.
One of the wasps had been skulking somewhere, and its foot-
long stinger jabbed where my head had been a second
before. No one else was anywhere close. The Witches were
dismantling the upstairs workshop, salvaging what they
could and consigning the rest to one of many fireplaces.

I landed with a thud, dodging the wasp's next strafing

run. Damn it. I'd assumed they had no intelligence of their own. I'd been wrong. My power was sluggish, slow to respond to my call. Big surprise. I needed blood. I'd expended gobs of magic tonight.

Fuck.

It wasn't night any longer. Streamers of daylight jutting into the house were a big part of my problem. I'd been too lost in my personal pity party about Mistral to even notice. Shame on me.

Conan ran to my side, barking and snarling at the wasp. I sent a pathetic jot of power into the air, but the wasp skittered sideways. My destructive enchantment drilled a hole in a nearby wall.

Magic sheeted from the wolf, turning the air a glistening blue. When it cleared, a gigantic eagle soared upward. Far more maneuverable than the wasp, it caught the unnatural insect in its talons and dashed it into a wall where its gray body broke apart, splattering everything around it with stinking innards.

Letting go of the remains of the wasp, the eagle flew to my shoulder, digging his talons in to steady himself. Now was as good a time as any. We were alone, but I still resorted to telepathy.

"Thank you," I told my closest friend and ally. *"There are things you don't know about me, and—"*

He clacked his beak; it sounded like a cannon going off next to my ear. *"Quiet. Nothing you could say would drive me back to the guardians. There is much you do not know. It was wrong of me to shield what I was, but you heard that perversion of a Sorcerer once he saw me in Ascent. If anyone got wind one like me was loose, I'd have been hunted the same way I was when I ran away the first time."*

"Friendships are built on honesty," I said. "I haven't been forthcoming, either."

The eagle detached from my shoulder. He shifted back to his dire wolf shape midair and came to rest in front of me. "All that matters to me," he said, "is the years we have been together. No matter how grateful I was that you rescued me, took me in, and found the Sorcerer who restored my magic, I'd have left if you'd given me reason."

Before I could reply, Conan kept talking. "I've sensed dark, hidden places within you. They're not as pervasive as they once were. My wish is for you to heal, not revisit a place and a time where you failed."

For the second time in as many hours, my eyes filled with tears. What the unholy hell? I'm not the crying type. No Vampire is. I crouched and held Conan's face between my hands. "Thank you. For everything."

"We owe one another nothing," the wolf said, quiet dignity streaming from him. "We chose each other."

Perhaps we had. I'd wondered many, many times whatever had possessed me to stop and take a closer look when Conan's puppy anguish enveloped me. I'd been drawn to him from the first moment I found him, half hidden in the recesses of a shallow well.

Vampires might not keep pets, but I couldn't have walked away and left him if I'd tried. The pull was that strong. Besides, I'd never viewed him as a pet, always as a companion. Our relationship one of equals.

I dug my fingertips into his thick pelt. "According to

Fairclaw, Vampires aren't high on your list of favorite supernatural beings. Weren't you frightened of me?"

His amber gaze bored into me. "No. You have a pure and shining spirit. You were worried about me, willing to sacrifice yourself to protect me. When you first knelt by me and scooped me up, I didn't even realize you were a Vampire."

Memories dragged me back to that night and the scrawny, trembling puppy I'd gathered into my arms, draping my shawl around him to keep him warm. The first thing I'd done was find a secluded glade in the nearby woods and kill small rodents for him to eat.

I smiled. "You were a greedy little thing."

He licked my chin. "And you kept the food coming. I ate so much I fell asleep."

"You did. Gave me an opportunity to feed myself without scaring you."

"You must have known I was magical," Conan said.

"I did, but I had no idea what you were. It was why I brought you to the Sorcerer. They don't like Vampires any better than your people, but he was entranced by you." I nodded. "I suppose he knew exactly what you were, but he never told me."

"Or anyone else," Conan said. "I made sure of it."

News to me. "What did you do? Last I checked before we left that village, he was alive and well."

"Nothing dramatic. I erased the tiny part of his memories where I resided. Couldn't risk him talking with anyone."

"But we spent months with him."

Conan made a whuffly noise in the back of his throat. If

he'd been a cat, it might have been a purr. "And I made alterations in his memories every single time. He remembered you and me and what he and I were working on, but not what I was."

The scope of Conan's power was mindboggling. "Glad you're on my side," I murmured.

"Always."

I dropped my hands into my lap and rocked back on my heels. "Do guardians have a primary form? And is it only the ley-lines and the realm of the dead—?"

Conan barked. It effectively shut me up. Just because I knew more didn't give me the right to quiz him. "Sorry." I offered a soft smile. "But I am curious."

"Our primary form is human, but mostly we're wolves. It's more convenient in the channels between worlds. Fur protects far better than skin." I must have looked like I had a million more questions because he shook his head. I understood his meaning. He'd tell me what he wished me to know.

Peppering him with questions wouldn't do anything but piss him off. Except I did want to know one thing. "It's none of my affair, but how did you end up alone and on Earth?"

"Stupidity. Hubris. Not in any particular order. When I've thought about it—and I have—I must have been meant to find you."

"Any idea why?"

"Not sure. That part of our tale has yet to unfold."

I crinkled my forehead as I thought about it. We might be the poster children for supernaturals getting along with one another. But Conan and I had been together for centuries, and the war with mortals was just now heating up.

Magic doesn't have timelines, I reminded myself. Not recognizable ones, anyway.

Dahlia came around a corner flanked by Cerys, Dee, and Percy. More Than Never sat on her shoulder, cawing. "We've closed all the drapes and blinds we can," she told me. "There's still daylight sneaking in, but you can mostly avoid it."

"Ewww. What was that?" Dee pointed at the squished wasp. Its stinger was still pulsing with a nacre glow. Magic takes a long time to die.

"Last of the wasps, I hope." I pushed to my feet. "What's left to do here?"

Nickolas scooted into the room, neatly sidestepping a sliver of sunlight. "Clive and I finished cleaning up the downstairs. Got all the bloodstains out and burned everything we needed to hide."

I raised one eyebrow. "Sheesh. Must smell like a crematorium from outside."

"No. Percy and the other Sorcerers have mage fires happening in the backyard. Some of the Fae constructed a ward. Our activities are probably fairly invisible."

"Any idea who owns this place?" I asked Dahlia.

"Yeah. Percy hacked into the county database. It's a real estate group that specializes in long-term rentals. The house was rented to a Jonathan Smith."

"Pfft. Wonder how he got that pseudonym past all the paperwork?" I muttered.

"Same way I got phony identification?" Nickolas suggested with a jaunty smile.

"Probably so," I agreed. Mortals' penchant for paperwork would be their undoing since there were so many ways around it.

"Alrighty." Dahlia was nodding. "We sanitized the third floor. First floor is done. That leaves the middle one. I assigned a few Witches to make certain we didn't leave anything for the paranormal police task force to gloat over."

"Is there a basement?" Nickolas asked. "Or an attic?"

"No attic," Cerys said. "Only a crawlspace, and I checked it."

"Want to hunt for a basement?" Nickolas asked me.

I grinned. Couldn't help myself. "Basements are a natural for us," I quipped. "It's where we keep the coffins."

After an uncomfortable pause, the Witches laughed along with us. "Not used to you being quite so blunt," Dee said, "but I rather like it."

"Maybe not so much blunt as poking fun at some of the stereotypes people have about Vamps," I said.

"Are we opening the club tonight?" she asked me.

I nodded. "We are. The gateway is closed. Not much chance of a repeat from last night. That stupid ass police officer can give himself points for being right about disaster not striking twice in the same spot."

"Hopefully, after last night, they'll have rethought arresting any of us," Percy muttered.

"If they'd wanted us, they wouldn't have been so helpful last night," Dee said.

I tended to agree with her assessment. Cops were never

nice to people they thought they'd have to arrest at some point. "Circling back to tonight," I said, "we'll offer cut rate booze, and I'll call a few musicians. Nothing like cheap liquor and free music to draw a crowd."

"We could help with the music," Cerys offered.

It surprised me, given her obvious antipathy for Vampires. "That would be amazing," I told her.

"Lots of us play," she informed me. "I'll get a group together. What time would you like us to show up?"

"How about eight thirty?"

"You got it." She held out a hand. I shook it.

"I'll pay you," I told her. "*Ascent* offers union rates."

She shook her head. "Wouldn't dream of it. This is our gift to you and Conan for closing off the portal. Not that darkness can't find another way in, but it will take them time. They lost a lot of magical power when we killed all those Sorcerers."

"It was more Conan and his tribe who altered the ley-lines," I clarified.

"Yes, but if it weren't for you, Conan never would have been there at all," Cerys said and inclined her head to the wolf in a sign of deep respect.

And there it was. My link with Conan was important. It was turning into the leading edge of something larger than all of us. The revelation excited me and iced my Undead bones at the same time.

He woofed gently in appreciation.

"See you tonight," I told her and Dee. "Get some rest."

"You too," Dee told me. "You look like hell."

Before I could retort Vampires always looked gorgeous as sin, Nick asked if I was ready to hunt for the basement.

When I nodded, he said, "I found a back staircase system. It will limit our exposure to daylight."

Conan fell in next to us.

"Any more surprises up your furry sleeves?" Nick asked him.

The wolf made his purring sound again as we barreled down a spiral staircase that appeared to stretch from the top floor to the bottom. It came out in a garage so pristine I felt certain no one had ever used it.

I headed for a door leading back inside. It was locked, but a touch brought the tumblers into line. Cautious about light, I cracked the door and shut it fast when the glare nearly blinded me.

"Fuck. Guess the kitchen doesn't have blinds," I said.

"Let's be smart about this," Nickolas suggested. Enchantment gleamed around him as he sent threads of seeking power downward. His green eyes widened. "Who would have guessed. There's something just below us. It's more a staging area than a basement, but my bet is it's how they traveled back and forth, leveraging energy from the ley-lines."

"Where is it?" I asked.

"Hang on. I'll show you."

Strands of coppery hair fell into his eyes. He pushed them aside, and the feel of his magic—blood and bone and thunder—swept Conan and me into a quick transport spell. The garage vanished, replaced by a rounded room maybe a hundred feet long by half that wide.

It reeked of sulfur, skunks, and sewage. The overall miasma was so noxious it made me glad I wasn't the breathing type. Conan had begun examining the lower edges of the room, where the walls met the floor.

He barked, followed by, "Here. There's still a weak place in the weave."

I trotted to where he stood. Nickolas stood just behind us. It didn't take much testing to locate what Conan was referring to. The wolf sneezed. My bet was the reek was damn near killing him.

"What do you think?" I asked both of them.

"Seal it with magic," Conan said. I noticed he'd shifted to taking shallow, panting breaths.

"Easier to blow the whole thing up," Nick muttered.

"But wouldn't we take out the house?" I asked.

"No," Conan said. "This place isn't part of Earth but a section of the conduit they built."

"Even better," Nick said. "I was assuming we'd have to be careful."

"Let's do it," I told him, suddenly anxious to return above ground. Something about this confined space made the fine hairs on the back of my neck stand on end. Another very un-Vampirelike reaction.

"I will craft the destruction," Conan said.

"I'll get us out of here," Nick offered. "Tell me when." Power formed a vortex rising from his outstretched hands. As I watched, it shaded from gray to violet to blue.

The air thickened with the clean smells of good magic. It was a welcome change, but it didn't come close to obliterating the raw sewage taint.

Conan moved a few feet from us. I'd grown used to how he manipulated magic, so I noticed the differences now that he wasn't hiding what he was. Enchantment spilled from him, forming a thick red line that followed the contours of the room.

He bolted toward us, shouting, "Now."

Nick loosed his transport spell. His timing was perfect. I saw the red line blossom into mini explosions that shook the place just before we got the hell out of Dodge.

Back in the garage, we looked at each other, bleary-eyed. "Are we done?" I asked.

"Think so." Nick nodded. "We can put the ritual farewell for Lorenzo off until tonight."

"Good idea," I said. "That way we can offer him a better farewell. My reserves are shot."

Conan shook himself and sneezed twice more, probably to clear residual stink out of his nostrils. "Time to hunt," he announced. "Let's go home."

Running on auto-pilot, I started to draw a teleport spell together. I was too done in to go to *Ascent* and collect the car. I'd worry about it later today. But then, I looked at Nick. "Where will you go?"

He smiled. "I have a place I've been staying."

His clothes were in my machine. I needed to put them in the dryer, and I could just bring them to *Ascent* later, but I wanted to do more. I might regret this, but over the course of the very long night that had bled into today, he, Conan, and I had begun to feel like a team.

I pushed my tired shoulders straighter. "No shenanigans,

but if you want a place to bed down for the day, you can come home with us."

"It's kind of you—" he began.

"Bullshit," I spoke over him. "I'm a lot of things, but kind isn't one of them."

He caught my lower arm in his hand. "You were there. Weren't you?"

"Huh? I was where?"

"You were part of Clan Hawke when Mistral was beheaded. At first, I was convinced you had to be too young, but now I'm not so sure."

Shock churned through me. How could Nickolas possibly know about me and Mistral? I dropped a brick over my incriminating thoughts. "I was part of Clan Hawke then," I said, feeling as if I had marbles in my mouth. "Why?"

"What happened must have branded you, left a huge impression on a young, Vampire. It's what has made you so..." He seemed to be struggling for words and finally came up with, "unvampirelike."

"Not sure what I am or not," I said stiffly. "Conan and I are leaving. You know where I live if you want to show up. Otherwise, I'll see you later at *Ascent*."

"Wait. I didn't mean to hurt your feelings," Nickolas said.

I looked right at him. "I'm a Vampire. I don't have feelings."

"That's a lie. You were crying in the place between worlds. Ariana. Please don't shut me out."

I was too tired and too confused and too relieved Nick

didn't know about my connection to Mistral's untimely end to do anything beyond teleporting the fuck out of there. Blood and rest and I'd be better equipped to pick up the tattered edges of my false front.

My home formed around Conan and me. I plopped onto one of the overstuffed couches in my living room. Conan stood over me, looking worried. "Are you all right?"

"No. But I will be."

"Why'd we leave Nick?"

I considered lying, but Conan deserved better. "Because he came too close to a truth I've been hiding forever."

"Was that the thing you wanted to tell me?" the wolf pressed. When I nodded, he woofed and then said, "Don't. I don't want to know. It's long over and done with."

"It is," I agreed, "but Vampires have memories as long as our lives."

He laid his snout alongside my cheek. "You'll figure it out," he said. "I have faith in you." Turning, he faded through a wall as if it weren't there.

"Good hunting," I called after him and dragged myself to my feet, dropping clothing around me. Everything could stand to be washed, including me. And I needed to feed.

I'd play things with Nick by ear. Maybe if I pretended to still be distraught about Mistral, he'd get the memo and leave it be. It was a flawed plan, one that meant I'd have to keep him at arm's length. Vampires were relentless when they got their fangs into something. Even if Nick was convinced my days at the Clan Hawke manor had traumatized me, he wouldn't back off until he was satisfied he'd done all he could to mitigate the damage.

I'd just have to make certain that day came sooner rather than later.

And I'd have to make double damn sure not to fall into his arms in a weak moment. Not entirely pleased, but understanding I was as close as I was likely to come to a resolution of the Nick problem, I scooped up my filthy garments and walked to the laundry room.

It was much easier to think about Conan and the miraculous creature he was. I'd always known he was special, but I'd had no idea how far that specialness would extend. In truth, I was a little in awe of his new status, except it was only new to me. He'd held onto his secrets forever. It gave me hope I might hang onto my own.

I switched Nick's clothes into the dryer and started a new load in the washing machine. I'd stop by the freezer for a quick infusion of blood, and then I'd run a bath. Warm water all the way to my chin would do as much as anything to ease the ache in my Undead soul. I'd finally found a Vampire I could love, but he wasn't for me. I'd sealed my fate the day I slew Mistral.

I shook my head. If Mistral was somewhere out there, he was laughing his head off. I may have ended him, but he'd had the last word. I bent and adjusted the temperature of the water gushing into the copper tub.

Eh. Mistral only thought he'd had the last word. Alone wasn't so bad. I'd done all right for myself. Conan and I would form the core of a resistance. Somehow, we'd break through the harsh line mortals had carved in the sand. Earth was big enough for all of us. There had to be a way to convince them of that.

And I wouldn't give up until either I had—or we'd lost so comprehensively there was no hope left. I didn't care for option two. Giving up—losing—wasn't part of my makeup. I sank into the tub and shut off the water before it slopped over the rim.

I'd take this a step at a time. One of the big advantages of immortality is I didn't have to rush anything. Not Nick. Not finding a staged solution to the war. As close as I was likely to come to allaying my assortment of worries, I closed my eyes and let the hot water ease the kinks out of body and mind.

You've finished *Harsh Line*, first of the Cataclysm books. Ariana's problems are about to get worse, but so are Nick's. That's the thing about knowledge. It's a two-edged sword. Once you have it, what in the hell do you do about it? Please take a moment to leave a review for *Harsh Line*. Doesn't have to be fancy, a line of two will do it. Curious about *Warped Line*, next of the Cataclysm series? Keep right on reading for a sample.

BOOK DESCRIPTION, WARPED LINE

I chose stasis—a long sleep—for me and two of mine. Hard to time these things, but we woke in the eye of a cyclone.

When I went to sleep—to avoid being drained of magic and blood by dark Sorcerers—Vampires weren't exactly on the endangered species list, but not many of us are left. No one ever accepted us. Not mortals and not others with power, either. At least one of those dams has developed a few cracks. Supernaturals aren't quite welcoming, but they'll take help from any quarter.

Mortals have declared war on magic, and they won't rest until we're all sitting in iron-clad prisons. What a bunch of cowards. If they weren't hiding behind false humanitarian walls, they'd be honest about their intentions and kill us outright if they could.

The world turned into an alien place while I slept. Not

much point returning to my clan house in Italy. It's probably long since disbanded. Besides, fate tossed me squarely in Ariana's path. She's like me, a Vampire, but I hunger for her in a very un-Vampirelike way.

She's done her damnedest to chase me away, but I'm tough to dissuade. She doesn't know it, but I won't back off until she's mine.

No matter what it takes.

WARPED LINE, CHAPTER ONE, NICKOLAS

$\mathcal{I}$ stood in the garage after Ariana's abrupt departure wondering what to do next. I'd clearly trodden on unholy ground when I'd blurted out my question about Mistral. She'd been in the Clan Hawke seethe when he was murdered. At least I knew that much.

Murdered is a bit of a misnomer. As head of Clan Hawke, Mistral was centuries dead, but his Vampiric existence had been cut short—presumably by one of his minions. No one else would have been able to get close enough to a master Vampire to do that level of damage. Back when I was newly made, I'd snuck away from Clan Giovanni more than once, intent on locating the assassin who'd ended Mistral. If I'd found him, I'd have been a hero in Vampire circles. As I hunted, my fantasies vacillated between ending him myself or hauling him in to face justice.

Never did fully decide, and it was a moot point because I never located his killer.

Ariana had done her best to mask her emotions, but she'd been visibly upset when I'd asked about her master. He was probably who'd turned her, which meant she'd have had a special bond with him. I wasn't used to tiptoeing around other Vampires. Most of us lost our reactiveness along with our humanity when we joined the ranks of the Undead.

Ariana was definitely different.

I hadn't realized I'd begun pacing, skirting the rays of daylight filtering around an enormous metal door at one end of what looked like a storage area, but a damned clean one that was absolutely devoid of any contents.

If I was honest with myself, I wasn't the same Vampire who'd chosen stasis to escape dark sorcerers out for my blood. Literally. Something about Vampire blood bolstered their magic. At the time, I didn't know they also murdered humans, absorbing their psychic energies to strengthen themselves.

For some reason that seems far worse to me than stealing the occasional sip from a willing mortal.

Prior to choosing a long sleep to vanish from sight, I'd been as accommodating as the next Vampire, which is to say, not accommodating at all. It was my way or nothing, and I didn't particularly care whose toes I stomped on. Other magic wielders don't like us because we're at the top of the food chain, and they're jealous of our strength and speed and our genuine give-a-fuck attitudes.

My interpretation.

If you were to ask any Witch or Sorcerer or Fae, they'd label us insufferable, lean closer, and whisper our magic wasn't up to par, either. They're entitled to their opinions.

Now that my views have had a chance to ripen, I can appreciate their line of arguments. We can be pretty damned arrogant, and our brand of magic is different. It's designed to hypnotize prey, so we always have enough to eat.

Beyond that, we don't actually require magic for much. Cheap parlor tricks are a waste of time and energy. I was on my tenth transit of the garage and not one step nearer to figuring out what to do next. Ariana had invited me to her home, but that was before I'd made the mistake of bringing up Mistral. She and Conan, her shapeshifting dire wolf companion, had vanished damned fast after that.

"There you are." Clive, another Clan Giovanni Vampire, trotted into the garage from a door that led into the house. Daylight streamed through the door in the brief moment it was open.

"How'd you manage to transit the kitchen?" I asked.

He blinked owlishly out of bloodshot dark eyes. "Not easily, mate." He examined his hands, the only part of him that wasn't covered. "Don't think I got burned." His accent was pure upper crust British. Blonde hair spilled down his shoulders. Like all of us, he was one striking specimen. His tall, broad-shouldered, slim-hipped build was draped in cheap garments we'd stolen from a secondhand clothing store soon after waking from stasis.

Clive was here. His presence settled things. He and I would retreat to the cave where we'd slept a hundred years away and wait out the day. At least I could stop perseverating about whether or not to teleport to Ariana's house.

"Where are Ariana and Conan?" Clive asked me.

"They went home." Something about my tone alerted him enough to shoot me a curious look, but I outranked him. He knew better than to mine for details. "We've put off the farewell ceremony until tonight."

"For Lorenzo?" He quirked a blond brow.

I nodded. "Too much was going on, and then we lost the night."

"Probably for the best," Clive said. Making a conscious effort, he inhaled and blew out an unneeded breath. "It's all right. The ritual was just to assuage my guilt. We don't have to give him any kind of sendoff. He doesn't really deserve it. Not after how he acted."

I tended to agree. Another member of Clan Giovanni who'd joined me in stasis, Lorenzo had engaged in group sex play with three mortal women. He probably would have gotten off clean, except he'd glommed onto one and drained her. The other two women panicked, and the story blew up all over the place.

"Good for us to remember," I muttered.

"What? To keep our dicks under wraps?" Clive's words were laced with sarcasm.

"I was thinking more about our fangs." I stopped for a moment before adding, "One of the biggest changes while we were asleep is how fast news travels. Computers can broadcast anything around the globe in seconds. It was how the police found out about Lorenzo's swan dive from grace so fast."

"I still think we should go home."

My face must have taken on an odd expression because Clive made come along motions with one hand. "What aren't you saying? I mean I get it we'd have a hell of a time crossing the ocean. I'd need those identification items you just got, but we'd figure it out."

"Runs deeper than that. Ariana showed me what Castelrotto looks like today. Sibiu too, which was where she and Conan were before coming to North America."

"You have to say more than that, mate," Clive urged.

"It's not just different," I told him. "It looks a lot like this place, except the buildings are older. If our clan is still in that region, my bet is they've moved out of the city. Not so sure they'd welcome us back. All the woods where we used to find game when we couldn't locate a willing mortal are gone."

Clive took a step away from me. "All of them?" he choked out.

"Most, yes. What trees remain wouldn't offer much in the way of cover."

He frowned. "What do you mean, she showed you?"

"Her computer has pictures from everywhere in the world."

His eyes widened. "We shouldn't have slept so long."

"Hard to second-guess these things," I said and shrugged. The strips of light oozing around the door were growing. I set a spell in motion and whisked us to the cave that was the closest thing we had to a home here. We're not exactly cold-blooded, but we don't feel the chill like a mortal might.

Once we were back underground, Clive settled on his haunches with his back against a wall. "Is our plan to remain here, then?"

"It's my plan"—I stressed the my part—"but if you want to return to Italy, I'll help you finesse how to manage it."

He was silent for a while, probably running options and prospects through his mind. When he looked up, he said, "I appreciate the freedom, but I'll remain with you. If I return to the clan house alone, I'll have a massive amount of explaining to do. Hell, for all I know, they'll think I did you in just like one of Mistral's minions did to him, and—"

"So long as you brought it up," I cut in, "do not ask Ariana about Mistral. She was there when the incident occurred, and it still upsets her."

Clive cracked a grin. "I'm guessing you already fell into that pothole."

"You'd have guessed right."

"What do you think about Conan?" Clive changed the subject rather abruptly.

It was a reasonable question. What did I think about the shapeshifting dire wolf who wasn't a wolf at all but a guardian?"

"It isn't so much a matter of what I think," I began, "but of all the questions I have. His kinsmen clearly want him back, but he has no interest in returning."

"They must have done something," Clive said. "Alienated him somehow."

I nodded. "Beyond that, they didn't look for him very hard."

"We don't know that," Clive said. "His magic is the strongest I've run across. If he didn't want to be found…"

"Presumably the other guardians' magic is on a par with Conan's," I tossed out. My tone might have been sharp because I don't take to underlings correcting me. I needed to get over that. In the Old Country, I'd outranked Clive, but I had to move past antiquated thought patterns.

"True enough." Clive grinned. "That Ariana. She's really something. Hell, mate, she's as tall as we are. And all that hair is so black, it almost glows blue. Her eyes remind me of blue pearls, and—"

"Enough." I cut him off midsentence before he started in on her high, full breasts and to-die-for ass. As it was, my cock had already begun to thicken.

"I get that she'd not for me," he said and slitted his eyes my way. "You want her for yourself, don't you?"

I could bluster my way through a lie, but Ariana wasn't someone to lie about. My attraction to her felt almost sacrosanct, not to be trifled with. "Yes, I do, but she and Conan are sufficient unto themselves."

His smile faded. "You're not suggesting they're lovers?" Something about the specter of cross-species breeding— beyond Vampires and mortals—apparently bothered him.

"No. Not at all. They're friends. Companions. He never takes human form. Until we ran into the other guardians, I wasn't sure he even could."

"Mmph. Interesting. Since we're staying here. What happens next?"

It was a reasonable question. For one thing, we needed more clothes. And something beyond this cave so we could clean up. "I'm committed to working off my debt at *Ascent*. Once it's been discharged, I plan to locate lodgings."

"Working there the other night wasn't bad," Clive said. "Never did time in a public house before, but I can wash glasses and buss tables with the best of them. Do you suppose she'd offer me the same deal she did you?"

"She might. You'll have to ask her. And *Ascent* is a nightclub, not a public house or pub."

Clive made a face. "Hate to volunteer for chair time, but maybe you could show me the library where you did all that reading. Soon as I open my mouth, I'm bound to make a mistake, and whoever I'm talking with will figure out quick enough I'm not from here."

"Sure. I can do that. We'll stop by there once it gets dark. And then maybe another quiet visit to Salvation Army once they close. I wouldn't worry so much about idle conversation. Your accent is pronounced. People will just assume things are different where you came from."

"Heh. They don't know the half of it. What happened to your accent, while we're at it?"

"The Scottish brogue disappeared during all the time I spent in Italy. It left my English quite bland."

"Aye, but how'd you get from Scotland to Italy? Were you turned before or after?"

It was a personal question. The old me would have told Clive it was none of his affair. In Vampire circles, I knew everything about those I'd turned, and everyone younger than me in the clan. By contrast, those older than me remained mysteries.

"Sorry," Clive mumbled. "I misspoke."

"Yes and no. If we were still in the clan house, I'd have deigned not to answer. This is the leading edge of a new existence for us, though." I settled onto my favorite flat rock, facing him.

"Our trip to the States to find fresh recruits for Clan Giovanni was far from the first such venture the clan underwrote. Different from the other clans, we've always prided ourselves on our diversity. We've established it by traveling to distant locations and unearthing mortals who were interested and willing to transform themselves."

I leveled my gaze at Clive. "You know this part because you were chosen. Unlike other clans who pick a mortal, drain them, and then offer up a wrist—which the mortal is able to refuse, if they're strong enough—for us, the turning part is a foregone conclusion. We know before we settle in to bleed a mortal to the point of death that they wish to become part of Clan Giovanni.

"I may have been born in the Highlands, but I was conscripted into the English king's army when I was but eleven. By my sixteenth birthday, I'd been knighted. It was what made me attractive to the Clan Giovanni scout."

"So you were selected." Clive nodded slowly. "Just like me."

"In a manner of speaking. Night had fallen after a particularly bloody battle. and I was surrounded by corpses, including my horse. Felt damned bad about losing him. He was the best warhorse I'd ever ridden. My armor had protected me from the worst of things, but that day I'd viewed my future with a clarity that had eluded me before."

"That you'd keep right on fighting," Clive said, something akin to hero-worship shining from his dark eyes.

"Exactly. And sooner or later I'd be killed. Very few knights saw their twenty-fifth year. I was still lying where I'd fallen, not far from my dead destrier, when I heard rustling.

At first, I was concerned it was one of my companions coming out of a period of unconsciousness. Before I rolled over and got to me feet, though, I tried to see what was going on."

"Bet all that armor was heavy as fuck," Clive murmured.

I snorted. "You have no idea. Anyway, I managed to position my helmet so I could see better. Vampires had closed on the field. Not many, only four, but they were systematically moving from corpse to corpse."

I straightened my shoulders. "I wouldn't have admitted it then, but I was scared. Every rumor I'd ever heard about the Undead blasted into my mind, and my heartrate soared. I started panting inside the helmet, and knew I had to get my body under better control.

"If the Undead were feasting on corpses, they'd have a heyday with me. I was quick about quieting my mind and did a decent job pushing my fear to a distant place. My eyes were shut, and I was barely breathing."

"Like that would make you invisible to us," Clive blurted.

"Yes, well, you know, and I know now, but all I had to go on then were myths and legends."

"One of them approached you, didn't he?" Clive leaned toward me, fascinated by my tale.

"Of course, except it turned out to be a woman. She squatted next to me and said, 'I know you're not dead, knight. Sit up so we can talk.'

"I floundered about, making enough racket to wake the dead—probably not the best example under the circumstances. Eventually, I managed a sit. The woman was smiling. Her fangs were on display; blood streaked her chin. I should have been disgusted, but she was so beautiful, I forgot to be terrified."

"She had you in thrall." Clive's words held such certainty, they made me smile.

"She did, indeed. She explained she'd been on the sidelines from dusk onward, watching the tail end of the battle. She complimented me on my bravery, and sketched out the basics about becoming a Vampire. The whole time, she was clear it was my choice. If I decided against the transformation, she'd erase my memory of her, and it would be as if our conversation never happened."

"What decided you?" Clive asked.

"Immortality." I shrugged. "The rest is history. She turned me, and—"

"Did it include fucking?"

He was so direct, I laughed. "It did, indeed. You know her. Roseann was part of the clan when we turned you."

"Ooooh. She's one hot babe. I tried to get into her bed a time or two, but she never gave me the time of day."

My laughter deepened. "She wouldn't have. To her, you were a youngster."

"So were you that night on the battlefield." Clive's statement held defensiveness.

"True enough," I agreed, "except there might have been a fifty year difference in our ages, not a three-hundred year one."

"Thank you for trusting me with your origin story," Clive said, his tone formal.

"You're quite welcome. I'm going hunting. I'll bring us back whatever I find."

"Someday, I won't be as sun-sensitive."

"Someday, you won't," I told him. "Rest up. I'll be back before it's time for us to go to the library."

Before he could protest it wouldn't take all those hours to hunt for carcasses we could drain, I got to my feet and launched a teleport spell. At some point during our conversation, I'd decided to drop in on Ariana and Conan. Mostly, I wanted to apologize for upsetting her.

More than that, though, I needed to see her with an intensity that was a physical ache in my guts. Fuck. What was wrong with me? A smarter man would steer well clear unless I was at work.

Fine, I told myself. *I'll apologize, and then I'll leave.*

Even I know a raft of crap when I hear it, and that one was riddled with enough holes to sink itself. I had to be very careful. If I wasn't, I'd throw my arms around Ariana, crush her to me, and bury myself in her body.

Ever enthusiastic, my errant member shot to full attention, readier than ready for action. I'd have to get rid of my hard-on before knocking on her door. A slight alteration in my casting ensured I'd emerge a good league from her cabin. I'd stroke myself into a hasty climax, and then I'd offer my apologies for prying into her private life.

Depending on her reaction, I'd either stay longer, or remain true to my commitment to beat a hasty retreat. We may have won a battle last night, but there was a lot more to do. I couldn't afford to dilute our efforts with a spate of unwelcome advances.

She and I had to work together. With staunch instructions to keep my eye on the bigger picture—the one that included mortals who wanted to slaughter every immortal—I emerged into a forest and grappled with the zipper on my trousers.

Clive understood Ariana wasn't for him. She probably wasn't for me, either, but I could fantasize. Imagery of her, head tossed back, neck corded with passion played through my thoughts as I stroked myself to a mind-bending climax.

ABOUT THE AUTHOR

Ann Gimpel is a USA Today bestselling author. A lifelong aficionado of the unusual, she began writing speculative fiction a few years ago. Since then her short fiction has appeared in many webzines and anthologies. Her longer books run the gamut from urban fantasy to paranormal romance. Once upon a time, she nurtured clients. Now she nurtures dark, gritty fantasy stories that push hard against reality. When she's not writing, she's in the backcountry getting down and dirty with her camera. She's published over 75 books to date, with several more planned for 2020 and beyond. A husband, grown children, grandchildren, and wolf hybrids round out her family.

Keep up with her at www.anngimpel.com or http://anngimpel.blogspot.com

If you enjoyed what you read, get in line for special offers and pre-release special reads. Newsletter Signup!

Rebel Reaper

Untamed Reaper

GenTech Rebellion

Winning Glory

Honor Bound

Claiming Charity

Loving Hope

Keeping Faith

Ice Dragon

Feral Ice

Cursed Ice

Primal Ice

Rubicon International

Garen

Lars

Soul Dance

Tarnished Beginnings

Tarnished Legacy

Tarnished Prophecy

Tarnished Journey

Soul Storm

Dark Prophecy

Dark Pursuit

Dark Promise

Underground Heat

Roman's Gold

Wolf Born

Blood Bond

Wolf Clan Shifters

Alice's Alphas

Megan's Mates

Sophie's Shifters

Wylde Magick

Gemstone

Lion's Lair

Unbalanced

STANDALONE BOOKS

Branded, That Old Black Magic Romance (paranormal romance)

Edge of Night (short story collection, paranormal and horror)

Grit is a 4-Letter Word (nonfiction)

Heart's Flame (post-apocalyptic romance)

Icy Passage (science fiction romance)

Marked by Fortune (post-apocalyptic coming of age story)

Melis's Gambit (historical paranormal romance)

Midnight Magic (paranormal romance)

Red Dawn (post-apocalyptic paranormal romance)

Shadow Play (historical paranormal romance)

Shadows in Time (Highland time travel romance)

Since We Fell (contemporary romance)

Warin's War (paranormal romance)